Best Wishes
always!

Praise for the Book

I am a great admirer of Aparna's illustrious journey from a small town girl to becoming a known name in the literary circles of the country. 'Between U & Me' is a memoir that resonates with the life experiences of ordinary yet accomplished people who are capable of infusing life into the imagination of the leaders of tomorrow. This book will serve as a lodestar as it promises to radiate the same motivating aura as was seen during her visit to Lovely Professional University. God speed to her constant endeavors!

Rashmi Mittal,
Pro Chancellor
Lovely Professional University, Phagwara (Punjab)

Stephen Covey has said, "I am not a product of my circumstances. I am a product of my decisions."

No matter who you are, what you do, where you are from, you are the outcome of your decisions and, in turn, your actions. However, your decisions are themselves reflections of your thought process, your perceptions and your beliefs. So what are the thought processes, perceptions and beliefs that can lead one to success?

Although the lives of successful people may inspire us, we may also be intimidated by them and write them off as 'gifted' or 'special.'

However, Aparna Sharma's book 'Between U & Me' is an inspirational memoir with a huge difference! Breaking the trend of drawing inspiration from celebrities and the who's who, she gives us 14 real-life, inspiring stories of the people who are a part of her life – her teachers, friends, colleagues, mentors, and subordinates – people who made a difference to her life! She has gotten into their life stories and unfolded their thought processes, perceptions, and beliefs for the benefit of the reader.

She effectively brings out their aspirations, their challenges and the lessons they learnt as well as words of wisdom for the reader, all in their own words.

A wonderful book about how best to live your day-to-day life!

Ranjit Shahani,
Former Vice Chairman & Managing Director
Novartis India Limited

If we are asked to name the people who have inspired us, many of us shall probably come up with some well-known names. How many of us would name someone around us, someone whom we know and is a part of our daily lives? The very idea that inspiration is to be drawn from the who's who is a tunnel-vision approach.

I love that Aparna has broken this norm through her book 'Between U & Me!' This motivating book is a compilation of stories of not one, not two, but fourteen people from all walks of life. Stories from those who have inspired, motivated and made a difference to Aparna's life as they went about their own daily tasks.

Written in lucid language, the book showcases the beautiful stories of these people, giving us glimpses into their personalities, their challenges, their triumphs, and most importantly, the lessons learnt that we can draw inspiration from. A must-read for people of all ages!

Robin Banerjee,
Managing Director – Caprihans India Ltd.
Author: Business book: WHO CHEATS AND HOW

It is said that all the knowledge in the world can be contained between the covers of books, and that the person, who does not read a book is no better off than a person who cannot.

The author, Aparna Sharma is herself a person of considerable accomplishments and her own story is an inspiration. In this book, she has gone one step ahead and sought to capture the inspirational stories of 14 other accomplished people such as her. The best part of the book is that it can be read time and again, whenever one is in need for some inspiration in one's own life. I wish the readers an accomplished life as much as the stellar examples contained in the book.

P. Venkatraman,
Chief Running Evangelist
YouTooCanRun, Author: From Sofa to 5K

Having known Aparna for many years, I am still always amazed to see the tenacity and grace with which she has approached every new endeavor, including this book. The lives of amazing people give us insights into the trials and travails that nature and circumstances place in front of us every day. Studying these patterns gives us enormous insights into the psyche of such distinguished people who have touched the lives of many in different ways. These nuggets of wisdom in this book, brought together by Aparna, are a guide in the journey towards her own self-discovery.

Dr. Sumit D. Chowdhury,
Managing Director & CEO – Gaia Smart Cities
Author: Rules of the Game: Discover, Learn, Invent The Art of Speeding Up Your Career

With light-hearted and illuminating dissections of the lives of inspirational people, the book provides a fascinating opportunity for the readers to identify with and possibly emulate and better their own lives.

The book also helps provide a benchmark for us to see the world through the eyes of similar yet different people profiled in the book, to better our own perceptions of ourselves. In order to change a given situation, we must change ourselves, and in order to change ourselves, we must be able to change our perceptions.

The book is useful not just at work but at home as well. Whether you want to improve relationships with colleagues, managers or have more fruitful social relationships, the book bestows serious lessons through the people it profiles and their achievements.

Anand K Padmanaban,
COO and VP India (PowerOne)

It is fascinating to see how these achievers have battled life's 'normal' challenges, using persistence as a weapon. Aparna has turned the single-minded focus she brings to her own life into the task of her writing to incredible effect. In fact, she often reminds me of Jonathan Livingston Seagull.

Molly Thambi,
Former Managing Director & CEO,
Calcutta Stock Exchange

Between U & Me

Ordinary People – Extraordinary Lessons

Aparna Sharma

Between U & Me
Ordinary People – Extraordinary Lessons

1st Edition Published in India by Vishwakarma Publications in May, 2018
© **Aparna Sharma**
For feedback or comments:
Email: aparna@aparnasharma.in ; betweenuandme2018@gmail.com
Website: www.aparnasharma.in

ISBN No.: 978-93-86455-62-8

All rights reserved.
No part of this publication will be reproduced, transmitted, or stored in a retrieval system, in any form or by any means, electronic, mechanical photocopying, recording or otherwise, without the prior permission of the Publisher.

Disclaimer
The views and opinions expressed in this book are the author's own and the facts are as reported by her, and the publishers are not in any way liable for the same.

Published by:
Vishwakarma Publications
34 A/1, Suyog Center, 7th Floor, Gultekadi Marketyard Road,
Giridhar Bhavan Chowk, Pune - 411 037, Maharashtra, India.
Phone: +91-20-20261157/9168682200
E-mail: info@vpindia.co.in
Website: www.vishwakarmapublications.com

Consultancy & Co-ordination:
Word's Worth Literary Consultancy

Cover Design & Layout:
Word's Worth Literary Consultancy

Printed At: Repro India Ltd., Mumbai

Price: ₹ 320/-

This book is sold subject to the condition that it shall not, by way of trade or otherwise, be lent, resold, hired out or otherwise circulated, without the publisher's prior consent, in any form of binding or cover other than that in which it is published.

This book is dedicated to my loving parents...
for their belief in me, understanding, and patience all along.

Thank you for bringing me into this world... am so grateful to be a part of you! Appreciate all the time we have spent together and even the time we could not; you are always an integral part of my 'BEING' and 'BECOMING'.

...Mamma & Papa, thank you for this wonderful gift of LIFE...

With Love, from Appu

Foreword

"Keep your mind, eyes and ears open; inspiration is all around you."

The most-needed ingredients for a good living today are positivity, strength of mind and ardent perseverance. As life becomes more and more complex, yet comfortable with the growth of technology, so are humans becoming lonelier in their ivory towers. This is the time when each of us is becoming increasingly vulnerable to feelings like insecurity, self-doubt, guilt, lack of confidence, lack of faith, etc. In each one of us exists the inherent need to draw courage, faith, confidence, and inspiration from someone.

At such a time, Aparna Sharma's book **'Between U & Me'** grabs our attention like a silver lining shining through a dark cloud. While people look up to me as a 'celebrity' and are inspired by my achievements, it is also true that they often ignore the strengths, determination and positivity that exist in the people around them whom they meet daily.

These outstanding qualities are not the birthright of the more educated or people from the affluent classes. They exist in everyone and help people overcome the day-to-day problems and challenges they face, whether they are for sheer survival or self-improvement. Kudos to Aparna for identifying such important qualities in people around her, irrespective of their age, status, educational and social backgrounds, and professions, to have looked up to and learnt from them – a true sign of a brilliant HR professional who has won numerous prestigious awards and has an experience of over 21 years to her credit!

In 14 short stories, the people who have inspired Aparna and continue to do so candidly talk to the readers about their life stories – their successes, failures, their learnings and finally, give readers food for thought through their valuable experiences. Their learnings and lessons are relevant to everyone – no matter what area they work in or where they live and what their backgrounds are. The lucid language and real-life incidents shall grip the readers as they relate with the various situations the characters (real people) reveal while they understand how these people have made a difference to Aparna's life.

The lesson this book drives home is that you don't need to be inspired only by celebrities or the privileged. One can derive inspiration and learning from anyone irrespective of what they do, who they are, where they live, what their social status is etc. The need is to have an open mind and a zeal to better oneself.

I hope readers will enjoy reading this book and the stories of these 14 people will inspire and motivate them as have they inspired Aparna!

I congratulate Aparna for coming up with the innovative concept of this book – **'Between U & Me'** and wish her and the book great success!

Dr. Devi Prasad Shetty
PadmaBhushan, PadmaShree,
Founder, Chairman & Senior Consultant Cardiac Surgeon,
Narayana Hrudayalaya Ltd.,
Bengaluru, 2018

Preface

I had to get this book out someday... not for **ME**, but for **YOU – the readers!** The need to motivate ourselves and face every day with renewed enthusiasm is more evident today due to the fast-changing world around us. There is no time like the present to share firsthand, the extraordinary experiences of 'ordinary' people, who have chased their dreams relentlessly and realized them.

'Between U & Me' speaks to everyone, about the world, as seen through the eyes of 'ordinary' people, and the hard work and ups and downs behind the magic they have created in their lives; 'ordinary' people, who have discovered greatness, yet, remained down-to-earth and humble.

This book encompasses the journey of people across various generations – from baby boomers to millennials. What is common between all of them is that they are all known to me personally and have hugely inspired me and impacted my life positively. Hence, I requested them to chronicle their journeys. Some of them are, in fact, octogenarians now... so they have loads of experience and lessons from life to share.

The purpose of this book is to inspire common people who have dreams, but are hesitant to pursue them, hindered by the limitations of their own mindsets. The beliefs, attitudes and learnings that are part of this book, are real-life examples, which will, hopefully, impact the lives of billions of people across the planet, who are in the quest for achieving greatness.

You can read these stories at a stretch or standalone; in either case, I urge you to spend time over the learnings and the 'Words of Wisdom' that each story brings out. This will help you draw the maximum out of each story while giving you valuable insights that you can apply to your own unique circumstances.

The process of writing this book has given me a deeper understanding of the lives of these 14 people, their hopes, their aspirations, their successes and failures, and their struggle to make a mark in their chosen fields. I realized that not only did these people excel in their own lives, they also carried themselves in a manner that served as a role model for others, to imbibe their lessons and emulate them in their lives. The wisdom that I have gained from these people has helped to change my perspective about life, increased manifold the respect that I had for them, and made me wish that someday, I, too, could elevate myself, if not to their level, at least somewhere close by.

The six-year-long journey of writing this book came with its own set of challenges. Writing the stories of these people entailed the challenge of working around the time constraints and schedules of each, sometimes across different time zones. At the time, I was working full-time and was simultaneously occupied with the writing of my first book, 'Reality Bytes – The Role of HR in Today's World.' Balancing personal pursuits and professional responsibilities was a tightrope, and though eager to share this wisdom with the world, sadly, I was forced to put this book on the back burner. I was able to revive and pick up the work of this book only last year. Today, with the publication of this book, I am immensely satisfied that my long-standing wish has been fulfilled. I am grateful to all my 'inspirations' for taking out time from their busy lives for repeated interactions, to give me a peek into their personal trials and tribulations, and to share their nuggets of wisdom that have made this labor of love worth its while.

Finally, I take your leave by handing over to **YOU – the readers,** this book, with the sincere hope that it will help renew your determination to break free of your limitations and pursue your goals. May it help you find in its pages, encouragement that you can look up to, anytime you feel lost in this journey of life!

Aparna Sharma
Mumbai, 2018

Contents

1. Making a Difference through Media
   Smt. Vimla Patil — 17

2. Achieving Heights in HR with Humility & Harmony
   Dr. T. V. Rao — 32

3. The Endearing Educationist
   Dr. Faiqa Saulat Khan — 52

4. The 'Chanakya' Coach: Balancing Strategy, Spirituality, and Success
   Dr. Radhakrishnan Pillai — 72

5. Hello – Health and Happiness!
   Dr. Sarah Musavi — 88

6. The Resilient Regulator
   Shri Raj Khilnani — 106

7. A Cheerful Crusader
   Vandana Jadhav — 122

8. Transforming Tresses the Tanveer Way!
   Tanveer Shaikh — 132

9. A Tale of Turnarounds & Transformations
   Ashwin Pasricha — 147

10. Doing One's Duty the 'Shant Advait' Way
    Dhyanshree Shailesh — 167
    (Mahamandleshwar Shaileshanand Giri) (Guruji)

11.	Lessons from a Life Well-lived **Shri Pheru Singh Ruhela**	185
12.	An Unconventional Odyssey **Prakhar Sharma**	200
13.	A Life Signifying Simplicity & Sensitivity **Arun Kaimal**	216
14.	Substance & Simplicity – A Powerful Duo **Smt. Sarita Deouskar**	232
15.	Packing a Punch with Positivity & Persistence **Aparna Sharma**	243
	Acknowledgments	260
	About the Author	261

1
Making a Difference through Media

Smt. Vimla Patil

Dear Vimlaji,

You have been a true inspiration for me for over a decade since the time I first interacted with you. In spite of your seniority, we quickly became very good friends. Humility, empathy and affection are synonymous with your accomplished personality. Three words which come to mind when I think of you are passion, commitment, and perseverance.

Your passion and enthusiasm about both, work and life, in spite of age-related health challenges you face today, are highly infectious and rub off onto others as well. Your focus is always on how to help others grow and develop, and your illustrious career reflects a steadfast commitment to these causes. This commitment is also reflected in your personal life.

When things have gotten tough, I have seen you persevere in the face of significant obstacles. Difficulties have only strengthened your passion and commitment to your goals. Whenever I have asked you if I can be of any help or do something for you, your instant response with a smile has been, 'Please be HAPPY always.'

Thank you Vimlaji, for inspiring me always and loving me selflessly!!!

Yours Affectionately,
Aparna

About Smt. Vimla Patil...

Smt. Vimla Patil is one of India's most senior journalists, author and media person. She has had a long and illustrious career spanning 25 years as the Assistant Editor and Editor of Femina, a top women's magazine (Times of India group), and that too, at a time when the concept of a working woman was anathema to our society. She built this first English women's magazine into an international brand. She used the medium of Femina to strive continuously for the rights of the girl child and women's emancipation and was successful in changing the status and mindset regarding Indian women, to create the persona of the modern, educated Indian woman. She unified the women of India through Femina, using common topics of relevance to them.

She has traveled worldwide and met and worked with personalities as varied as foreign dignitaries, politicians, Indian Prime Ministers like Indira Gandhi, Rajiv Gandhi, and Atal Bihari Vajpayee, top classical singers and film stars. She conceptualized the 'Miss India' contest for Femina and made it the popular event it is today.

She has authored numerous features on a wide range of topics like lifestyle, travel, wildlife, archaeology, women's concerns, celebrity interviews, and art and culture pieces about India. She has contributed to many leading papers in India and Asia. She has written scripts and done the artistic direction and music design for Son-et-Lumiere (Sound and Light) shows for the Ministry of Tourism, Government of India. She has also written for websites. She lives in Mumbai, India and has a son and daughter, both very accomplished and settled abroad.

"Success is the fruit of tireless efforts and the art of making the most of changing circumstances." – Smt. Vimla Patil

Unusual Upbringing

My unusual family circumstances helped me nurture atypical dreams.

I began my studies in a hostel at the tender age of six, when most young girls were still playing with their dolls. Boarding in a convent meant that there were girls from diverse communities and religions in the dormitory. Very early in life, I understood that my childish demands would be pushed aside for the larger good of the group. Each of us was given responsibilities and was expected to fulfill them meticulously. While corporates today generally conduct trainings to promote team building, manage conflicts and improve relationships, my convent years provided me a natural learning ground to imbibe these qualities. My journey to become an 'individual' in my own right, had begun from a very young age itself.

Childhood Chronicles

My childhood and school years were interesting because I was brought up jointly by several aunts and my father as my mother was ill most of the time. My upbringing was, therefore, an eclectic mix of orthodox values as well as forward-looking rational thought. While most families of the time were strictly traditional and tried to fit into the tightly woven societal fabric, my father had broken traditions and challenged customs when he married my mother, a child widow, in the 1920s.

I lived in South Mumbai where the Independence movement was at its peak. I observed leaders like Gandhiji and Chacha Nehru and sometimes even worked as a student volunteer. Though my school belonged to the Church of Scotland, my teachers were dedicated to the Independence Movement and taught us the glorious chapters of India's history and Sanskrit with great enthusiasm. These events shaped my thinking to a large degree and taught me the importance of standing up for a justified cause. My father, who always wore a khadi kurta and hand-spun dhoti, followed the careers of Gandhi and Nehru with passion, joined the Quit India

Movement and burnt British textiles at Flora Fountain (Mumbai). The seeds of my 'stepping away from the ordinary' were sown largely because of his towering presence in my life.

Thank You, Teacher!

In school, I was clear about the subjects I loved and, therefore, topped. I believe that being clear about one's goals is the first prerequisite to achieving success. I was fortunate to study my favourite subjects under some of the best teachers in Bombay.

> I believe that being clear about one's goals is the first prerequisite to achieving success.

I remember that I had gone to my Sanskrit teacher, after the result of the S.S.C. (Class 10) examinations, to tell him that I had scored 96 percent marks. I expected him to congratulate me. To my utter surprise, he asked me, "What happened to the remaining four percent marks?" His blunt question shook me out of my bubble of joy. Initial indignation was replaced with gratitude when I realized the two-fold lesson that he was trying to teach me. The first, that I had the capability to achieve much more, and the second, to not become complacent about my achievements, but rather, to analyze how I could do even better. A little like the 'What Went Wrong, What Went Right' analysis used in today's industry to overcome project shortcomings and better the achievements. Such defining moments came over and over again into my life and taught me many useful lessons.

My father and my teachers respected my every desire to learn. I played netball with passion, learnt classical music from some of the best teachers of the era, and listened to the best musicians – Pandit Ravi Shankar, Ali Akbar Khan, Pandit Omkarnath Thakur, Faiyaz Khan, Bade Ghulam Ali Khan and many others – all alongside my schooling. This exposure to various fields during my schooling days helped me become the multifaceted personality that I am today. Such exposure on multiple fronts is very important, to not just develop an all-rounded personality but also to help one find one's hidden talents and abilities. I was lucky to have had access to such company because of my curiosity and was even pampered by some masters owing to my enthusiasm and willingness to learn.

> They say that the best way to build your personality and become a sterling person is to be in the company of great people, great achievers, and great artists.

Daddy's Daughter

Through the various stages of my life, I followed my dreams, with complete support from my father, many times against the prevailing societal norms. Seeing my grades and liking for social work, he sent me to college saying that he was happy for a daughter to be successful. After I completed my B.A. (graduation) in English Literature and Indian Culture, I enrolled at the Govt. Law College and completed my L.L.B. too. At this juncture, my father started to dream about making me appear for the IAS (Civil Services) examination. But fate had other plans. I was destined to be a media person. My English teacher persuaded me to take up literature and creative writing.

To my father's credit, he agreed and sent me to London – alone and just 21, which was brave in those days – to study journalism. This was at a time when most girls were automatically married off in their early twenties. My colleagues at the college in London were from various countries, and this gave me a rare opportunity to understand other cultures. I spent holidays at the homes of my pals and introduced Indian cooking to their families. They also helped me see plays, music shows, and beautiful fairs and exhibitions.

Before returning to India, I went on a tour of European countries and saw their marvellous capital cities. The dual advantage of this three-year study was that I qualified as a media person and met my future husband, whom I married on my return to India.

I had got a first class in creative writing, and my family, particularly my father were overjoyed with my achievement. His faith in me and encouragement to walk on new paths led me to be independent. With support from him and my aunts, I set up my first married home. My in-laws were happy for me though they did not share my ambition. I could balance work and home because of my supportive husband, my father, and my aunts who cared for my children while I worked.

Fate, Fortune, Femina

It was fate that landed me my job at Femina. At a conference, I met Mr. J. C. Jain, then General Manager, Times of India, who offered me an opportunity to join the new magazine, Femina, from its first issue. I accepted with élan and never looked back from there. Armed with the confidence of my degree in journalism, I worked with dedication and enthusiasm to do my best, under the guidance of Frene Talyarkhan, the first editor of Femina. Two years into the job, I excelled at writing features, interviews, speeches, and summaries of major events. Those were the days when John F. Kennedy's charisma was sweeping the world. India and the USA were finding new cultural bonds. New horizons beckoned, and I was offered an opportunity to work with the US Information Service, where we would facilitate visits of celebrities and write for various papers.

Here, a new world opened up to me when I met stalwarts like John Kenneth Galbraith, Pearl Buck, Red Nichols, Arthur Schlesinger, and many other top names from USA. I was part of the cavalcade when Jacqueline Kennedy came to India on a goodwill visit. I traveled extensively to write stories about the collaboration efforts of the Peace Corps and the US-India collaboration. This was a steep learning curve in my career, and my stint in London during my education helped me appreciate and adjust to the various cultural, lingual, and other differences during my travels.

However, new challenges lay ahead, with new milestones to be achieved. The Times of India asked me to return to the Old Lady of Boribunder (The Times of India) as Assistant Editor of Femina, and in 1973, I became the Editor of Femina.

Motherhood Moments

While the work front was packed with visits to dignitaries and foreign countries, back home, a sweet discovery that I was expecting, put me on cloud nine. I remember vividly the moment when I brought my lovely twelve-day-old son home from hospital. I agree with what Gail Sheehy says in her book 'Passages,' "Once you are pregnant, you are 'pregnant' all your life." Motherhood has made me complete and taught me many valuable lessons.

My greatest challenge was to build the careers and characters of my children within the time available to me. I worked maniacally hard to make a success of both sides of the coin – work as well as home. As a young working woman and mother, my family taught me that mutual dependence was the mantra of progress. I had always looked after, supported, and loved the elder women relatives in my family, and they, in turn, helped me bring up my children. This allowed me to walk the tightrope between work and home that every working woman faces today. Every modern woman must learn that 'public relations' and 'team building' begin within the family. I am glad that my children are honest, hardworking, and successful people today, as a result of the 'community upbringing' they got from my family and me.

> Every modern woman must learn that 'public relations' and 'team building' begin within the family.

Fostering Femininity through Femina

It is said that, 'With great power, comes great responsibility.' It was when I started on my journey as the Editor of Femina, that

I perceived the profound truth of this statement. Sitting in the Editor's chair on day one, realization struck me that I not only had the opportunity to build my career in Media, but also had the responsibility of changing the lives of countless women through my work.

We, an all-woman staff, were convinced that this first English woman's magazine had a great role to play in changing the lives of all Indian women. One of the major social issues Femina dealt with was the status of the girl child. In a male-dominated society, Femina set out to promote a life of dignity for women, starting with the girl child and her rights. From then on, for more than half a century, Femina has worked for the empowerment of Indian women. In the following 20 years, till I retired, we fought many word battles with various social and political agencies of the government to help change Indian laws wherever they were discriminatory to women. Many times, we were discouraged by the regressive attitudes and the magnitude of the tasks before us. But, picking ourselves up, motivating one another, we carried on with this herculean task of bringing Indian women on a more equal footing.

My time at the Times included the years of the Women's Movement for equality all over the world. I had the opportunity to see it as I was invited by the US Government for a program of meetings. I got all the books written by Kate Millett, Germaine Greer, and Simone de Beauvoir who started this movement in Europe and the US. In India too, Indira Gandhi passed the equality law in the 70s. This helped media persons like me work for a more equitable deal for women, which preceded religious laws.

Till the 50s, women could neither open their own bank accounts without the signature of their husbands, nor could they take a loan without a sanction from their husbands. Dowry was a huge burden on families, and few women had access to higher education because getting married was considered more important than getting a university degree. But all this has changed gradually over the years. Slowly but surely, step by tiny step, we were successful in sometimes denting, sometimes transforming attitudes and mindsets, and bringing in the change that we had set out to bring.

Most importantly, since Femina was an English fortnightly and went to every corner of the country, we had the opportunity to try and create the identity of an 'Indian' woman. Hitherto, there were distinct categories of women in India – the South Indian, the Punjabi, the Bengali, the Maharashtrian or the Gujarati – this is how people identified themselves. They never said they were 'Indians.'

> I think my greatest achievement was the work I did in changing the perception of women as belonging to one country, as opposed to belonging to different communities.

Femina brought about this radical change by unifying all women under the three F's of top interest to them – Food, Fashion and Furnishing a home. We succeeded in creating the persona of the Indian woman through these and more ties, offering women financial self-reliance, education, an inclusive Indian personality, and pride in their heritage. We tried to spread women empowerment to the grassroot level by making it in an all-inclusive phenomenon. I remember we had an advertisement where a tribal woman was shown dancing, and the copy said, "We know she does not read Femina. But the woman who will change her life does, and that's what counts."

We also successfully set up the Miss India contest, which has today become a very prestigious national event. Fashion shows and modeling were, at the time, not viewed as respectable career options for women. But I chose to look at this contest not merely as a fashion show but also as an opportunity to provide women a chance to express their talent and develop their personalities. Many super successful women were groomed in their early years through the Femina Miss India Fashion Show, which I conceptualized in 1966 and led up to 1993. The Miss India contest became an annual event that drew the media and the public on a very large scale. Beauty finally gained an 'OK' from the connoisseurs and the market.

Another great bonus in my career was the opportunity to travel the whole world to learn from women of many countries and give them a glimpse of an Indian woman's life. I traveled to the UK, all countries in Europe, and exotic countries like the Fiji Islands, Venezuela, Yugoslavia, USSR, Japan, Maldives, Mauritius, the whole of USA, and many other countries. Being the editor of a successful magazine for women, I met game-changer celebrities like international orators, actors, writers, artists, Indian Prime Ministers – Indira Gandhi, Rajiv Gandhi and Atal Bihari Vajpayee – as well as the Shah and Shahbanoo of Iran. I also met some of India's great masters, among whom were Late Pandit Ravi Shankar, Pandit Jasraj, Late Sitara Devi, Late Pandit Bhimsen Joshi, Lata Mangeshkar, Late Homi Bhabha, Late M. F. Husain, Late S. H. Raza, Late Rajesh Khanna, Amitabh and Jaya Bachchan, Hema Malini, Late Dev Anand, Dilip Kumar, and scores of other luminaries, who added a little glitter and a soft glow to my life too.

Laugh Your Way to a Long Life

Humor is an essential part of our lives. As the editor of Femina, in 1975, I took a Fashion Show group to Bangkok, Singapore and Kuala Lumpur (KL) to promote Indian textiles. I had three models with me and we carried a tape of the music track as a spool. Since I was the organizer, the master tape and the copy were always with me.

On our way to the hall in Kuala Lumpur (KL), where the Indian High Commissioner to Malaysia was hosting the show, a male colleague, wanting to be kind, offered to carry my bag of tapes. Imagine my panic when I discovered that he had left it behind in the taxi, by mistake! Despite our herculean efforts to trace the taxi, we were unable to do so. Some quick thinking was required on our part, to carry off the show successfully. I went to the local drummers and convinced the *dholak* players to perform during the folk dance intervals in the show. We used the hotel's in-house music tracks for the model entries. As I sat at the console, signaling to the *dholak* players and the music system controller, I couldn't stop laughing at the situation because the audience enjoyed the show, without realizing that this was a stop-gap arrangement and not part of the regular show! The next day, we air-dashed a copy of the tape and carried on the show in other cities.

> In spite of one's planning and best efforts, unforeseen and even unpleasant incidents do occur in life. The important thing is to not spend time in a blame-game, but rather to focus on finding a solution.

From 'Working Woman' to 'Working for Women'

In the 70s, we were known as the astonishing all-woman group from India at several fashion fairs in Yugoslavia, Fiji, Senegal, and Australia, and got more publicity for being a woman-managed group than the groups from developed countries like France and Italy. The fashion show business is BIG today and there is much technology involved in conducting shows. Ours was, however, a callow but pioneering group that took the first steps in taking Indian designs and fabrics to many countries in dazzling shows. I am extremely proud of this achievement.

I was the Assistant Editor of Femina for 7 years and it's Editor for 20 years. The biggest challenge in my career was to convince the Indian society that 'women's liberation' was not a socially destructive movement for India. I can proudly say that I successfully turned the magazine into a movement for women's empowerment. As the editor of Femina, I was able to put the spotlight on Indian textiles, food, fashion, and lifestyle, which are an international rage today. I was able to create opportunities for women and to impress upon them that work, when done with dignity and pride, yields fabulous results. By the time I finished my stint at Femina, the magazine was selling brilliantly and earning fabulous ad revenue.

I am pleased that I chose Media as my profession. My work has given me everything I possess. I would not change my job or the way I 'lived' it, even if I am given an opportunity to do so today – except that I would bring it into the current era, where opportunities bear faster fruit. I used everything I learned to build my career – music, archaeology, culture, history, law, theatre, and many other things – to live a multi-channel life, and enjoyed my work. They say you should work as if you don't need the money. I admit, passion was enough to drive me.

> The biggest challenge in my career was to convince the Indian society that 'women's liberation' was not a socially destructive movement for India.

Rejuvenating Retirement

When I retired in the 90s, satellite TV, computer journalism, web writing, website building and information technology became the new tools and numerous opportunities came my way. In fact, I had more work and opportunities after retirement, than during my regular job! My generation had neither seen computers, nor had they learnt information technology in their schools or colleges. Although I did overcome this challenge, it made me realize that a scientific bent of mind is as necessary in life, as devotion to fine arts and literature!

I edited house magazines, wrote for innumerable publications and websites and started my own website too. I traveled to Iran, Sri Lanka, Britain, Ireland, and, of course, the whole of India as well, as the world became a closer community because of swift communication.

I am grateful that life gave me the opportunity to be 'mini-immortal' in a small way, by writing and doing the artistic direction and music design for two prestigious sound and light shows that are seen by thousands every year – one in the Somnath Temple in Gujarat, and the other on the banks of the Ganga in Haridwar. I can never forget the joy I felt while doing research for the script and the music. I also scripted a sound and light show for the Udaygiri/Khandgiri caves in Orissa.

In Retrospect

Meanwhile, both my son and daughter have made their careers in the UK and Ireland respectively. My four grandchildren were born over the years in those countries, and they were the bonus from my son and daughter to me!

I used almost all the opportunities offered to me by life. While I would have liked to devote more time to writing scripts, novels or stories, instead of doing daily journalism and newspaper stories, I feel I have done the best under the circumstances.

I have been a proud Indian throughout my life and always say that if God were to grant me one blessing, I would ask that all my countrymen have all the food they want, satisfying work, and a home to be proud of. This, I believe, is the key to removing the rich-poor divide and to bring down the caste and community barriers, which I think are artificial and based on false notions of superiority. Education should be the birthright of all Indians and I would create a system, which would deliver this to every child in our country. As a matter of fact, going back in time, I would devote more time from my busy career towards these objectives.

Rocks... Steady

Throughout this exciting journey of mine, there were three 'rocks' who stood by me steadfastly. The first is my father who was way ahead of the times and encouraged me to dream big, in an age when daughters were just expected to grow up and get married. The second is my maternal family, who did not put any conditions upon me and supported me at every step of my career. For instance, my Masi (mother's sister), who brought up my children, insisted that I go to Bangladesh during the 1971 war to report the sorrow of the women of that country, reassuring me that if something unfortunate were to happen, she would bring up the children. And last, but the most important, is my husband, who applauded every achievement of mine and supported me wholeheartedly through good and bad times. Without all these wonderful people who shared my dream with me, I would not have been able to do what I did, in an age when 'working woman' were almost derogatory words!

Life Lines

- The body is a vehicle that helps us achieve our goals. We should keep it in good condition with proper diet, exercise, and lifestyle.
- Women must learn to build their wealth and manage their finances. It is not enough to depend on the male members of the family for financial well-being.
- The past must never come in the way of the present or future. Compassion, love, and forgiveness cure all ills of life.
- Giving credit where it is due makes one feel light to go forward in life.
- Problems are to be solved through dialogue or actions. When they are unsolvable, one must take a 'bend in the river' and move on, just as water changes its course to overcome obstacles.
- Don't take life too seriously. A certain element of 'silliness' is also essential in life to make it enjoyable. My friends and I too shared such goals – walking up to the Valley of Flowers in the Himalayas within a fixed time frame; waking up at 3 am to listen to music or sitting by the Ganga in the freezing cold – all just for fun!

Words of Wisdom

I would pass on my experiences, rather than advice, to all of you. The courage to live 'out of the box' lives, to make one's own choices for the future, to have the right attitude towards one's family, and most importantly, to listen to one's heart while making decisions are some of the lessons which I have learnt. Also, it's important to respect others' hard work and appreciate their success without envy and ill will. Finally, having goodwill towards the world makes your skin glow and gives you excellent sleep.

In the end, I think my life is a mix of funny incidents, hurtful experiences, lovely memories, hard work, and outstanding success. When all these are strung together with a sense of balance, life becomes a complete experience!

2

Achieving Heights in HR with Humility & Harmony

Dr. T. V. Rao

Dear Sir,

Our association is for over 20 years and goes back to the time I started my corporate career. You have been a knowledge partner on the projects we worked together on, as well as a mentor for life. Besides being a pioneer on many topics in HR, the depth of your knowledge has given you an iconic stature. I truly admire your straightforwardness, humane approach, and above all, your humility in spite of all your accomplishments.

You embody the 'Human' and 'Resources' parts of the HR profession as a genuine 'Human Being.' This quality of yours makes you absolutely unique. You clearly 'walk the talk' and 'practise before you preach/teach.'

There's just so much to learn from you and integrate into our personal and professional lives. Truly admirable!

Yours Affectionately,
Aparna

About Dr. T. V. Rao...

Dr. T. V. Rao is a teacher, social entrepreneur, and institution builder. Considered one of the Fathers of HRD (Human Resource Development) in India, his contribution to HRD spans over four decades. Born in rural India and brought up by his mother and grandparents, he completed B.Sc. (graduation) from Andhra Loyola College, B.Ed. from Regional College of Education, Mysore, M.A. in Psychology from Osmania University, and Ph.D from Sardar Patel University. He started the Departments of Psychology at Andhra and Udaipur Universities and the Education & Training Department at the National Institute of Health Administration & Education, New Delhi.

Dr. Rao has worked as Visiting Faculty at the Indian School of Business (ISB), Hyderabad and as HRD Advisor to the Reserve Bank of India. He assisted the Administrative Reforms Commission in reviewing the personnel management practices for civil services, and also served as member of the HRM (Human Resource Management) Review Committee of Public Sector Banks set up by the Ministry of Finance in 2009-2010. Dr. Rao worked as a short-term consultant to UNESCO, Bangkok; USAID Indonesia for the Ministry of Health, Indonesia; NERDA, Malaysia; FAO Rome; and the Commonwealth Secretariat, London.

He joined IIM-A (Indian Institute of Management-Ahmedabad) in 1973 and taught there until 1994 as a full-time Professor and subsequently until 2014 as Visiting Professor. While at IIM-A, he chaired the Post Graduate and Doctoral Programs, Public Systems Group, and the Ravi Matthai Centre for Educational Innovations.

He has so far taught several thousands of students, executives, CEOs and institution builders on self-leadership, personal and managerial effectiveness, interpersonal competence, entrepreneurship, performance management, and HRD. He has assisted over a 100 organizations in implementing his thoughts and designs in utilizing and developing human potential. He believes that we are all born talented and we can make an impact by drawing the best in us by helping others. With this belief, Dr. Rao founded the National HRD Network and the Academy of HRD, which are now renowned institutions in the field of Human Resources.

He has authored around 60 books including 'Managers Who Make a Difference'. He is the honored recipient of several awards from various professional bodies and institutions for his outstanding contributions in HRD, the latest being the Ravi Matthai Fellow Award by the Association of Indian Management Schools. He set up TVRLS (T.V. Rao Learning Systems Pvt. Ltd.), a research based consulting company in 1996, of which he is currently the Chairman. He is a member of the IIM-A Society and part of the Board of Governors.

"Human Resources is a philosophy and a way of life. It is not merely systems and processes. It is learning and developing oneself and others." – Dr. T.V. Rao

Childhood Challenges

When I was young, I used to feel that my life was almost like a Bollywood movie. My mother came from a family of daily wage laborers and palm tree trimmers (Gowda community). My grandfather barely earned enough for having three meals a day. My mother was so beautiful that she had offers to join films. However, she never did so due to the social taboos in the early 1940s.

A handsome, young, and rich man from another community (Choudhury or Kamma) in the village fell in love with her and they got married secretly. After I was born, my father was forcibly brought back to the village by his community and they married him to another rich woman from his community. After this, my mother returned to my village and was immediately married off to an old man. Apparently, she never lived with him and decided to stay with my grandfather in the same village where my biological father lived. Many people suggested that she take legal action against him.

However, she refused and brought me up on her own. Although she was not educated herself, she went through tough times and struggled to get me educated. She played multiple roles in her life. She was first a daily wage laborer in the fields and then went on to become their leader. She then became an Ayurvedic practitioner, later a rice merchant and finally, she joined politics and even became the General Secretary of Andhra Pradesh Mahila Congress before she passed away in 2003. My mother's story demonstrates her hidden talent and the resilience of Indian women. She had a great entrepreneurial spirit, was continuously active, and an epitome of love and determination.

> From a very young age, I understood that you can learn from everything that happens to you. While my mother taught me how one should take things in one's stride and do the best one can, from my father I learnt how not to treat someone who loves you.

Engaging Education

I skipped studying in a primary school, went for tuitions, and got admitted directly into the sixth standard when I was just eight years old. I continued my studies and did reasonably well to get admission to Andhra Loyola College (ALC), Vijayawada for P.U.C. (Pre-University Course equivalent to Class 12) and then, B.Sc., 16 kilometers away from my village. My life at ALC from 1961 to 1965 was filled with guidance and mentoring from my teachers. I was only 14 when I joined the college to do my Pre-University Course and 18 when I graduated with Mathematics, Physics, and Chemistry.

Although I wanted to do my Masters in Chemistry, Rev. Fr. Douglas Gordon, the Principal of ALC guided me and prompted me to do B.Ed at the Regional College of Education, Mysore (RCEM). This program was started in collaboration with the Ohio State University by NCERT (National Council for Educational Research and Training). Fr. Gordon told me, "Apply for this course, and come back after completing it. I will appoint you as a demonstrator in the Chemistry laboratory, and then you can apply for M.Sc. Chemistry, as you are too young to do M.Sc. now."

> Teaching, disseminating knowledge and guiding the youth are noble and satisfying professions. Not only do we grow, but we also contribute to the growth of others.

After appearing in the selection tests and an interview, I got admission in RCEM. I was again the youngest of the lot, as almost all students were already working as teachers and some were post-graduates.

> Age has nothing to do with knowledge or capability. The urge to learn is the most important factor for your success.

Passion for Psychology

Professor Dr. Prafullachandra Dave (P. N. Dave) had come to RCEM that year after studying at St. Louis, USA. He taught us 'Psychological Foundations of Education' in a very interesting manner. He would get rats into the class and teach us how they learn to reach food in a maze. He also gave us many psychological tests. I constantly topped in the Psychology class. I finished my one year B.Ed and topped the RCEM Science stream. When the results were declared, I went to meet Dr. Dave. He asked me about my plans. I told him that there were already people from the village asking if I would join their school to teach, but that I preferred to join Loyola College as a Demonstrator in Chemistry and apply for a M.Sc. a year later.

To my surprise, Dr. Dave advised me that I shouldn't take up Chemistry, as I had a special aptitude for Psychology. He suggested that I do my Masters in Psychology. In those days, one needed a B.A. in Psychology even to apply for an M.A. I told Dr. Dave that no one would accept me for M.A. Psychology as I didn't have a Bachelors degree in Psychology. But Dr. Dave knew that this was the right path for me. Not one to give up, he said he knew a professor of Psychology at the Osmania University in Hyderabad, and as RCEM was an experimental college with an unusual syllabus, the Professor might agree to treat it as equivalent to B.A. Psychology. He wrote a personal letter and told me give it to the Professor at Hyderabad.

> Many people can teach, but it takes a guru to direct a pupil towards his true calling.

What happened next was exactly what Dr. Dave had hoped for. Dr. E. G. Parameswaran (EGP) was the HOD in the department of Psychology in Osmania University. He admitted me without hesitation after reading Dr. Dave's letter. In the Psychology Department, we were a like a family. Shalini Bhogle (popular commentator Harsha Bhogle's mother), was our senior. I topped the University and even created a new record. EGP encouraged me to apply for a Ph.D in the US and work with Dr. Udai Pareek, who was, at that time, working in the University of North Carolina. While I was corresponding with Dr. Udai Pareek and others to try for my admission in the USA, the Andhra University (AU) was opening a department of Psychology and Parapsychology and was looking for lecturers. EGP suggested that I join the Andhra University to develop the department until I got admission for Ph.D. He wrote to Dr. Ramakrishna Rao (RKR), who was heading the Psychology department in AU, recommending me.

Teaching Tales

Impressed by my academic record, Dr. Ramakrishna Rao (RKR), without hesitation, offered me a position as an Assistant Lecturer on an ad-hoc basis and said that he would get it regularized once the appointments were announced. He decided to pay me from his Parapsychology Fund until then. Parapsychology dealt with paranormal phenomena like telepathy and clairvoyance. I registered for my Ph.D to work on 'Dreams' at AU, with Dr. Ramakrishna Rao as my guide. RKR even got special equipment from Germany to study dreams using tachistoscopic exposure of certain stimuli. He gave me all the freedom to design and start the M.A. Psychology course in AU. Within six months of my joining AU, I came to know that Dr. Udai Pareek was returning to India to work in Delhi. I decided to go to Delhi and work with him as I had my share of discomfort with Parapsychology in which AU was beginning to specialize.

Dr. Udai Pareek was a social scientist, an institution builder, author, researcher, and a great human being. He turned into a friend, philosopher, and guide in the later years. A few months after he recruited me to work with him as an Assistant Research Officer, we came to know that the National Institute of Health Administration and Education at Delhi (NIHAE) was looking to recruit an Assistant Professor of Education and Training –

someone with three years' experience and a background of B.Ed. Although I did not qualify in terms of experience as I only had a year's, Dr. Pareek thought me well suited for the post. Perhaps he was impressed with my hard work or the unusual combination of B.Sc., B.Ed, and M.A. Psychology.

The selection committee of the Ministry of Health was then chaired by the celebrated Dr. Ramalingaswamy. Dr. Pareek drove to his residence and handed over my bio-data, enabling me to be called as a contact candidate – a provision available in those days for appointments in the Government for those who did not exactly meet criteria but were considered suitable by the selection committee. This was the fourth time that one of my mentors had guided me towards the right path.

> If one is hardworking and committed to one's work, one automatically reaches one's chosen path.

I was selected and appointed as Assistant Professor of Education and Training in 1969 by NIHAE. This coincided with my marriage, and my wife Jaya, since then, has been a lifelong companion and has supported all my subsequent endeavors. Dr. Pareek also asked me to co-author some of the books he was writing and initiated me into a lot of the activities he was involved in. We partnered on many books and worked together in Delhi, Udaipur, Ahmedabad, Indonesia, and back in Jaipur as long as he lived, i.e., until 2010.

Initiation at IIM-A

Ravi Matthai (RJM), whom I met in 1973, a year after he stepped down as Director of IIM-A, wanted to work with education and other sectors to professionalize their management. I was writing a book with Dr. Pareek on 'A Status Study of Behavioral Science Research in Population' to be published by Tata McGraw-Hill and sponsored by the Family Planning Foundation (of the Tata's). Dr. Pareek joined IIM-A as a Professor in early 1972 and I joined him in Ahmedabad to complete the book in the summer of 1973. At

Dr. Pareek's suggestion, I expressed my interest in joining IIM-A as they were planning to start work on Education Systems with Ravi Matthai as the focal point. Ninety percent of the faculty at IIM-A at that time had Ph.Ds from abroad while I had completed my Ph.D from Sardar Patel University, for which I worked from NIHAE as a part-time student. I didn't think IIM-A would be interested in an Indian Ph.D.

I met Ravi, then Samuel Paul and Dwijendra Tripathi who were at that time, respectively, the Director and Dean of IIM-A. Our discussion largely focused on my Doctoral thesis, which was on medical education. I jokingly said that in the thesis I had proved that medical colleges spoil medical students. We also had an intense discussion on college climate and how it affects student values.

I was selected, and thus, my long sojourn with IIM-A started in December 1973. Joining IIM-A and working with Ravi Matthai and professors with degrees from famous US universities were the most significant events in my life.

Ravi's advice was, 'Always keep your gun loaded so that you have the choice whether to fire it or not' – meaning, equip yourself with knowledge at every possible opportunity. He believed there is nothing like a menial job. He used to drive a truck from Ahmedabad to Jawaja in Rajasthan himself and transport villagers and all of us from one place to another, stay in villages, eat food he had never eaten before and learned to apply management in sectors that we had never worked with. Whenever I was unhappy with any of my colleagues at IIM-A, Ravi would advise me, "Remember T.V., all are God's children." From Ravi, I learnt an important lesson.

> All professions are good, and all jobs can be made great. It depends on you. You can achieve marvels anywhere and make a difference to yourself and others.

Distinctive Work with Dr. David McClelland

The first project I was involved in at IIM-A in 1973-74 was evaluating the Entrepreneurial Development Programs (EDPs) in Gujarat. A large number of EDPs were conducted in Gujarat using Dr. David McClelland's achievement motivation and entrepreneurship models. We evaluated the value addition of the Behavioural Science components in these programs. When I was presenting a paper at a seminar at the India International Center, New Delhi, Dr. David McClelland (a renowned American psychologist from Harvard University) happened to be in town and attended my presentation. He invited me to collaborate with him as a short-term Research Associate at Harvard University to work on a new tool on 'Psycho-social maturity' that he was developing. Working with him and his associate Abigail Stewart to develop the Stewart Maturity Scale and subsequently, on a collaborative project at IIM-A, was a great learning. I owe a lot of my later work on Leadership styles and the 360 Degree Feedback tools to Dr. McClelland's work and the Stewart Maturity Scale. A lot of Daniel Goleman's (a well-known psychologist and author) work on Emotional Intelligence is based on the psycho-social maturity concepts of Dr. McClelland and Abigail Stewart. I conceptualized three leadership styles commonly seen in India (Benevolent, Critical, and Development) on the basis of this work and developed tools to measure leadership styles of Health and Educational Administrators besides corporate sector executives. These later become popular tools in the 360 Degree Feedback as well.

Encouraging Entrepreneurship

Around the time I was working with Dr. McClelland, I was invited by East-West Center (EWC) Hawaii, for a workshop on Entrepreneurship. During the three weeks of my stay at EWC, I made friends with a number of scholars from Malaysia, Indonesia, and the Philippines. During this workshop, we conceptualized an Entrepreneurship Development Organization (ENDEVOR). My Malaysian friends later converted it into the National Entrepreneurial Development Association (NERDA) and initiated a number of Entrepreneurial Development activities in Malaysia. This body was supported by the then Deputy Prime Minister of Malaysia, Dr. Mahathir Mohamad and remained active until the Government of Malaysia took charge of promoting entrepreneurship in a big way in Malaysia. With the help of NERDA, we introduced EDPs at various institutions in Malaysia between 1976 and 1980.

Evolution at IIM-A

IIM-A was a great platform to learn, write, teach, research, manage, influence, and earn. As a result of a consulting project undertaken through IIM-A, we started the first Human Resources Development department in 1974-75 in Larsen & Toubro (L&T) and created history in HRD. We started many courses and made HRD popular. We started a course on Laboratory in Entrepreneurship and laid the path for subsequent development of entrepreneurs in IIM-A. I started the National HRD Network (NHRDN) in 1985, which is a popular professional body in India, and invented a methodology for developing leaders, which became popular as '360 Degree Feedback' as named by the American scholars in the 1990s.

I enjoyed the IIM-A professorship, both full-time and later as Adjunct Professor or Visiting Professor. It gave me immense pleasure to design new courses, new programs, test them out, offer them to students and executives, and influence their thoughts. I still cherish the freedom and self-regulation, excellent colleagues to work with, mutual respect, and collegiate culture with first name basis at IIM-A. I found OCTAPACE (Openness, Collaboration, Trust, Authenticity, Pro-action, Autonomy, Confrontation and Experimentation) values in full operation at IIM-A.

Contributions and Concepts

My work with Ravi and Dr. Pareek provided me with rich experience, and I feel that they have a major role as mentors in many of my accomplishments. If someone asks me what my important contributions in the last four decades are, my answer would be my writings. This includes my books, articles, and talks reproduced in the form of articles. They are reflections of my thoughts, ideas, philosophies, actions, beliefs, values, experiences, and a lot more, including sometimes, my life itself. Some of my writings are not entirely my own; they are products of shared thoughts, ideas, opinions, models, and conceptualizations along with a few others with whom I interacted, worked, learnt, and articulated.

I have over 60 books – some edited, co-edited, authored, and co-authored. Some are research reports, text books, and new conceptualizations in various fields: entrepreneurship, education, health and population, psychology, and human resources development.

Each book is a product, and writing a book is like making a movie. It varies from a few months to a few years of work including thought, gathering of knowledge, writing, testing, and final production, including release and launch. I am very proud of my books as many people have told me that they have been positively impacted by them. Most impactful among them in my view include Effective People (Random House India, 2015), Managers who Make a Difference (IIM-Ahmedabad Business Books, Random House India, 2010, 2016), Hurconomics for Talent Management (Pearson Education, 2011), 100 Managers in Action (Tata McGraw-Hill, 2012 with Charu Sharma), Future of HRD (Macmillan, 2003), HRD Audit (Sage, 1999, 2015), The Power of 360 Degree Feedback (Sage, 2005 and 2014 with Raju Rao), HRD Score Card 2500 (Sage, 2008), HRD Missionary (Oxford & IBH, TVRLS 1990, 2010), Designing and Managing HR Systems (with

Dr. Udai Pareek, 1982, 2003), Performance Management (Sage, 2004, 2016), Pioneering HR System in L&T (AHRD), Nurturing Excellence: IIMA (with Vijaya Sherry Chand, Macmillan, 2010), Human Resources Development: Experiences, Interventions, Strategies (Sage, 1996).

Each book has a story, a meaning, and a definite contribution to the body of thought and knowledge in that field. The timing of each book has a story behind it. For example, the first HRD book, 'Designing and Managing Human Resource Systems' was written in 1978 after my experience in Bharat Earth Movers Limited in implementing HRD. We first tested it out in a workshop at IIM-A in 1979. Dr. Pareek wrote the conceptual part and the first three chapters and I wrote the experience part of it and we shared the rest. It was meant to give the right direction to the new HR Function. It was first published in 1982 and won the ESCORTS award as the Best Management book by All India Management Association (AIMA) and went through one revision every decade. It became a text book to introduce HRD and HR in many institutions.

Almost every book is an outcome of serious thought sharing, application, and finally, a reflective production. Also, quite a few of my books in HRD are emotional outcomes and even outbursts out of my observation of the wrong use of HRD or wrong understanding or incorrect interpretation.

> Thoughts and ideas are for sharing. If I have an idea or a thought, I am restless until I share it with others. I share it, talk, give speeches and get it further reinforced and then write to make it a paper, or eventually, a book. I do not copyright my ideas and therefore, many of my ideas get copied and presented as someone else's. I feel happy if someone acknowledges my ideas and, of course, feel equally happy if someone uses them and they get accepted even without acknowledgement.

Innovative Initiatives

I was also blessed to have undertaken many innovative initiatives. One such initiative was the first program designed and offered at IIM-A in 1986, on 'Leadership Styles and Organizational Excellence.' The special attribute of this program was that it required the top-level managers to register three months in advance and give us a list of those who worked with them and whose views they valued. The program was run very successfully. Subsequently, this methodology got to be known as '360 Degree Feedback Methodology.' The design that we had evolved in 1986 is by and large, the same design of leadership development that the Hay Group and many others use. They have evolved it on their own, and so have we, and it is surprising that the rationale, the thought and the methods are similar.

The second was the concept of 'HRD Network' and the building of NHRDN and Academy of Human Resource Development (AHRD) in the last 20 to 30 years. There are many innovations in these institutions. We undertook many innovative practices to popularize a lesser known 'HRD Network.' For example, we got the newsletter sponsored by corporates (like L&T, State Bank of Patiala, Indian Oil, Hindustan Petroleum Limited-HPCL or Sundaram Clayton or Materials and Minerals Trading Corporation-MMTC) and got their HRD practice profiles published, printed 2000 copies, and mailed it to all possible HRD managers and CEOs free of cost. The costs of printing and mailing were met by the sponsor and the inputs by HR professionals and academicians were free. The newsletter was run for several years by the Center for HRD (CHRD) at XLRI and later, by the NHRDN. We created the concept of 'Member Honoris Causa' and many CEOs became members of NHRDN.

There was no membership fee when we started NHRDN for the first two years. Neither were there any entry restrictions. For example, even secretarial staff became members. Our argument was that HRD is for all and the body will have anyone interested as a member.

In AHRD, we had two innovative programs. The Diploma in HRD offered by AHRD in the early 90s had an innovative methodology of the candidate having to apply the knowledge after learning each concept and writing a review of the practice followed at his/her company. This built a strong database at AHRD and also got the candidate's companies involved. For example, those candidates learning about the significance of induction had to send a review paper reviewing their own induction program and suggesting improvements and were even required to share these with their bosses.

Similarly, the doctoral program using an eight-week compulsory course work along with a series of papers and thesis was an innovation. I was struck by this idea when I was on the Planning Board of the Indira Gandhi National Open University (IGNOU) in the mid-eighties. I suggested to the first Vice Chancellor of IGNOU, Dr. Rami Reddy that managers were sitting on bundles of data and if only we could help them learn research methods, those who were already post-graduates could use the data and come up with many research findings and revolutionize the field of management research.

Once we started the program, in the first 7 to 8 years, there were over a 100 students who registered and about 25 students who completed their Doctoral fellow program and went on to become CEOs, faculty of IIMs, IITs, XLRI etc.

Unfortunate Failures

When an infrastructure facility is committed to an institution and the institution is moved from one city to another and then the commitment cannot be honored for some reason, it shatters not only the people behind the institution but also the institution itself. And if this happens in the early stages of the institution, it is the worst thing that can happen. The people involved lose the initial enthusiasm and face turmoil on various fronts. This is what happened to AHRD. There were not one, but a series of mishaps and unfulfilled promises. As a result, AHRD was never the same as it was originally meant to be. When land was bought to establish the Mudra Institute of Communications (MICA) at Ahmedabad, we rushed to buy the neighboring land. However, the price had increased several times and we could not afford it.

Subsequently, an industrialist promised us some land in a hilly region outside Hyderabad, closer to what is known as the Ramoji Film City today. We got him on board, visited the hills, and were planning to shift AHRD from Ahmedabad to Hyderabad. But while we were doing so, he put conditions like, we should complete the construction of the building and the campus within the year, get the PM to inaugurate etc. There was no way we could do it. He wanted to use AHRD to make plots and develop his property. This was a painful discovery.

At this time, another industrialist came to our rescue and promptly donated land. However, even he withdrew after we shifted, forcing us to invest in a small piece of land. This land also got into legal disputes. Finally, we had to shift AHRD back to Ahmedabad.

> Land and infrastructure need to be ensured first before you start any institution. You need the support of a good industrialist or a philanthropist to build institutions. Academicians have serious limitations in building institutions.

Missed Missions

I wanted to globalize the HRD Network. The mission was to spread the philosophy of HRD. We had the talent and opportunity. There should have been NHRDN in Sri Lanka, Malaysia, Indonesia, Philippines, China, Japan, Vietnam, Thailand etc. Eastern countries are already aligned with the HR philosophy. We were only trying to take this philosophy into the corporate life and influence the organized sector.

> After all, what is HR philosophy? Sow your own seeds and grow yourself by creating an environment for growth. Self-development is the best and facilitators and gurus help you to recognize your talent and use it for the benefit of yourself and society.

The dream was to make CHRD at XLRI, a center for learning in HRD across India, and to make AHRD a place where most people across Asia could come and spend time learning and teaching their own philosophy of HR. So, globalizing the HR network was possible. However, circumstances and the people who mattered had a different vision. It was partly my failure that I didn't push these institutions to think in this direction. Thus, my dream remained a dream.

> Howsoever committed and powerful you may be in relation to a cause, there are always others who are more powerful than you with their own visions, agendas, and commitments. At times, one has to be prepared to be a mere co-traveler than an influencer and change agent.

Exit IIM-A

After completing 20 years at IIM-A in 1993, I felt that my life had become predictable and routine. I wanted to do something different; however, I did not have the slightest idea what that would be. I was confident that I wouldn't have any problem earning my living, as I had been assisting many companies in designing, auditing, and establishing HR Departments or in PMS (Performance Management System). The day I got my twenty-year service medal, I announced that this signaled that I should do something different. That is when I sent my resignation and the course of events that followed was not predictable in any way. Many thought that I would shift to Hyderabad. However, the next two years were busy stabilizing the AHRD as an honorary

Director, while simultaneously earning my living. I decided not to take salary for the work I did for the AHRD as I was a 'Trustee.'

> I strongly feel that Trustees should not expect to get a salary; rather, they should donate their time for the benefit of the institution and build it up.

T.V. Rao Learning Systems Pvt. Ltd. (TVRLS)

I started TVRLS, my own consulting firm in 1996. This was more of an accident. Never in my life did I have any dream of starting a consulting firm. Although I am more of a research author, I think that I might have got this entrepreneurial streak from my mother. Another contributing factor would be McClelland's achievement motivation concepts and entrepreneurial thinking. Perhaps, they suited my background and aspirations.

TVRLS is a research-based consulting firm that was started to promote the best HR practices in the industry, with a view to facilitate talent discovery and its development at individual and organizational levels. With Talent Management and Organization Development as focus areas, TVRLS offers various industries, tools such as PMS, Competency Mapping, 360 Degree Feedback, Psychometric Testing, and many others.

Although people perceive entrepreneurs as money-makers, making money is not the only objective of TVRLS. Once my company became well-known, I had lucrative offers to sell it and make money. However, I refused to do so as I knew that once it was sold, it would no longer do what it had been started for.

Becoming an entrepreneur gave me the freedom to use my time and resources the way I thought best. Now that I was not tied down to a job, I could freely use my time to further the causes that I felt were priority, which would have been impossible in a regular job. For instance, no institute can promote only one methodology. However, in the past 20 years, TVRLS has worked with over twenty thousand people for '360 Degree Feedback' and made a huge difference. I have also been able to devote time towards disseminating knowledge through my books. I have written many more books after I became an entrepreneur – to the extent of writing a book almost every year.

HR is all about making a difference, and through TVRLS, I believe that I have been able to contribute in my own little way towards making that difference!

In Retrospect

As I look back, I feel that the contributors to my success are – the people around me – my mother, teachers and well-wishers who encouraged and guided me, my own hard work, drive, ambition, commitment to all that I got involved in, be it education systems, entrepreneurship, consultancy, health and population, or any field, and my desire to share knowledge.

Life Lines
- Document your experiences and your points of view. This is what you can leave behind for the next generation.
- Learn from others – your seniors, juniors, colleagues, strangers, competitors, and collaborators. Everyone can teach you something.
- No one is small, and every small will be big; if not today, then tomorrow. Respect the smallest of all. 'Do unto others as you would like them to do to you.'
- OCTAPACE (Openness, Collaboration, Trust, Authenticity, Pro-action, Autonomy, Confrontation and Experimentation) values are the most important. If every person is honest, transparent, proactive, trusting and trustworthy, and has a positive outlook, the world will be a great place to live. We all have the responsibility to make it so.
- Hard work and sincerity always pay in the long run.

- Give your views, but don't waste your time criticizing others. Leave it to them once you speak your mind.
- Learn to enjoy every moment that you have with your family as they are a great source of unacknowledged support for all your work and accomplishments.

> *Words of Wisdom*
>
> *There are no limits to growth. When you share, you grow. Share your ideas, experiences, thoughts, problems, solutions, and all that you have and lay the path for your growth. By listening, you learn. Listen to others – friends, colleagues, strangers, people you like, and even those whom you may not and gain from their thoughts. You are creating milestones in your own life to grow. Besides, you may be creating a turning point in someone else's life. Best wishes for your journey!*

3

The Endearing Educationist

Dr. Faiqa Saulat Khan

Dear Faiqa,

You are a true champion! A woman of substance, you are full of life, exuberating warmth and affection. I wonder how you manage to be so positive in everything you do and maintain the poise and grace of an elegant self, in the most turbulent times!

You are the strongest pillar of support for all your near and dear ones including me, and yet, never let anyone worry about your own struggles. You are like a candle that brings light into the lives of others, dispelling darkness and bringing hope.

I am so proud that you have carved a niche for yourself through perseverance and persistence and inspire everyone who comes in contact with you to excel in life. You leave no stone unturned to do your best. You walk the talk and are an angel at heart.

You truly are my inseparable soul-sister!

Yours Affectionately,
Aparna

About Dr. Faiqa Saulat Khan...

Dr. Faiqa Saulat Khan is a well-known name in the field of education. With an M.A. and Ph.D in History and numerous national awards to her credit, she is credited with introducing many novel techniques in the educational field, at times when such concepts were unheard of. Her stellar contribution to the field of education has helped shaped many young lives. As the Founder and Director of Trailblazer's International School, she has ensured that students are provided with holistic growth, integrated and experiential learning so as to prepare generations of responsible and happy people that balance material success with humane values. Not one to rest on her laurels, she constantly endeavors to bring in innovation to enhance the quality of teaching and make a positive difference to the education system.

"Strive to always give your best, and God will take care of the rest."
— Dr. Faiqa Saulat Khan

Initial Influences

The eldest of three sisters, I was born into a conservative *jagirdar* family from Bhopal. My sisters and I inherited a rich heritage from both, my father's as well as my mother's families. I was deeply influenced by my maternal as well as paternal grandmother.

My maternal grandfather was the Nawab of Porla, a town near Nagpur. My maternal grandmother, the Begum of Porla, like most grandmothers, would tell us stories that would transport us into the world of fantasy. She was an absolute no-nonsense person and a woman of grit. Widowed at a young age, with six children to look after, she managed to educate her children well, all on her own. It was she who took all the important decisions in the family. She always advised us to carry ourselves well. She taught us that we must strive to be unique. She would say, "The cows and the sheep all walk in herds. But the tiger always walks alone. *Sher bano. Tum mein sher ka dil hona chahiye!*" She cheered us to be on the right path and be honest and truthful always.

From my paternal grandmother Shehzadi Amna Sultan, I learned the equally important lessons of humility. *"Jitne bade bano, utna jhuko. Jo nahin jhukte, woh toot jate hain!"*, she would say. She often gave us the example that trees that are laden with fruit are the ones which are bent the most. Only by being humble can one remain grounded. She, too, was a strong woman in her own right. She was a cousin of the last Nawab of Bhopal. She was actively involved in her family business, loved social work, and inculcated positive values in her family. Thus, from a young age itself, I learnt that one had to be strong, independent, yet humble and be able to hold one's own in life.

A lot of our family friends were IAS officers and I was influenced by them too. One of these, Shri A.V. Singh, retired as the Chief Secretary of Madhya Pradesh. His wife, Kiran Vijay Singh, was the Additional Secretary of MP. Both of them created a deep impression on me and helped shape my views. It was as a result of this influence that I started nurturing the dream of becoming an IAS officer. I was ambitious, and like them, I wanted to serve my country.

Destiny Diverts

It is said, 'Man proposes, God disposes.' This is exactly what happened to my IAS dreams. Destiny had something else in store for me. When I was in the 11th standard, at an age when most students plan their further studies, I was engaged to be married. This was an arranged marriage. The marriage was to be held immediately the next year, once I turned 18.

This took the wind out of my sails. I was really upset and did not want to get married so soon, but was compelled to agree owing to family pressure. Thus, in 1991, I was married off after I completed my Class 12 exams and turned 18. I thought I would not be able to even continue my education, leave alone appear for the IAS. Although my father-in-law encouraged me to continue my studies, he was of the firm opinion that I should not appear for the IAS as it was a demanding career and one that would involve routine transfers.

Once more, I was totally disillusioned! My long-cherished dream, for which I had been preparing since Class 8, was shattered. I internally fumed at the thought that though capable of doing so, I would not be able to pursue my dreams. The fact that someone else could thus control my future was a rude shock for me. However, I was determined not to give up hope so easily. I accepted the situation, while nursing the thought that I might eventually take up IAS studies after graduation.

However, the Mandal Commission was introduced at that time, and my IAS hopes went down the drain. The temporary suspension of the IAS exams, the uncertainty and large-scale self-immolation by students was very demotivating. Fate had dealt me another cruel hand. This setback to my dreams was very frustrating. I saw my life stretching out before me, meaningless and without any purpose. I had never imagined myself doing anything other than

IAS. After much inner turmoil, however, I finally decided to make peace with my fate. I accepted the situation and decided to move on and completed my graduation in 1994 from Maharani Laxmibai College in Bhopal.

> Life is a journey and not a destination. It can't be bound to just one goal, one place, one person, or one dream. Even if you don't achieve your most important goal or dream, you have to still keep moving ahead and find others.

Chance Calling

After my post-graduation, the Principal of my college recommended my name for the opening of a Lecturer in History at the Government College of Excellence, to teach History in the Hindi language, as I had topped the University. Since I had always been interested in History as a subject, I took up the offer. However, as I discovered that it was not possible for me to teach History in Hindi, this proved to be short-lived, and after teaching for a few months, I gave it up.

> When you realize that you can't do justice to a particular task in spite of all your efforts, it's time to reassess whether you are the right person for the job.

When I was a student at St. Joseph Convent School, Sister Francis Joseph had been the Principal as well as my English teacher in the 11th and 12th classes. It was she who taught me debating, due to which I won many prizes in debate competitions. This was a skill that really helped build my confidence. Being able to confidently put across one's viewpoint in the face of opposing views is an essential requirement in today's world. It also requires one to think about a subject comprehensively and formulate one's thoughts clearly, rather than rashly putting forward half-baked opinions. These skills have stood me in good stead throughout my career and personal life as well. In 1996, Sister Francis Joseph called me and told me that she needed someone trustworthy to work with her and I accepted her offer. Thus, it came about that in October 1996, I joined my alma mater as the class teacher of the 5th class.

I was very excited to work as an educator in my own alma mater, and it was no surprise that I absolutely loved my job. Somewhere, I felt assured that this was my calling, and felt compelled to give my best at all levels of teaching assigned to me.

Role Reversal & Realizations

This role put me on the other side of the table. When I sat in the teacher's chair, I realized that traditional teaching methods and techniques could not be used to teach the students of today. I could relate to the students, who went through their entire school life learning Physics, Mathematics, and other seemingly important subjects, without a clue as to why they were doing so. This was because the focus was on rote learning and scoring marks, rather than on understanding and application of the subject. Besides, technology had started spreading its wings. Students were becoming more and more tech-savvy, while the teachers shied away from it, leading to an increasing generation gap. There was a pressing need to use technology like computers to engage the students.

I decided that I would address this lacuna by improving the techniques used for teaching. Children, by their very nature, find studying a mechanical and boring activity. I have always felt that it is the responsibility of the teacher to make studies interesting for students.

This was the turning point in my life. There was no looking back now. I got down to work with enthusiasm and passion. However, I also realized that knowledge of proper teaching methods was essential in order to improve my teaching skills. Sister Francis also made it mandatory for the school teachers to be qualified as Bachelor of Education (B.Ed). So, while still working, I enrolled for and completed my B.Ed in 1997, in Social Studies and English

Literature. I also enrolled for a Ph.D in History. I continued my work in full swing at the school.

Occupational Opportunities

The year 2003 was a year of numerous happy tidings for me. I completed my Ph.D, while continuing my career. Dr. Mrs. Rita Noronha, who was a Professor of History at the Government Girl's Nutan College, was my guide. The subject of my thesis was, 'The History of Bhopal, Nawab Shahjahan Begum and her times – 1845-1901.' This was a golden age in the history of Bhopal. There had been four female rulers in Bhopal under the British rule, who had done a lot of work for the empowerment of women and the abolishment of the 'purdah' system. Being able to bring out the achievements of these women and the contribution of Bhopal gave me a feeling of pride. Many among us may not be aware of the fact that Bhopal has the distinction of being the first city to have a Post and Telegraph. Besides this, one of the Begums of Bhopal was the first Chancellor of the Aligarh University.

This was also the year when I became the HOD of the Social Science Department. I set up a Social Science Lab, which was welcomed by the students. I also started organizing Career Fests that would give students an idea of the various career options they had in Social Sciences.

During the same time, I also got many opportunities to participate in programs that helped me develop my skills as a teacher. The NCERT, in collaboration with the Commonwealth of Learning, Canada, had organized a pilot course in Career Counseling. This was an International Diploma in Guidance and Counseling, and was to be conducted at the Regional Institute of Education, Bhopal. I was lucky to be among those selected for the program. Here, we learnt to handle various challenges the students faced and to act as career counselors, guiding them in their career selection, based on their skills and abilities. On the successful completion of the program, I decided to organize Career Fairs that would give students an idea of the various fields that they could take up as a profession. Luckily, I was encouraged by the Principal of our school in implementing this novel idea. Today, we have numerous career fairs and aptitude tests, but during those times, there was a lack of such guidance where students could get knowledge about and explore occupations besides the standard ones like becoming doctors or engineers. I wanted to change this. According to me, one needs to find out what one's strengths and weaknesses are and where one's interests lie, and choose a career path considering all the above, rather than just beating the well-trodden path out of peer pressure or due to monetary considerations.

> I believe in the saying by Confucius, "Choose a job you love and you will never have to work a day in your life." Steve Jobs, too, has said, "Your work is going to fill a large part of your life, and the only way to be truly satisfied is to do what you believe is great work. And the only way to do great work is to love what you do."

Remarkable Recognitions

During my childhood days, I had learnt shooting from my father. I had been influenced by the story of Arjuna from the 'Mahabharata', who, during an archery competition, when asked by his guru as to what he could see of the target, replied that he was able to only see the eye of the bird that was to be hit. Shooting helped me develop a razor sharp focus and I won many prizes at various shooting competitions, the latest being the Arjun Singh Memorial Cup Championship in 2015 in the Ladies category. This focus had extended to the other parts of my life as well, and was responsible for my success. Whenever I decided on a goal, I would ignore all obstacles and focus only on the end result that was to be achieved.

I received my first award as an Educator in 2007, while teaching the 10th, 11th and 12th classes as the Head of the Department

(HOD). I had identified that although the students did well in other subjects, the History curriculum of the 10th class included a chapter on identifying national monuments, in which the students, even brilliant ones, were unable to score marks. I was determined to change this scenario. The standard methods of teaching were not helping.

> As a teacher, I realized that I needed to adopt a different, proactive approach that would make the subject interesting and engage the children, rather than just blaming them for not understanding the subject or for not studying well enough.

This got me thinking of a way to overcome this problem. Luckily, I had learnt to use computers and my husband had a laptop. I borrowed it from him, and prepared a PowerPoint presentation which gave a description of the various monuments along with colored pictures from various angles, which the students could go through. Using technology as a tool for learning was a novel concept at the time. I faced a lot of criticism from the other teachers, who commented that this was unnecessary and a waste of the students' time. However, I was certain that this method would create curiosity in them and help them understand the subject better. This feeling was reinforced when the children got excited on seeing the laptop itself and went through the presentation with great enthusiasm!

On hearing the results of the Board Exam, my happiness probably exceeded that of the students! My efforts had borne fruit. The students excelled in History and five of them had scored cent percent marks! This was a benchmark for the school. This achievement was also recognized by the CBSE that awarded the school for the best performance in the subject of Social Studies, and in turn, the school felicitated me for the best subject performance in the 10th CBSE Board. I learnt the truth of the maxim, 'Where there is a will, there is a way.' Rather than just accepting the *status quo*, I had introduced a novel learning method that enhanced the quality of teaching and helped the students understand the subject better. For me, the high marks scored by them were a by-product of their enhanced understanding, and not an end in itself. It was something like Aamir Khan's dialogue in one of his popular movies, wherein he insists on improving capabilities as a sure step to success.

During this period, Air India used to conduct RANK and BOLT Awards for students and teachers. The Broad Outlook Learned Teacher Award (BOLT) was given by Air India in collaboration with the newspaper, 'Nav Bharat,' as part of their social outreach program. They had advertised about it in the form of an all-India competition, and I enrolled for it. At the District and State levels, the interview panel included distinguished people such as board members of banks, professors, directors, and school principals. This panel picked up city and state winners, who were then sent to the national level. I was lucky to qualify as the winner from the city of Bhopal, for the year 2007-2008. I was also successful in becoming the state winner for Madhya Pradesh. This cleared the decks for me to participate at the national level. Along with me were other state winners at the national level, which included teachers as well as students from all the states of India. As part of the final competition, all state level winners were to be taken on a week-long tour to Singapore.

In spite of initial family resistance at the thought of my traveling alone abroad, I was determined to make the most of this opportunity and felt that one should not compromise on what one felt was right. The fact that I was financially independent and that this was a tour for a championship also helped me take a firm stand.

Here, I would like to share an important learning with the women of today. Although I came from an affluent family, I had a meagre salary. However, it was this salary that gave me the feeling of independence. The fact that I could decide how to spend my money, gave me a lot of confidence. This was an investment in myself. I could do the things I wanted. I could control my resources and finances. Similarly, every woman needs to be independent. I was never short of money, but it was only because I earned my own money that I could have a say in how I wanted to spend it.

> No matter how well-off your family is, till you don't earn your own money, you cannot become financially independent.

Singapore was a learning experience like never before! We visited the best of universities, and also went sightseeing. It was very enriching, as we got exposure to international universities like Nanyang Technological University and learnt about their education system. Based on these visits, we were given various tasks related to teaching that we had to complete each day. A panel of Air India staff was to judge our performance in these tasks. We were also evaluated on the basis of our behavior and attitude. At the end of the trip, I returned to India, fresh with the knowledge of the education system at the international level and the enthusiasm to implement it at my school. The final interview was to be held at the Air India Headquarters in Mumbai. The panel of judges included eminent personalities like Shobha De, Amin Sayani, Lara Balsara, and Priya Dutt.

The date of the final interview drew near. Finally, D-day arrived. The interviews were going on since morning. Though confident about my interview, I found myself a little nervous. I couldn't wait for my interview to get over. As luck would have it, however, my interview was scheduled for the last. By the time I finished, it was almost 8 pm. As the judges and I were coming out of the Air India building, I remarked casually to Lara Balsara, "It has got pretty late, hasn't it?" She replied, saying, "Yes, we saved the best for the last." This comment of hers really made my day.

I went on to become the National Award winner for BOLT and there were six runners-up! This was really a high point in my career that gave me both, exposure at the international level and recognition at the national level. The award ceremony was to be held either in Mumbai or in Delhi, where the award was to be given at the hands of President Kalam. Sadly, the ceremony did not take place due to the Taj shootout and the fact that soon, Air India fell into a crisis.

But this award had, in a way, opened up many possibilities for me. St. Joseph Convent School has branches all across the world. In 2008, I got a golden opportunity to attend a conference at the United Nations Headquarters, New York, as part of the Congregation of Sisters of St. Joseph (CSSJ), along with 20 students and Sister Lily, who was the Vice-Principal of St. Joseph Convent School, Bhopal. There were groups from other continents like Europe, Africa, and Australia. However, our group had the distinction of being the only one to represent the entire Asian continent. During this visit, we were able to witness a session of the General Assembly in the UN. This gave us a wonderful insight into its working. A special session on climate change and the role of students was organized for all the delegates of CSSJ at the UN headquarters. Here, the students learnt a lot about the important aspects of climate change and how they could impact and reduce our carbon footprint.

During the drought in Bhopal, the Chief Minister of Madhya Pradesh had called for the deepening of the lake and voluntary contribution of labour for this cause. At the time, I had led the students of the school for the same. This made the students realize that they could actively contribute to resolving the problems of global warming, pollution etc. At one of the sessions at the UN, our group was lucky to be able to share this experience, as well as our views on global warming. This was a firsthand experience for us, and we were able to sensitize the students towards the need of environment conservation.

Apart from these remarkable awards and opportunities, I also won various awards like the Best Educator Secondary School TCS Education World Award (an award sponsored by TCS in collaboration with the Education World Magazine) at Ahmedabad in 2009; the Education Quality Foundation of India (EQFI) award in 2010 and the Best Educator National Award as a secondary school teacher. Mr. Vineet Joshi, the Chairman of the CBSE board at Delhi, presented this award to me at a function held in Delhi by EQFI.

In this manner, every year from 2007-2011 in a row, I won seven national awards. It was not as if this success had come easily. But though faced with challenges on the personal and professional fronts, I was determined to succeed. That none of the awards were merely honorary or nominations, but were competitions where my work had been scrutinized and found noteworthy, was very gratifying to me.

Brickbats

This success, however, came at a price. Joining my alma mater, I had felt blessed to be colleagues with my own teachers. But now that I was gaining such recognition and awards, these very colleagues became my competitors. I had to face hostility from the other teachers, who resented my success. The fact was that whenever I learnt about any competition, I informed and encouraged them to participate in it as well. But since they never even filled the form for the competitions, it was a foregone conclusion that they could not win. How then, could they grudge me my achievements? But, this did not stop their antagonistic attitude. As a result, I had to face various challenges like rivalry and procrastination in any work to be taken up. However, I did not allow their attitude to deter me. I decided that my work and the results would speak for themselves.

> One loses energy in giving explanations. If one gets embroiled in arguments and small issues, one loses focus and the enthusiasm to do something new. Therefore, one needs to save energy and enthusiasm by not reacting to such negative situations and people.

One should learn to be like the deaf frog in the well. This little frog was climbing the wall of the well, trying to get out. The other frogs at the bottom were calling out and dissuading him, saying, "It's way too difficult! You will never make it to the top!" Yet, this frog kept on trying, and finally succeeded in coming out of the well. It turned out that this frog, being deaf, was unaware of the criticism around him. So he kept up his efforts and eventually succeeded. I decided to apply this principle in my life and be deaf to the pessimistic and scathing comments around me. I learnt not to let such people get to me. At rare times, though, when I get bogged down due to the negativity, I recall the mantra, 'The more resistance there is, the more resilient I am,' and pick myself up.

Harmonious Horizons

From 1996 to 2011, I had contributed significantly to developing and enhancing the education system at the school. I had also received recognition of my work in the form of awards. But now, I began to feel saturated. I felt that I had proved my merit and done all that I could here. I wanted to do more as an educator. So, in 2011, I quit as the HOD of Social Sciences and decided to take a break and do something more worthwhile.

Mr. G. Balasubramanian, who is a prominent educationist, is my mentor and guide. He is the ex-Academic Director of the CBSE Board. He told me about the Global Indian International School (GIIS) - a chain of Singapore schools in India. They were launching two schools in Delhi and Indore as pilot projects. He was their Academic Director. He approached me to become the Founder Principal of the school at Indore. New horizons beckoned. The chance to set up a school right from scratch was a God-sent opportunity.

But this meant that I would have to leave my family in Bhopal and shift to Indore, a three-hour drive from Bhopal. Naturally, I faced a lot of resistance from both, my maiden and marital homes. Caught in a dilemma between my career and my family responsibilities, I went through much emotional anguish over my decision, something that I am sure working women today face at various points in their careers. But eventually, I decided that family discord and differences of opinions would be a part and parcel of life. Looking at the bigger picture, by remaining in Bhopal, I would only be fulfilling my responsibility of doing the best for my children. But by taking up this opportunity, I would be instrumental in contributing to and shaping the lives of thousands of children.

This thought made me resolute and so, braving all opposition, I decided to move to Indore. This decision proved to be one of the best that I had taken. It also helped that my son was to join the Daly College in Indore.

Being the Founder Principal of GIIS was a steep learning curve, which gave me rich experience and immense exposure to the various issues involved in running an organization. I got the opportunity to augment learning using tools and techniques like video conferencing, something that I had always felt needed to be a part of the learning methods. Our school had the distinction of being the first to implement this revolutionary learning technique. We were using technology to connect with our counterparts in branches of these schools located abroad, like in Japan and Singapore. Festivals, debate competitions, conferences, education, and extra-curricular activities were conducted for the students through video conferencing with students in Tokyo and Singapore. We all were lucky to be part of this new technology.

This exposure vastly improved students' understanding of the world and their cognitive learning. It also helped broaden their outlook as they were exposed to diverse cultures, festivals, and accents too. I feel that traveling is the best educational exercise. The only difference was that here, instead of physically traveling, students were traveling virtually. That children from a small town like Indore were talking to children from Tokyo reinforced the fact that the world had indeed become a global village. It gave me immense satisfaction that in my first job as a Principal, I was part of creating this global community, and this made my sacrifice of leaving behind my family worthwhile. I was indeed lucky to be a part of this school.

Over the next three years, I continued my efforts to implement and set up a stable and robust setup. I had now been an educator for around 16 years, and a Principal for around 3. Now, I held dreams of starting my own school. So in 2014, when I quit the school in Indore and returned to Bhopal, I registered my own education society. However, many challenges lay ahead. There were a lot of funds required, and I did not have a tie-up with any institution. So, in order to raise sufficient funds, I decided to join the NRI Global Discovery School as the Founder Principal, for two years. This is an Ahmedabad-based chain of schools, which had set up a franchise school in Bhopal. I gave the management there a clear idea of my plans and they too, agreed. I had set myself a target of October 2015, when I would start my own school. So I set to work immediately and established a successful setup here too.

The Trail of Trailblazers

Now the time had come to focus on my dream – that of starting my own school. But I was still short of funds. To overcome this constraint, I decided to set up the school in a part of the premises of my own house. Thus, the Trailblazers International School was established with humble beginnings. In the process, I also realized that at the time, good schools in Bhopal were located very far off, in the outskirts of the city. Children had to travel long distances to reach schools. This would drain their energy, leaving little enthusiasm for studies and extra-curricular activities. However, as my school was located within the city, most of the children could reach school in just 5 to 10 minutes. Thus, a lot of their time was saved, which they could utilize for other activities.

Typically, the class strength in any school is 65 students per class whereas my school has only 25 students per class. This helps the teachers to pay individual attention to each student. I poured my life's learning into establishing a model school that would be one of the best. I ensure that the best facilities are made available to the students to create a global connect. I have built my school with great hopes and the dream that it should be a national level school that would provide quality education to students. The differentiating factor is that my school would be a generator of 'happy, satisfied, evolved, and responsible human beings.'

> The education style in other schools laid more focus on academic achievements that were necessary for materialistic accomplishments. However, merely providing the next generation with the education to be economically sound is not enough. A student who scores cent percent marks may not necessarily become a happy and responsible citizen! It is equally important that one teaches children to be happy, yet to behave responsibly towards the environment, towards the society, the world, and inculcates human values in them. The education system of today is sorely lacking in this aspect.

In our school, learning towards human values is imparted on a daily basis. This has been a long process and one that requires constant reinforcement. Alongwith the subject matter, a school also needs to instill values in children. For this, however, first, teachers need to walk the talk, and be role models for children. They need to live with those values, and not just believe in them. Children learn best by observing and emulating others around them. Teachers need to sensitize children first in order to inculcate values in them. Today's teachers are detached. I realized that I first needed to groom the teachers to inculcate the values in themselves and deliver content in the manner I wanted, and then, when the students saw it being practised, they would take it up.

We also made efforts to take up integrated learning in all subjects. We have introduced concepts like Color Days for the preparatory classes. For example, on the Blue Color Day, the songs sung by the children have some mention of the color blue; in the Maths class, the teacher would ask the students to count the number of blueberries, and so on. These small innovations make learning much more interesting for students and help reinforce concepts through integrated learning and boost cognitive growth.

My aim is to give the right environment to children and to remove the unhappiness and materialism prevalent in society today. We are bringing up children to be grateful, happy, satisfied, and contented. I have spent considerable time and effort in this direction, and I am satisfied that these efforts are paying off. The generations coming out of our school will be more balanced people. This is because they have been taught that the process is more important than the outcome. So, instead of mugging up subjects, the focus is on learning and understanding the topic. This approach extends to the other parts of their life as well, so that we produce youth who truly want to make a positive difference to society, rather than merely participating in the rat-race. I continue to be motivated to bring in more innovation to enhance the learning experience, while enhancing the value system, so that we can produce more of such responsible citizens in the future.

In Retrospect

I feel contented that I have utilized my experience and learning not just to shape my own career, but also the lives of thousands of children in a meaningful way. Although I have faced numerous hardships in this process, all of these have helped strengthen me as a person.

Although I had been yearning for recognition from my own people, my opinion had never mattered. But, proving my merit on national and international levels gave my self-image a boost that no trophies or certificates or recognitions could. Through the awards, I had created a platform for myself. People now recognize me in the education field. Students come up to me and say, "You have made a difference to my life." The fact that I have touched someone's life gives me the satisfaction of having achieved something beyond money. And this achievement is not due to my heritage or family background, but because of what I have accomplished as an individual. I derive motivation from this beautiful quote by Allama Iqbal -

> "Khudi ko kar buland itna ke har taqdeer se pehle,
> Khuda bande se ye pooche, bata teri raza kya hai."

Life Lines

- Always remember that in life, nothing is permanent. As the saying goes, 'This too shall pass.' So in one's happy moments, enjoy the moment, remain humble, and thank God. And in bad times, don't lose hope.

- Along with material success, it is equally important to become a good human being. One needs to look at the bigger picture. Otherwise, one becomes selfish and thinks only about oneself. One should try and do something that can bring people together for a positive cause. That way, one can contribute to society and maximize the positive effect.

- Nurture a hobby. This gives one an outlet to express one's creative side. In my case, my hobby of shooting helped me develop the quality of being focused. Gardening helped me develop an appreciation for and gratitude towards nature.

- A mature person does not get affected by negative people. Rather than just blaming the other person, he or she will analyze why the other person is behaving in such a way. This helps one remain objective about the situation, rather than reacting emotionally.

- While making a decision, one should carefully think about all the concerned people who are going to be affected by it. Take a measured decision, rather than a rash one.

- The next generation is a trigger-happy one. However, maturity lies in being able to absorb shocks. Think bigger, think happy!

Words of Wisdom

My advice to all women is to find a field of their liking, and make efforts to pursue it and create a world for themselves outside of their homes. This gives one an outlet for one's talents and increases one's confidence. More importantly, it shifts one's focus from the small and inconsequential things in life to something more meaningful.

Our children are our investment for tomorrow. We need to invest sufficient time to groom them, not just to excel in materialistic achievements, but also in human values. Our efforts in nurturing them today will bear fruits in our later days, and instill us with a sense of pride at having brought up a responsible, well-balanced gen-next.

A successful teacher is one who is able to guide a student to realize his or her inner talents and potential, and pursue the same. That I was instrumental in doing so and shaping my students' lives gives me a feeling of immense satisfaction.

As of now, I have just scratched the surface. There is so much more to accomplish...

"Sitaron Se Aage Jahan Aur Bhi Hain
Abhi Ishq Ke Imtehan Aur Bhi Hain...
...Tu Shaheen Hai Parwaz Hai Kaam Tera
Tere Samne Asman Aur Bhi Hain."

~ Allama Iqbal

4

The 'Chanakya' Coach: Balancing Strategy, Spirituality, and Success

Dr. Radhakrishnan Pillai

Dear Radha,

I remember our first meeting at a program based on your first book. Known as the 'Chanakya Guru,' you are a person with remarkable achievements as an author, professor, speaker, and strategic thinker, and yet, are so simple and humble! Your drive for results with constant focus on excellence is absolutely contagious and your ability to wear multiple hats and juggle various roles seamlessly is truly noteworthy.

You have been a true guide to me with practical tips for my book as a debut author. I have learnt so much from you and continue to do so even now. Am so short of words to "Thank you, Radha!"

Yours Affectionately,
Aparna

About Dr. Radhakrishnan Pillai...

Dr. Radhakrishnan Pillai is a well-known management trainer, author, and consultant. A certified Management Consultant, his varied qualifications include a degree in Management, an M.A. in Sanskrit and a Ph.D on the 'Arthashastra.' Fondly known as 'Chanakya' Pillai, he has devoted his life to studying and spreading the teachings of Chanakya, the master economist, philosopher and kingmaker, who lived in 3rd century BC. His bestselling book, 'Corporate Chanakya,' has sold over three lakh copies, has been translated into as many as ten regional languages, and has been made into a film as well.

He has contributed significantly in making the knowledge of the 'Arthashastra' available to thousands of people across the world in a simple yet effective manner. He has conducted seminars, lectures, training programmes, radio shows and trained several lakhs around the world till date. His sessions have helped people transform their businesses and lives in a significant way. He has taught at the Oxford and Cambridge Universities, the London Business School, Heidelberg and Cologne universities in Germany as well as in Dubai, Muscat, Singapore, China, and Indonesia. He has also written more than 200 articles in various newspapers and magazines. His life is a perfect blend of spirituality and material success. A recipient of the Sardar Patel National Award in 2009 for his contribution to the field of Management and Industrial Development, he grooms future leaders and politicians of the country through the Chanakya International Institute of Leadership Studies (CIILS) at the University of Mumbai.

"There is a difference between telling others you are spiritual and telling yourself you are spiritual." – Dr. Radhakrishnan Pillai

"What is Life? Who am I? What is the purpose of my birth?" Although such philosophical questions often arise in our minds, we tend to neglect them and say, "These are meant to be answered in one's old age. Why worry about them now, especially when I am at the peak of my youth and career?"

Spiritual Start

In my case, however, not just did such questions enter my mind; rather, they were asked and discussed deliberately since my childhood, especially by my father. I would say that I was born into a spiritual environment. My parents were involved in the *seva* (service) in the Chinmaya Mission, a spiritual organization founded by the world-renowned spiritual leader, Swami Chinmayananda.

While my childhood was filled with wonder and curiosity, trying to understand the workings of the external world, my father also taught me to think about the world within. Through the stories of the 'Ramayana,' the 'Mahabharata' and the teachings of the 'Upanishads' and various Indian scriptures, I understood that one is not born just to exist and go through a routine; rather, there is a higher purpose to life. My journey on the path to spirituality thus started at a tender age. This influence shaped me and my outlook towards life.

Whenever we visited my native place in Kerala, my mother took me to various temples. Temples, to me, were not just monuments, but were living examples of the great Indian culture that had survived the test of time.

There is an old saying in India in Sanskrit, 'Your mother takes you to your father and your father takes you to your spiritual guru.' This proved true in my case too. It was on an auspicious *Mahashivratri* day in 1987 that my father took me to the temple of the Chinmaya Mission located at Powai, Mumbai. Little did I know that this was to be the beginning of my spiritual journey, which was to change my life forever.

The Charm of the Chinmaya Mission

With my increasing involvement with the Chinmaya Mission, the spiritual atmosphere at home got extended to all parts of my life. In the Chinmaya Mission, we had weekly spiritual classes, camps, projects and various activities. I found that the Chinmaya Mission was not just another organization, but the place that I really felt I belonged to, a second home, so to say. The best times of my childhood and youth were spent there. I grew along with the Mission.

My best friends on both, personal as well as professional levels are from the Mission. My partner in my first business, Venkat Iyer, is a friend from the Mission. When we started the Chanakya Institute of Public Leadership, at the University of Mumbai, Department of Philosophy, the co-founder Director, Ranjit Shetty was also from the Chinmaya Mission. On the home front too, I got married to Surekha, whom I met at the Chinmaya Mission. She too has been an active member of the Chinmaya youth wing, called Chinmaya Yuva Kendra (CHYK). Thus, the influence of the Chinmaya Mission and its teachings have been an all-pervading and an inseparable part of my life.

Earn & Learn

I started working immediately after Class 12. I was studying and working right from 1992 onwards. I completed my B.A. (Bachelor of Arts) in Sociology in 1996. I also completed two management diplomas – a Diploma in Industrial Management in 1999 and a Diploma in Management Consultancy, later in 2008. In 2004, I also did an Interdisciplinary Sanskrit course in Indology from the Chinmaya International Foundation (Chinmaya University), did M.A. in Sanskrit in 2010 and completed my Ph.D in 'Leadership from the Arthashastra by Chanakya' in 2015. Currently, I am doing my D.Litt. in Law and am also guiding Ph.D students. The reason I have studied such varied subjects is my love for venturing into unknown territories. Needless to say, the knowledge of all these subjects lends new dimensions to my thought process.

> Working while you study is a good way to keep yourself grounded. Instead of taking your parents for granted and demanding that they fulfill your expectations, you understand early in life the effort that goes into earning every single rupee.

The Dot-com Disaster

The first turning point in my life came in the year 2001. Working in a company in Bangalore at the age of 26, life was rosy and the future looked bright. I was the epitome of the perfect young man who had it all – good education, a cushy job et all. But I was in for a rude shock. The dot-com bubble burst, and as a result, my company had to shut down. I, along with many others, suddenly became jobless. This was totally unexpected.

> Life has a way of changing its trajectory when you least expect it to.

Although I was shaken, I did not give up hope. I knew that this was not the end of the world and was positive about finding myself a better job. I returned to Mumbai, my home town, and started attending interviews. Being in Mumbai, I naturally turned to my spiritual anchor, the Chinmaya Mission. Swami Chinmayananda had, sadly, left his mortal coil in 1993. Now, the organization was thriving under the able leadership of Swami Tejomayanandaji, the then head of the Chinmaya Mission. I met Swamiji who asked me, "What are you doing nowadays?" I replied, "I am in search of a job, contemplating which company to join."

Swami Tejomayanandaji smiled and said, "Swami Chinmayanandaji used to say, 'My youth should not look out for jobs; instead, they should create jobs!'"

Business Beginnings

My conversation with Swami Tejomayanandaji was a turning point in my life. His words, "…create jobs!" struck me like a bolt. On the lookout for employment myself, the idea of being a generator of jobs had not even remotely occurred to me. Being a job provider instead of a job seeker would be a quantum shift! Although I did not react, I knew I had food for thought. Creating jobs meant that I had to think like an entrepreneur and become one! I spent days and weeks contemplating what kind of jobs I could create. I was only 26 years old at the time.

> In life there are times when one feels one knows exactly what one wants and where one wants to go. However, sometimes, a casual conversation or a subtle shift in circumstances give life a different direction.

Spirituality being my guiding light since childhood, and travel my passion, it was natural for me to choose the field of spiritual travel and tourism as my business. I named my company 'Atma Darshan.'

Though eager to start with this new venture, doubts assailed me. Where would the initial funding come from? Was there any future in this sector? Although spiritual tourism was already a part of the Indian culture, it was more of a family affair. There were no professionals in this field back then. What if I failed? How would I manage to run my household?

In doubt, I recalled my guru's teachings and gathering courage, decided to take the plunge. I realized that had this not been meant to happen, Swami Tejomayanandaji would never have spoken to me of it.

The initial period was a steep learning curve. I was a first-generation entrepreneur and since neither I, nor anyone in my family had prior experience of being an entrepreneur, I had to learn the nitty-gritties of running an organization the hard way.

The next challenge was, how would I take my business to thousands of people when I was all alone? I knew I had to find an innovative solution. Then I remembered Chanakya's teaching – never enter into a battle alone! In spite of the dot-com disaster, I realized that this was great technology that nobody was using much at that time. I put this technology to optimum use and created a website for my company. A novel idea at that time, this instantly made my business global.

My efforts paid off and I was lucky to get over 15,000 tourists in the very first year itself. It is said that if you take just one step, God takes the next ten for you. The next ten years were spent in a whirlwind of activity that took me to different parts of India and the world. I traveled across the length and breadth of India, visiting various temples, ashrams, meeting saints and sages and reading spiritual literature.

India and Indians were an undiscovered goldmine. I saw India from a very different standpoint – that of a great spiritual country. I feel satisfied that I enabled thousands of people to travel along with me to 'Discover Spiritual India', as the tagline of 'Atma Darshan' goes.

I was also blessed to be accompanied by spiritual masters like Swami Ishwaranandaji, Swami Sacchidanandaji and many others from the Chinmaya Mission and other spiritual organizations. This was a happy union where I was able to pursue my business as well as my spiritual calling. I learnt a lot from these formal and informal interactions. I was steadfastly progressing on my journey towards knowing my inner self.

Chanakya Calling

Though my business was doing well, I wanted to grow it further. But for this, I needed to do something different. Realizing the rich heritage of India, I went through various Indian books on management, looking for the pearls of wisdom that our ancient Indian culture held. This was when I came across the 'Arthashastra,' a book written by the mastermind in economics and politics, Chanakya, who lived in the 3rd century BC. This was to prove the second important turning point in my life, when I decided to study the 'Arthashastra.'

In 2004, I had organized a tour to Kailash Mansarovar, led by Swami Ishwaranandaji, from the Chinmaya Mission. The serene atmosphere and natural beauty of Mount Kailash brought me inner peace and stillness. In this divine atmosphere, at the abode of Lord Shiva, a strange thought came to me, "Dedicate your life to study and apply the teachings of the 'Arthashastra.'" I was sure this was not my own thought. It was a divine indication from a higher being, guiding me on my life purpose. I was stupefied! I had done some initial reading of the 'Arthashastra,' but to dedicate my whole life to it was a strange idea indeed! But when God decides, who are we to resist? I decided that this was where my future lay.

When I came back from Kailash, I had two major responsibilities. One, to run my company in a more efficient way, and the second, to study the 'Arthashastra.' Regarding the first, I was fortunate that with my partner – Venkat Iyer at 'Atma Darshan,' business started flourishing. But the second was more challenging. I was not sure how I would be able to make time to study the 'Arthashastra,' which has 6000 *sutras*. It is a vast book whose knowledge cannot be assimilated only by reading it. It had to be studied in detail under the guidance of an able teacher.

As always, Chinmaya Mission came to my rescue. I came to know that Chinmaya International Foundation (CIF), the research wing of the Chinmaya Mission at Kerala, was dedicated to the study and research of ancient Indian scriptures. In December 2004, I got a chance to study the 'Arthashastra' at the CIF. Swami Advayananda, the in-charge of CIF, was kind enough to accept me as a student. But his condition was very clear. I would have to stay there, research and study the 'Arthashastra.'

For a person based in Mumbai, that too, an entrepreneur, married, and with many responsibilities, taking time off to study in an ashram in Kerala at the peak of my career seemed impossible. Numerous doubts crossed my mind. "How will my business run in my absence? What about my household responsibilities?" But again, my business partner, Venkat, and my life partner, Surekha, came to my rescue. With their strong support, I finally went to Kerala to study the knowledge of one of the greatest strategists on earth – Chanakya.

> Concentrate on the purpose of what you are doing; time will manage itself.

Swami Advayananda was more than just a great scholar. He not only knew that I had to study the 'Arthashastra' within a limited time, but also that I required personal attention. Among the panel of scholars at CIF, he spoke to Dr. Gangadharan Nair, the then dean of Adi Shankara Sanskrit University. Dr. Gangadharan readily agreed to teach me the entire 'Arthashastra' and Swamiji gave this research an academic status. He said, "This is a research program and you are a research scholar." It was a 'One teacher, one student' program, specially designed for me. Thus, I began the journey of a lifetime that was to be devoted to the study of the 'Arthashastra.'

The time I spent in Kerala was the best part of my life. I had full freedom to study the way I wanted. But as it is said, "With complete freedom, comes complete responsibility." I knew I had to complete my study at the earliest. Besides, I could not just be studying the 'Arthashastra.' I had to go back and immediately apply it in my business. So I put in almost 16 - 18 hours per day to study. As I delved into the depths of this great text, I marveled at the genius of this great teacher, economist, jurist, and royal advisor, whose works went beyond time and are referred to by scholars even today.

This was probably when I learnt to multitask. Although it may sound unbelievable, I am currently working on 125 projects at a time!

Dr. Gangadharan Nair and his wife were like parents to me. I went to their house every evening to gather gems of knowledge. The remaining part of the day was spent in the library of CIF, researching the thousands of books on Indology. Towards the end of the course, I had to write a research paper. The paper, 'Management Fundamentals in Kautilya's 'Arthashastra,' that I produced during this period, gave me an academic standing. The paper has become very popular both, nationally and internationally. It has inspired many other scholars, students and teachers to look at the 'Arthashastra' as a book on Management.

The Chanakya Charisma

Armed with this precious ancient knowledge, I finally returned to Mumbai after a hiatus of two months, eager to take up my next challenge of applying these learnings in my business. I began work in full earnest. I was totally focused on running my business more efficiently using these principles. However, with my research paper on the 'Arthashatra,' came my first experience of popularity, and with it, various other opportunities as well. The Times of India group was then starting a newspaper called the 'Mumbai Mirror.' I got a chance to be a weekly columnist with the group. I wrote for the Mumbai Mirror as a columnist for over four years and went on to gather a huge fan following for my column.

When one gets popular as a writer, one also gets invited for various speaking assignments. Invitations for lectures, seminars, and talks became a part of my life. Well, all this was giving me a lot of popularity and fame. But my business commitments were going for a toss. I also had to earn money for my family. Walking this tightrope between my business and other assignments got me thinking of a way to balance both these fronts. It was then that the thought entered my mind, "What if I take up the learning and teaching of Chanakya's knowledge, full-time?" I was thrilled at the thought. 'Make your passion your profession,' is an oft-heard phrase nowadays. The idea of spending my working life doing something I actually enjoyed, seemed too good to be true. But then doubts on both, the personal and ethical fronts, started entering my mind. I did not want to make a business model of this ancient wisdom and turn it into a commercial venture.

At the same time, I was concerned as to how I would be able to earn my livelihood. Caught in this *dharmasankat* (dilemma), I sent God a silent prayer for help. Muulraj Chheda came as an answer to my prayer. When I had first met Muulraj Chheda during a common management program that we attended, little did I know that it would turn out to be a relationship that would take Chanakya's teachings to the next level. The SPM group of companies, where he is a Director, was kind enough to fund and support my research work.

Chanakya in the Corporate World

Another milestone was when my first book, 'Corporate Chanakya' became a bestseller overnight. Till date, the book has been in the bestseller list for over 75 weeks without a break and ranks next only to the biography of Steve Jobs. It has also gone for 25 reprints and has sold over a lakh of copies in the first year itself. It has also been translated into ten regional languages in less than two years. It is also used as a text book in management colleges across the globe.

The success of the book got me many invitations for training programs across the globe. Shemaroo, the entertainment company, has made the film, 'Chanakya Speaks – the Seven Pillars of a Successful Business,' based on my book. With this film, I got an entry into the film world too.

My next major break was with the company Varroc, where I trained 10000 people, right from the Chairman to the contract workers. This was a golden opportunity for me as I believe it is important for any knowledge to percolate down to the lowest level for it to get implemented effectively. Even today, I find it unbelievable that an entire organization was trained in Chanakya's principles – a rare occurrence indeed!

Chanakya on the Campus

But the jewel in the crown was the entry into the University of

Mumbai. While I was doing various training programs with the corporate world, I also started working with the academic world. Dr. Shubhada Joshi was instrumental in getting a research project on 'Arthashastra,' with the department of Philosophy. Very soon, I started our own leadership institute named 'Chanakya Institute of Public Leadership,' with my friend from the Chinmaya Mission at the University with the aim of creating future leaders for the country, inspired by ancient Indian wisdom.

All these milestones happened in a very short period of time, i.e., in less than two years. This upward trend continued and in 2009, I became the youngest Indian to get the prestigious Sardar Patel International Award. Was it destiny? I would be happy to call it *Guru Kripa* (my Guru's blessings). I believe that this success was due to the grace of all my teachers and mentors, not to mention all the other people who supported me in every way.

> Although one should be proud of one's achievements, one should not forget that the success achieved is not due to one's efforts alone; rather, it is the collective result of the contribution of numerous people, in direct and indirect ways. So, one should remain grounded even at the peak of one's success and help others, just as others may have helped one.

At the University, we have a flagship leadership course where we train children totally free of cost. This is my way of giving back to society what I have received from it. Many big companies support us financially and morally. Even individuals have come ahead to take forward the work we are doing, of promoting Chanakya and his teachings in a modern way to awaken India to its past glory. I also realized that I was born to be a teacher. Teaching is my strength and my passion too.

Failure is Never Final

Most of us are agonized by failure. However, I think we should not worry too much about the little incidents but look at the big picture. Everything that happens is only for our good. But the fact is that, an incident not working in one's favor is only beneficial when one reflects on it and tries to look at its positive side.

To give my own example, as a young boy, I had dreamt of joining the Indian Navy. However, I lost the chance to clear the entrance exams by just two marks. I was very upset at the time, and it was with great resignation that I pursued a degree in Management. However, what I had thought of as a failure turned to be my biggest advantage.

Today, I train top officers from the Armed Forces like the Army, Navy, and Air Force of various countries. So, had I cleared the exam, I would have been a part of the Indian Navy. But instead, today, I teach war strategy to a large number of officers of the Armed Forces!

> There are no failures in life, only learnings. It is up to us to make good of the adverse events that we come across. One cannot control the events in one's life, but one can definitely control one's reaction to them.

Triumph with Technology

I feel there is one important dimension that our generation should be proud of – the rapid growth of technology that has allowed us to grow at the speed of thought. Internet, mobile phones, emails, social networking sites – all these have connected human beings from different corners of the world, with lightning speed. I have also used technology to reach out to the masses to teach the 'Arthashastra,' through video conferencing and virtual and digital classrooms. I remember when I had addressed a group of 2000 employees from Mahindra Satyam. I was in Hyderabad, while there were people from seven locations watching me 'live.' This would have been impossible without the blessing of technology.

As a trainer in the Indian Armed Forces, I undertake training programs for the leaders of the Army, Navy and Air Force. I often wondered how they came to know about me when they got in touch with me for the first time. Col. Sunil Nair, who organized my first lecture at the Defence Staff Service College (DSSC), said, "We found you on the internet while browsing about Chanakya." To imagine that my name would be linked with the great Chanakya, albeit, in the virtual world, was a humbling thought. Students from various colleges where I have delivered lectures have uploaded my videos on YouTube, Facebook etc. Again, technology has helped me cross the boundaries of time and place.

In Retrospect

I was blessed to receive guidance from Swami Chinmayananda on how to lead my life. He taught me that one should work towards multiplying the goodness within oneself. If one wants to be successful, one must single-mindedly keep doing one's work each day with devotion. I have been following his advice, and this is what has made a difference to my life. I deliver one lecture/talk every day. So in one year, 365 lectures. I have been doing so for the last 20 years, so one can imagine the number of lectures I have delivered so far.

> To keep doing what you do with passion, focus, and determination is the simple mantra for excellence!

Even today, people come up to me and say, "Sir, that lecture of yours that I attended many years ago has changed my life. It gave me a new direction." The feeling of satisfaction of having contributed to shaping someone's life cannot be valued in monetary terms.

God has been very kind to me and I can only thank Him for this stupendous success. I have traveled across the length and breadth of India and also to many countries abroad. I am on the Board of Directors of more than five companies. I have taught at many prestigious universities across the globe. Fame, money, glory – I have been blessed with it all without asking. I have a loving family and friends whom I can count on. But more importantly, I have spiritual guidance in the form of the Chinmaya Mission that has kept me grounded, both, in the heights of success and the depths of despair.

My parents and my wife have stood by me in good times as well as bad. Surekha is more than just my wife. She is my best friend, my greatest joy, and a companion with whom I can discuss everything. Someone asked Socrates about marriage. He said, "By all means, marry. If you get a good wife, you will become happy. If you get a bad one, you will become a philosopher." In my case, I am happily married and am teaching philosophy!

Life Lines
- The greatest joy is when one finds one's spiritual guru. It is the beginning of an unending journey to discover oneself.
- One must read a lot. Reading is not just about books. It is learning from the experiences of many others who have walked the path before you. Reading opens your mind to a new world of possibilities.
- It is important to cultivate and maintain one's relationships. Swami Chinmayanandaji once said, "A truly wealthy person is not one who has lots of money, but one who has lots of friends."
- The best advice I got from my guru Swami Chinmayananda is, "You are not the body – you are the self that can never die with the body." Death is only of the body, while your good work continues forever.
- Your family plays a very important role in your success.
- Happy people don't have more opportunities; they just focus on opportunities instead of their failures.

Words of Wisdom

What you have got from your country is a gift to you. What you do with what you have is your gift to your country. Work for your country and the good of the whole world. We need to bring back our spiritual glory, which is India's strength.

India is a great civilization, a great culture. It is a country whose thinking has survived the test of time. One wonders what is meant by the line 'Unity in Diversity.' In spite of differences in culture, eating habits etc., it is the spirituality of our country that keeps us united! We are lucky to be born Indians. This great nation has given us the message of spirituality. Now, it is for us to take it to the world.

5

Hello – Health and Happiness!

Dr. Sarah Musavi

Dear Sarah,

From being colleagues at work, to being thick friends across continents – you and I have traversed the whole journey! What inspires me most, Sarah, is your adaptability – whether it is working in various functions with people having different skillsets, or different cities in India, or now in a different country – you have experimented with your life and career in such a fulfilling way, that it has helped you, your family, and of course, friends like me. Thanks for being my 'go to' friend as a mentor, health coach, laughter specialist, or even a vent for the so-called 'silly things'. You probably don't know – you're an invaluable friend!

Stay the same, always!

Yours Affectionately,
Aparna

About Dr. Sarah Musavi...

Dr. Sarah Musavi is a Certified Health Coach as well as a medical and health writer in Ottawa, Canada. She has designed a flexible life for herself so that she can be the voice for healthcare practitioners and continue to support communities, especially teenagers, with their health. She started her health-coaching journey in 2011 as the CEO of My Health Alive, a health service that supports women to deal with weight issues using an alternative and holistic approach to health. After six years of working primarily with food, exercise, and lifestyle habits, Sarah is passionate about supporting teenagers discover their potential. Her goal is to strengthen this generation so we can have an energetic adult population in the next ten years.

Her Master's degree in Health Administration (MHA), coupled with a Ph.D in Biochemistry, gives her a strong research and scientific background to interpret and communicate healthcare data in order to bring about positive health outcomes. Appreciated by her colleagues for her focus and attention to detail, her tailor-made nutrition programs and coaching ensure that people become healthy and happy and are positively transformed. Her extensive travels have given her a wide perspective of various cultures. Passionate about health, education, and children, she seeks to help eliminate obesity in youngsters and also conducts coaching and workshops for children and parents to help them achieve their personal best.

Sarah has also taken up the task of simplifying medical terminology, concepts and health through her writing services. This idea was born out of a need for removing various myths, confusion and simplifying the health information available. Her 'funda' in life, 'to keep flowing,' ensures that she finds new ways to innovate in her work so that she can transform and touch people's lives in a positive way and make the world a better place.

"Health is not a destination. It is a multidimensional snapshot of our mind. It shows up in our words, actions, and choices for Sleep, Thoughts, Eating and Movement – STEM." – Dr. Sarah Musavi

I watch as Stella, my 81-year-old patient excitedly packs her luggage for a cruise to Russia. With our rigorous treatment plan and her physiotherapy, she has speedily recovered from her broken hip. What's more, she is also rid of her acid reflux in just six weeks! I am contented to see her healthy and happy! This is my life... this is my work.

The words that best describe me are 'Gypsy', 'Dreamer', 'Believer', 'Explorer,' and 'Traveler'. As one would gather from them, I have taken life as it came – in phases, like a journey, constantly moving, never stagnant. Movement allows me to let go of attachment to patterns. It gets me out of my comfort zone. I like making a new wave every now and then – that's me – FREEDOM personified!

Early Years

Born in the summer of 1968, I am the second child of a mathematician and a professor of wildlife. The stories from my parents that have had the most influence on me are those of bravery, patriotism, gratitude, hard work and holding high standards for service through the work they did.

My mother inspired me with childhood stories of her life in poverty after India's partition, when all their belongings were lost. To add to their woes, my mother lost her mother in her teenage. Though bereft of a mother's love, she and her siblings bore this loss bravely and focused on their studies, won scholarships and medals, often on an empty stomach. These stories taught me the important lessons of resilience and determination.

> Facing tough times and having one's back against the wall is an opportunity for one's inner strength to shine through, leading one to achieve extraordinary results.

My Fearless Father

As a zoologist, my father advocated that we must save our planet and wild animals from human activities. Apart from teaching at the university, he started a nature conservation club and signed up families to learn about the planet, all for free. Every weekend, we either watched a film show by BBC or went on a trip to appreciate the balance of nature. These excursions inculcated in me a love for nature.

My father started the first academic department for wildlife studies, with support from Dr. Salim Ali, the eminent Indian ornithologist. My father is one of the bravest social workers I know. Once, he got an opportunity to put forward his proposal for funding at a ministerial meeting in South India. This was a crucial make or break meeting. The bus journey took him through the sandalwood forests in Tamil Nadu, ruled at that time by dacoits. In the middle of the night, the bus broke down and the driver would not be able to start till dawn. This meant that my father would not make it to this critical meeting.

Without a moment's hesitation, he got off the bus and started walking in pitch darkness. He heard wild animals and knew that if any dacoits saw him, they might shoot him, but none of these factors deterred him because he was determined to attend the meeting. I believe it was his passion and conviction that positively influenced the ministers and finally earned the Department of Wildlife and Ornithology, university funding.

Teenage Times

An unforgettable incident from my school days is my first public speaking appearance at the age of 13. I went up on stage fully prepared with a topic. However, when I opened my mouth, I went completely blank and just stood there for a full minute. I desperately tried to recall my speech, but to no avail. Then, all of a sudden, a topic came to my mind and I started speaking. But this was not the topic I had prepared for! However, my thoughts were flowing out aloud, and I was on a roll. The audience was thrilled with my speech, and I actually bagged the silver prize! That's when I learnt something important about myself.

> I cannot be tied up in processes and details. The beast of freedom lies within my core and I have to nourish it each day, or I will turn speechless!

As a teenager, I had a dream of traveling to quaint and peculiar destinations. I didn't know how this would happen, but throughout my life, I kept my dream alive… so alive that not a day went by when I didn't imagine myself in one of those places. My dream was so real that all my friends, family, and later, my co-workers, knew about it and used to bring me resources on how to get there. I would joke about it, but in my heart, there was never a doubt about me achieving my dream.

> I believe in the words of Muhammad Ali, who said, "If my mind can conceive it, and my heart can believe it – then I can achieve it."

Rebellion and Revolt

As a youngster, although peer pressure tried to steer me towards the easy path of going with the crowd, I could not do so if something didn't make sense to me or if I got bored due to lack of creativity. At such times, I would find myself starting to do my own thing. Breaking the mould was, so to speak, my inherent nature. Thus, early on in life, I got used to being a lonely crusader.

One of these 'breakaways' was in 1987, when all my friends enrolled for the medical entrance exam and my parents brought a form for me as well. After five days of sitting with the form, I realized that I simply could not go through with it even though I was good at Science. This meant that I was faced with the herculean task of communicating this to my father, who, since the time I was six, had coached me to only think of Medicine as a profession. However, gathering my courage, I confessed that I had no interest in Medicine, primarily because even then I did not agree with charging poor people to get them healthy and somewhere deep down I believed that "food is our medicine." Though he opposed my decision, I did end up getting my way.

> Most parents have great hopes for their children and my father was no different. But the thought of spending my life doing something I wasn't interested in, solely to please him, seemed illogical to me.

Now that I was not writing the medical exam, I chose to study Biochemistry because I wanted to understand how the body worked and how we could make it more efficient.

Remorseful Retrospection

Although I broke away from the flow in my teenage years, I spent my early 20s following protocols and being in the flow, while always dreaming of a life outside it.

My dream was to travel, but back then, the Indian mindset did not allow for such adventures. My parents gave me the option of pursuing a Ph.D, which would allow me to travel under the safety of academia. I could not see myself completely in sync with this picture; however, I did not have any other choice. I tried to wriggle out of this and in 1991, secretly applied to a job posting by the British Airways for management trainees. I had to write a cover letter myself, for which I had no training, yet, I guess my passion to see the world showed through and I was selected for a three-day test and interview process. Now the challenge was to travel from Aligarh to Delhi without arousing the suspicion of my father, who was convinced that the world beyond academia was not safe for his daughter.

I convinced my mother to travel with me to Delhi on the pretext that I was going to see a doctor for my intestinal ulcers. What strikes me even today is that my passion could not be deterred despite suffering from bleeding ulcers for a year as well as typhoid and a kidney infection.

After many rounds of interviews and tests, I was shortlisted from among 8000 applicants and recruited for a salary of Rs. 4000 per month, plus travel tickets for the whole family every year. I remember feeling on top of the world that I had finally achieved my dream to work in an environment that resonated with my core being – fast, fun, creative, and lucrative and that would let me and my family travel the world for free.

When the letter with the BA logo arrived, my father enquired what it was. After I confessed all, he looked worried, but also knew that it was my dream. Finally, although he gave in once more, I knew he was not at all pleased. Torn between my love for him and my long-cherished dream, I was stressed with my decision. How could I give up that for which I had persevered so much, to the point of even attending the interview on the sly and overcoming intense ill-health? However, at the same time, I could not bear to see my father so unhappy. Finally, with a heavy heart, I decided to respect my father's wishes and sent British Airways a letter of regret, though it broke my heart to do so.

I would like to think that I made the right decision at the time, though sometimes I do wonder what turn my life would have taken, had I continued on this path.

A Purposeful Ph.D

In my quest to escape academia, I made several unsuccessful attempts, which included applying for Food Sciences in the Indian Army and to the Tata Institute of Social Sciences (TISS) in their Social Work post-graduate program. However, with all doors closed, my only option was to pursue a Masters and then a Ph.D in Biochemistry, which got delayed by a year because of a serious bout of typhoid. However, I managed to get a 92 percentile in the Graduate Admission Test and won a scholarship of Rs 2000 per month from the Indian Council of Medical Research.

Seeing my potential, my teachers arranged for me to meet a well-known scientist, Dr. Vishwanathan, in the Industrial Toxicology

Research Centre (now called the Indian Institute of Toxicology Research) in Lucknow, in 1992. I was happy to see the laboratory with a lot of modern equipment. Dr. Vishwanathan interviewed me and introduced me to his star scientist, Dr. Poonam Kakkar, who was looking for her first doctoral student. We got along instantly on many levels and she asked me to apply to the scientific committee for an interview. I worked hard on my biochemistry concepts and came out with flying colours at the interview. Thus, in January 1992, I started my Junior Research Fellowship (JRF), working on neurotoxicity due to sleep-inducing medications. From that day onwards, I worked tirelessly to get the project completed in the shortest time possible, helped my advisor equip the lab, and continued to apply for funding and publishing papers.

One of my strengths is that once I start something, I put my heart into it, focus on it, and get it done to the best of my ability.

The biggest challenge for me during this phase was battling my intestinal ulcers and weakness while working long hours in the lab. Finally, I found a *hakeem* (a practitioner of herbal medicine), who had cured many people through his multi-generational prescriptions and apothecary, who prepared medications from fruits, roots and vegetables. It took a whole year for my ulcers to heal completely and for me to finally get my energy back.

One day, a scientist in the lab told me about the Masters in Health Administration Program in Temple University, Philadelphia. I read the brochure and instantly fell in love with the course. From then on, in 1993, I had my heart set on pursuing this program. In any case, I could not see myself growing as a scientist. It was too isolated and slow for me.

> I realized the truth of the quote by Steve Jobs, "The only way to do great work is to love what you do. If you haven't found it yet, keep looking. Don't settle. As with all matters of the heart, you'll know when you find it."

For some years, I held onto the remorse of pursuing a doctorate degree in Biochemistry. Frankly, if I were to go back in time to my college years, I would not even have considered being a scientist. It was not a profession that suited my personality. I like to mingle with people and love to make real differences in real time. As a doctoral student, I only had test tubes and acidic solutions as my friends. I did my best, but I could not see myself going far in that field. In my view, this happened due to the boundaries of the society I grew up in. I don't blame my parents for taking me in that direction because they did it with the best of intentions, given their understanding of the world.

I count that time as a failure, in the sense that I spent five precious years of my life in the lab doing something I was never going to be excellent at. My heart was in healing real people with an understanding of their personal journeys.

From 1994-1998, with a dream of traveling the world, and especially the US, I focused on completing my Ph.D, making sure I learnt everything about neurotoxicity. If my experiments failed, it fueled me to put in even more time, including weekends, into my work.

When one has clarity of dreams and purpose, one relays this enthusiasm into the world. As a result, the universe conspires to move one along that path. Help and opportunities come as little hints knocking at one's door. With a deep passion and alertness to one's own voice, one is able to listen to these little messages.

In 1998, a very close friend and an eminent scientist, Dr. Saman Habib, told me of an opening at the Indian Institute of Immunology, New Delhi, and asked me to apply. My Ph.D fellowship had not ended and I was still trying to finish the last leg of my thesis. However, I listened to her, and even though it was not in my original plan to apply for a post-doctorate fellowship, I went ahead. After a month of my application and interview, I received confirmation, a full year before my research fellowship ended. This came as a surprise to my Ph.D advisor, who was expecting me to continue for another year and support the lab, but she understood my drive to move on. So, from there, I went to this completely new environment with very advanced molecular biology work.

Monsanto Musings

One day, in January 1999, a senior scientist in my lab told me of a multinational company that was looking for scientists. The advertisement, though intriguing, didn't mention the name of the company. However, my spirit of adventure kicked in and I applied. About three weeks later, I got a call asking me to attend an interview at Kolkata. Both, my father and my lab chief in Delhi were mad at me for agreeing to accept the plane ticket from someone I did not even know. But I was excited to see what lay ahead. I was asked to prepare a 20-minute presentation on my Ph.D thesis for the interview.

So off I went, defying everyone and every sensible advice. Though this was the first time I was flying alone to an unknown place to meet strangers, I was not at all scared. A couple of weeks after the interview, I heard from the HR Manager, Aparna Sharma, inviting me to join Monsanto in Bangalore as a Junior Scientist, starting March 1999. The salary was more than what my parents were earning as professors. I did not know anything about Monsanto; however, in line with my spirit of constantly exploring, I had decided that I would join them, even in the face of parental resistance. Only this time, the resistance was a little muted, may be because I was in my late 20s and because it involved Science!

Monsanto was a great experience! I took some professional risks and was rewarded for them. However, my dream of traveling and going to the US was still alive, so after a year of working as a database scientist, I grew impatient and applied for a post-doctorate at the Miami Medical School. This seemed to me the only choice left for going to the land of my dreams. I was exhilarated when I was accepted as a post-doctorate fellow in a very prestigious lab. I got my visa and let my team manager know that I would like to quit. However, Monsanto had other plans for me, as Aparna came in to talk to me. I explained my reasons and voila! I was offered a very lucrative role as a Communications Manager at the head office in Mumbai and was even promised a transfer to their office in St. Louis, Missouri, US if I performed well. Since it seemed a very good offer, I accepted to stay because it gave me a chance to move away from the field of academics.

On the face of it, it may seem crazy that I refused a visa to go to the US, after dreaming of traveling for 15 years. However, I think I was patient because I knew that there is a time for everything.

In October 2001, I resigned from Monsanto and decided to pursue a Masters in Health Administration. I spent a few months studying for the tough GRE (Graduate Record Examinations) exam, qualified for it, and was selected at many universities in US as well as Canada. I chose Dalhousie University in Halifax, Canada, with a scholarship and half the cost of studying in US. Though I was to pursue a new field, I was excited that my lifelong goal to positively impact people's health directly through the many opportunities that MHA would open up, was finally materializing.

When I left India in 2002, I knew I was changing the course of my life and my dream of seeing the world was now becoming a reality.

> If one really desires something, makes efforts to achieve it, and keeps one's faith alive, one will definitely achieve it.

Achievements Abroad

After settling in Canada, I successfully completed my Masters in Health Administration in 2006. In 2011, I started my health practice, 'My Health Alive'. After pursuing various careers in diverse fields, I now have a sense of contentment, of walking down the path that is in line with my life purpose. My health coaching practice is doing far better service to humanity than merely prescribing medicines, because the real crisis today is not infections, but chronic diseases that need holistic consideration. I am now able to coach people to evaluate their lifestyles and thoughts and the effects of both these factors on their health, instead of merely popping pills and following the quick-fix methodology of modern medicine that advocates 'a pill for an ill.' Together, we put under the lens each person's journey with food, physical activity, sleep habits, and most importantly, THOUGHTS, thus helping them truly transform their lives in a wholesome manner!

I even started a community organic garden along with help from a very energetic church pastor and two other 'green finger' ladies in the neighbourhood. Today, we have 47 families using this wasted land as an organic garden, feeding their families with nutritious vegetables, sharing with others in the under-privileged communities and teaching their children love for Mother Earth.

In my 15 years in Canada, I have experienced a different world, learnt a lot in terms of values, communication, and in the process, also learnt to appreciate Indian culture. My best lesson has been 'everyone needs love and that is what they live and die for.'

Travel Tales

My dream of traveling started to look up more after I met my husband, who, fortunately, is a travel bug as well. Together, we have a dream of traveling to the far and beyond. We relish our little booklet of '1000 places to see before you die.' There are still about 990 places to check off!

For the moment, we are simply developing our database and bank balance with a focus on our travel book. As of 2018, I have taken a road trip from the Eastern Standard Time to the Atlantic Time Zone and walked the ocean floor in New Brunswick, where the water recedes by 1000 ft every day during the low tide. I have walked through the Rocky Mountains, bathed in the hot springs of Alberta, walked on the Athabasca glacier and visited the coffee plantations of Coorg and tea estates of Coonoor in Karnataka, and taken a cog rail up 14,400 feet in Colorado.

> I look at travel as a means to broaden my mind and understand how I can bring value to my family, and more importantly, to the community I live in. I am eager to discover lessons I can learn from other cultures that I can translate into the lives of youngsters, especially teenagers, to give momentum to the agenda of a peaceful world.

Interestingly, although traveling to regular tourist places gives me a sense of my place in the world, the most pivotal learning comes each time I travel back to India, especially when I am going through villages on a road trip. I admire their resilience and sense of community. Life is more meaningful when it is filled with community, simplicity, freedom, service, connection with Mother Earth, and healthy eating.

Maternal Moments

My life has changed 180 degrees after being blessed with a son in 2004. I found meaning in my life due to him. Each day, I feel overjoyed to have this opportunity to nurture him, and I live to help him turn his dreams into reality and grow up to be a purposeful adult who can influence others' lives with love and health.

Motherhood also embarked me on a journey to learn the tricks of bringing up a child in a new environment. During my childhood, I had the security and belongingness of an extended family that included family and friends. However, in a new land, and with no immediate family, it takes much more effort to look after children and instill values in them.

I have always coached my son about the importance of healthy eating and sleeping habits. I am teaching him the importance of drinking water and steering clear of medications to stay healthy for life. I am very grateful for what Canada has offered my child and me. Today, he is a fit and healthy thirteen-year-old, competing at the provincial level in speed skating, doing well in school and having a clear understanding of how to stay healthy with food and other habits of sleep and exercise. The most important lesson he has learnt is that of 'healthy competition' with his colleagues at the speed skating club, where he is making small strides in helping other athletes stay healthy.

I will count it my success if my son grows up with values of honesty and respect for human beings, animals, and the planet and when, at the core of what he does to make a living, is the goal to be part of the solution to bring about world peace and an end to poverty, illiteracy, hunger, and disease. Soon, when he will be a young man, my advice to him will be to look for ways to stay positive, polite and to nurture his soul with good habits and good company. I hope that he will choose his friends wisely and that I will be able to inculcate a positive attitude in him to look at problems larger than himself.

My Health Alive - Holistic Health Solutions

Obesity is a global epidemic. I have two countries to call my own – Canada and India, and surprisingly, the diseases in both countries seem to be similar when it comes to chronic ailments. I would like to focus on coaching people in both these countries to eat and live holistically. This means that family, friends, and food must come together at the table!

My clients are already experiencing their desired weight, sleep, energy, and pleasure for life. I have named this system, 'Strengthen your STEM – Sleep, Thoughts, Eating and Movement.' I am rediscovering myself and find my need to help people get rid of chronic pain, a motivational force. I am discovering the power of the mind that we can tap into through meditation. I wake up each morning with an innovative plan to make a positive difference to the health of busy women by empowering them with self-awareness and the knowledge that their freedom is theirs to take. They do not have to be sick if they choose not to.

This is the first time in my life that I am enjoying my career so much so that it is not a career – it is my life!

I enjoy my work because it energizes me to see the changes in my clients' health and thinking, and the abundance they are creating for themselves with my support as a knowledgeable and caring coach. I am learning from each of my clients and growing as a person.

My most interesting client is Stella, an 81-year-old lady, who has been a widow for 50 years, living by herself in Canada. She asked if I could help her with her an acid reflux problem she had had for 50 years. She signed up for 12 sessions, and every week she would show up on time and follow every plan we would come up with. When winter came, I offered to meet her in her home and was blown away with how well kept her two-bedroom house was – all maintained by herself, including cooking and hosting a paying guest. Stella even volunteered at a hospital and a nursing home, helping people with their needs. She has an undying love for life that can put even youngsters to shame. When she fell down and ended up with a broken hip, she hobbled on her feet and her biggest complaint was that she could not go swimming. Soon, following her physiotherapy exercises and our plan, she was able to get off her crutches. Not just that, she also got rid of her acid reflux in just six weeks, and went on a cruise to Russia. She was so excited to get on board without having to worry about acidity and an upset stomach! Stella constantly communicates with so many people who get inspired with her energy.

> Stella taught me more than I taught her – that age cannot be our excuse for health issues and that when we are in a mode to serve others, we stay the course and are not hindered by obstacles.

The Charisma of Conviction
Life is meant to be enjoyed through communication, travel, enjoyment, supporting others, and simplicity. We work to live

and not the other way round. I have learnt that it is important to put forth my view, even if it means going against the wishes of those I love. However, in order to do this, it is important to know what one wants to do as well as what one doesn't want to do. If one can present a compelling case with respect and kindness, then even the hardliners can be persuaded to see one's point of view. However, the feeling must be justified with facts and figures, and in a rational manner, if others are involved. Most importantly, communicating regularly is the key to an easy and pleasurable life. Proper communication helps build bridges where none exist.

In Retrospect

My childhood was a simple one full of family, friends, and food, together at the table. Fond memories of Sunday morning breakfasts on cold, sunny days in India with my parents, relatives, and friends sitting in our garden shall remain with me for the rest of my life. I am fortunate to be able to narrate these things to my son, who does not have the benefit of a large family.

> Some rare and precious moments that seem uneventful when they occur come back to haunt us once the time has gone.

If I could go back in time, I would like to assess my interests for my career, take time to research options, talk with my parents to weigh the pros and cons for the long term and focus on priorities in determining my career path. A 'give in' and ineffective communication do not work for me. It was a result of these that I ended up doing a Ph.D! I also gave into doing what my husband thought was best for me, while not taking the time to communicate to him what I really wanted to do. I tried to briefly convince him that I was committed to my son and family and that I didn't want to work just yet, but he thought that I was making a compromise and made sure that I continued with my career, which I did half-heartedly.

Looking back, I think it was my battle with my ill-health, both, on a physical and mental level, that was the inspiration for the work that I do today. As a health coach, I work tirelessly to understand my clients' symptoms at a biochemical level and connect it to the external and mental environment that may be producing the symptoms. I work out a plan to change their mindsets or habits and therefore, the change in food and lifestyle is gradual and exciting.

I am grateful that I live in the beautiful city of Ottawa, Canada, a family-friendly neighbourhood and a country that respects human beings regardless of their personal beliefs and the diverse cultures they come from.

Life Lines

The most important lessons for me have been –

- Communicate what you believe in. Share facts and figures to convince others. Do it with respect even if others have a different viewpoint.
- Surround yourself with people who energize you and are positive.
- Always treat your sleep and eating habits as top priority. Make meal times and sleep times well-guarded rituals because they feed your soul. Physical activity is the third-most important ingredient for a healthy life, after eating and sleeping well.
- Always engage in learning activities to grow your mind.
- Travel to explore cultures, and learn the best from each culture.
- Do not compare yourself to others because, as someone has said, "It is the most violent act you can do to yourself."
- As Steve Jobs has said, "Have the courage to follow your heart and intuition. They somehow already know what you truly want to become. Everything else is secondary."
- Keep life simple and keep silent when you are angry. Regular meditation helps us to use silence as our strength.

Words of Wisdom

I love to laugh, have fun, and connect with people. I believe that when women have fun in their lives, they can radiate it everywhere. They just need to learn to embrace it every day in their lives and not plan for it. This should be the normal way to live – with freedom and joy. This joy does not depend on material gains; it has to be explored, preserved, and treasured within our core. Our inner joy should guide us through life, and when we are able to do that, we let everyone else live joyfully. I have learnt that emotionally, men depend on women a lot more than the other way round, and only when we realize this, will we be able to welcome joy and peace in our lives and let them experience it too. We also need to realize the power of women connecting to each other and accept ourselves as leaders. The earlier we tap this resource and join hands, the better we will make this world.

I thank all the lovely women who –
a. Allow their inner joy to guide every action and decision.
b. Understand the power of holding hands with each other, because they will change the world.
c. Never try to compete with men to be equal because they are smart enough to understand that men and women are not competitors; they were created as the lock and key and are complementary.
d. Never get into the battle of comparison because by doing so they make a better and more pleasurable world.
e. Surround themselves with at least five positive thinking people because that way, they also move ahead positively.
f. Are on a journey to strengthen their STEM.

I would love to hold hands with all women who are waiting to unleash their inner joy and peace to make a better world by just letting go!

6

The Resilient Regulator

Shri Raj Khilnani

Dear Sir,

You are a father figure, a friend, philosopher, and guide. I have known you to be a law enforcing and a law abiding person – an absolute disciplinarian! You are a thorough gentleman with a warm heart who always lends a helping hand, whether in your official or personal capacity. I wonder if the Almighty makes people like you anymore.

Yours Affectionately,
Aparna

About Shri Raj Khilnani...

Shri Raj Khilnani is a policeman with a difference. Having a sound sense of discipline, he is also blessed with a strong spiritual foundation that helps him focus on the humane side of law.

Joining the IPS in 1977, he has worked alongside senior police officials like Mr. Julio Ribeiro who was the Police Commissioner of Mumbai and Mr. Ronnie Mendonca who was the Director General of Police (DGP), Maharashtra. Raj Khilnani assisted Mr. Ribeiro, along with the State Reserve Police Force (SRPF) to crush the miscreants in the Thane-Belapur industrial belt following which, Mr. Ribeiro became the Police Commissioner of Mumbai.

Raj Khilnani led many challenging assignments throughout his career. He clamped curfew and maintained a prolonged red alert preventing riots and security threats after the Babri Masjid demolition and the Bombay riots and bomb blasts. He was also assigned the responsibility of the preventive detention of Dr. Datta Samant that had to stand the judicial scrutiny of the High Court.

As Assistant Superintendent of Police (ASP) in Dahanu, Thane, he handled a very heavy charge beset with diverse problems. It was extensive, covering highly urban industrial areas touching Bombay and right up to Gujarat, covering remote tribal areas.

In 1981, he worked as Additional Superintendent of Police of composite Thane District. In the new Commissionerate, he continued as Deputy Commissioner of Police (DCP) for Thane, Bhiwandi and New Bombay. He worked extremely hard to curb the widespread organized bootlegging and gambling activities by creating terror among the anti-social elements not only in his zone, but also in Kalyan, Ulhasnagar, Dombivali, and Ambarnath.

As the Commandant in the SRPF, he again showed his charismatic ability to lead, and raise the morale of the battalion which was continuously deployed under adverse conditions to tackle the famous textile mills strikes in Bombay.

The professional competence and skill required of an Indian Police Service (IPS) officer have been amply demonstrated by him throughout his career with his special knack of promoting team spirit and leading the force by his sincerity of purpose and strength of character in both official and personal capacities.

Being a disciple of Meher Baba, his deeply ingrained spiritual outlook enabled him to set an example of high moral integrity. Thus, he was able to establish very high credibility amongst the officers and constabulary. He was eager to improve the image of the Police not merely through public relations, but also by an honest, impartial approach to work and empathy for the public. He had genuine concern about the well-being and welfare of his subordinates. As Superintendent of Police (SP), he organized many drama and orchestra shows to substantially augment the Welfare Fund.

Self-restrained by nature, he proved himself through his deeds, his reputation at the various places he worked, and his dedication which meets the highest standards expected of a senior police officer.

In 2010, he started Heart Quest Charitable Trust, symbolizing goodness and all that is positive and virtuous.

"When you are looking for an answer to something, look into your heart. The place that holds God is the heart. The answer that you get when you ask God who resides in your heart is the right one!"
– Shri Raj Khilnani

It was the year 1977 when I was training in Thane as an IPS probationer. I went into a building in a police jeep. When I entered the gate, I saw children playing. Although I was in civilian clothes, the children ran away as I approached. One little girl from the group was nonplussed. She started crying bitterly. I held out my hand to her. As she continued to cry, she pointed to the police jeep. She was crying because she was afraid of the Police!

I knew her fear was baseless. But how could I explain this to her? This incident shocked me to the core! Police are meant to serve a social cause. But how can they do it if people don't trust them?

Even before I had completed my training, this incident brought to my notice the negative image of the Police in the minds of citizens. That's when I decided, I would make a difference!

> As Mahatma Gandhi said, "You must be the change you wish to see in the world."

Blessed Beginnings

I was born in Pune into a family that had a mix of scientific and spiritual views. My grandparents, both paternal and maternal, were aristocrats in the Sind province of erstwhile British India. They lost their aristocratic status due to the Partition. However, they looked at this positively. The consequent turmoils that this created in their lives led them into spiritual quests. Both my grandfathers were spiritually blessed in their own way.

My mother's father who was a very eminent doctor had done his Fellowship at the Royal College of Physicians (FRCP) in London and had written two books sharing his spiritual good fortune and experiences. He invented the medicine for plague. When Ramana Maharshi was ill, it was my grandfather who gave him his last glass of fruit juice. My grandfather was also fortunate to have had the company of spiritual gurus. He also often took me to meet Saint Udasinji of Ramtekdi, Pune and have *prasad* (a religious offering consumed by worshippers after worship) from his hands. He had been to Phaltan and had met Upalekar Maharaj and had also been to Kolhapur to meet Shri Dattabal Maharaj.

My father's father was a barrister in London and was a follower of Sadhu Vaswani. He visited the renowned saint daily. I often joined him on these visits and heard the saint deliver discourses. Since both my grandparents were well-educated from England, they ensured that my parents too got excellent education.

Pious Parents

On shifting to India during the partition, my father started working as a judge. Having got into the bureaucracy, my parents had attractive opportunities to take to a life of material progress and restore their aristocratic lifestyle. However, since they had had a devout upbringing as children, they chose to pursue their spiritual aspirations.

They were ardently looking for divinity in the midst of a disturbed worldly life of enjoyments. It was not just a matter of seeking solace, but also a genuine urge to reach out to the reality in their apparently material life.

My father became a scholar on Maharshi Aurobindo's works, having studied the collection of books written by the seer. He had received a rose and an invite from the Holy Mother from Pondicherry in the mid-1950s. He also literally knocked at the doors of Guruprasad, at Bund Garden Road, Pune, where Meher Baba had started residing. Meher Baba was our mentor, Guru, and a very strong and positive influence in our lives.

Adolescent Ambitions

As I look back on my life today, I find myself truly fortunate on many counts. I wasn't very studious. I was very playful and devoted much of my time and energy to my many hobbies, particularly carpentry.

My maternal uncle was the first commander and trainer of the Air Bus aeroplanes. He had trained Shri Rajiv Gandhi. He became my idol and I decided to become a pilot.

Our family would visit Meher Baba quite often. Once, my brother asked him what he should study. Meher Baba told him to take up Chemistry. At that time, I had also accompanied my brother. When I asked Meher Baba what I should study, he said, "You are still young. I will tell you when the time comes." However, I persisted and said that I wanted to become a pilot.

But to my surprise, Meher Baba refused and said that I should not become a pilot. I was disappointed but determined that I would defy him and become a pilot no matter what. However, as a young child, I did not realize that when Meher Baba said 'no' to me, it was not his personal wish, but the divine knowledge that he had that my destiny lay elsewhere.

And so it came to be! At that time, I used to wear spectacles and as I grew, the power of my spectacles became four. This made me ineligible to become a pilot. Meher Baba had been right, after all!

My next choice was to become an engineer as I was fond of electricals and carpentry. In 1972, I joined Karad Engineering College. But my father was transferred to Mumbai and refused to let me stay in Karad on my own. He suggested I study law and become a judge.

But destiny had other plans. It's a mystery how, when things are destined to happen, they will happen no matter what you do! Throughout my growing years, I had closely seen many District Superintendents of Police like Shri S. K. Bapat, Shri S. K. Seth, Shri Baraokar, Shri Parthasarthy, Shri Ray, Shri P. S. Pasricha, and others and had been greatly influenced by them.

I was ambitious and at the age of 20, I decided that I wanted to get into the Indian Police Services (IPS). The Indian Administrative Services (IAS) and Allied Services Examinations were started soon

Aparna Sharma | 111

after independence in the early 1950s to replace the Indian Civil Service examinations of the British Raj.

Examination Experiences

I was wholeheartedly engrossed in studying Physics and Chemistry of M.Sc. levels and appeared for the IPS and IAS exams.

I had studied the question papers set by the Union Public Service Commission (UPSC) for the previous 22 years. I saw that in both Physics and Chemistry, although the standard was of M.Sc. level, there were lots of optional questions. A candidate had to answer 5 questions only out of 12, each of 40 marks. The questions were also repeated regularly and formed a pattern. I had solved all the question sets from 1951 to 1973. So when I appeared for the examination in 1974, I was pretty confident of making it into the IPS.

However, for the first time in the history of this examination, the pattern of the question paper was totally altered. There was not half as much option left in selecting the questions. What was worse for me was that instead of just 5 questions of 40 marks each, there were over a hundred questions of 1 or 2 marks each. The exam was a new ball game altogether, and this came like a bolt from the blue! Hardly anyone who opted for these subjects cleared the examination that year!

> No matter how much preparation you do, Lady Luck has the final say!

Appointment to IPS

However, I was determined to get into the IPS. So, I changed my strategy. Since my father wanted me to follow his footsteps, I studied law and prepared afresh with law subjects. I once again gave the exam, this time for the IAS and topped the list of successful candidates in the allied, i.e., Central Services. That was when I realized that Meher Baba had not told me to study for

IAS because then, I would have probably taken for granted that I would pass the examination and would not have made any efforts on my own.

The UPSC Board sent me a letter stating that I would have to appear for three eye tests and see three different eye specialists who would give my eyes a clean chit. My spectacles had the power four and it was the outer limit for a candidate to be selected. Even a power a little higher than this and I would not have been selected in the IPS!

> It's a mystery how, when things are meant to happen, they find a way to happen no matter what you do!

I was appointed to the Indian Police Service in the year 1977 on selection by UPSC through IAS and Allied Services exams. I was also awarded the Silver Medal for Law during IPS Training at LBS National Academy of Administration, Mussoorie.

A police officer's life can never be boring. Neither is it a 9-5 job, nor can one work at it that way. My work taught me a variety of lessons – some the hard way, some joyfully, and others, quite unexpectedly.

From Victim to Vandal

When I was the Superintendent of Police in Thane, I called all the Inspectors of Thane and asked them, "Who is the most feared *goonda* (miscreant)?" They told me it was 'X.' I told them, "I will give you time till tomorrow morning. Bring X before me by that time!" Horrified, they pleaded with me to not give such orders. But I was adamant. They asked me for 2-3 days, and I kept following up with them till they brought X to me.

When I saw X, I couldn't control my laughter! Even a high school boy shouldn't have been afraid of the thin, short chap sitting before me. I called for a cup of tea and sat him down. I asked him, "Why are people afraid of you?" And he told me his story.

Once, he had happened to see a man being murdered by a feared *goonda*. X managed to stop the murder. However, the murderer hurt X and in the tussle, X ended up killing the *goonda*. The next day's newspaper carried the headline, 'X murders a well-known *goonda*' along with X's photo. X was charged for murder.

When he was released, he went from pillar to post looking for a job to earn a living. But who would employ a murderer? He was left with no choice and had no means of earning an honest living. So, he took the newspaper that had carried his photograph and began to show it to people and threaten them to pay him money for their protection. Soon, he became an extortionist and created his own gang!

While it was true that X was a victim of circumstances, taking to crime to earn a living dragged him into deeper murk, from which it was impossible for him to get out!

> Life is a combination of what happens to you and what you make out of what happens to you.

The Tale of a Transfer

When I was the SP of Jalgaon, a Traffic Awareness Week was to be held for the benefit of the public. The Traffic Inspector came to me for guidance. As a leader, I told him, "Do what your heart tells you to do. I am with you!" To promote the event, he put up a stage and a traffic exhibition in one of the main *chowks* (crossroads).

At that time, a politician who held a high office in the Municipality of Jalgaon city was called to sit on the stage with me. There was a huge crowd and the press clicked my photos with him. The Jalgaon Municipal Elections and State Elections were to be held around the same time. The party workers of another political bigwig were disturbed to see my photograph with the politician from the Municipality. Perceiving a threat, the political bigwig asked officers at higher levels to have me transferred. Within a year of this incident, I was transferred.

Election Episode

It was quite surprising for me to know that Police could be used to fulfill political agendas. Once, the party workers of the same political bigwig came to me saying that they wanted the Police to help them. I said, "I will help you within the legal framework of my job." They replied, "Candidates are going to the Collector's office to file papers for the Municipal Corporation elections. But they are carrying knives. We want you to frisk them, take their knives and show their real face to the public."

I told them, "You have told me the problem. Now I will do my job." I made enquiries about those candidates and found that they were not carrying any knives. I told the party workers of the truth. I said, "If anybody is found with a knife, it is my responsibility. But I will not take action against innocents." Obviously, they were not happy with this answer. They wanted to use the Police and humiliate their rival party candidates and their workers.

> No matter how strong the provocation, one mustn't take action until one knows the whole truth.

Media Mayhem

When I was the Superintendent of Police of Gadchiroli in Chandrapur, Naxalites had attacked a police station and in the ambush that followed, I had happened to kill a Naxalite. As this news spread, a Union Minister called me and fired me on the telephone asking me what I thought I was doing. That's when I came to know that sympathizers of the Naxalites – journalists, advocates, and other activists had complained to him about my actions during this incident. However, when a journalist wrote a complementary article about me, the Jt. Director SIB for Maharashtra called me and told me that I was doing a good job.

> Not everybody knows the whole truth. What they know and believe is how the truth has been projected to them.

Aparna Sharma

Work Woes

It was very common for astrologers and ascetics to meet high officials, give their predictions and take pictures with us. From 1982 – 2013, I met them off and on. During these years, most of them continually told me – 'Many people gossip about you behind your back.' At first, I ignored this prediction of theirs. But later, I did think about what they were saying. Were people really talking ill about me? Although I was disturbed by this thought initially, later I realized that if indeed this were so, I was never going to know about it anyway! What I didn't know wouldn't hurt me. So why worry about it?

> Once you reach a certain position, people are going to talk about you. You can either pay attention to them or do your job. I chose to just go on doing my job.

Work is Worship

When I was the Superintendent of Police at Chandrapur, the Chief Minister (CM) of Maharashtra called me up. He asked me to come and meet him when I came to Mumbai. He appreciated my work when I met him. It was quite surprising that when I was transferred from Mumbai to Chandrapur, a lot of people had expressed their sympathy towards me, as though a lot of bad luck had befallen me. But here was the Chief Minister of Maharashtra appreciating my work!

"Sir, how do you know about my work?" I asked genuinely surprised. That's when he told me that two MLAs had brought a delegation of people from Chandrapur to him, asking for me to be transferred! The Chief Minister made his enquiries about them and about me too. He came to know that those people were running organized bootlegging and gambling clubs! Their economic interests were affected due to my work and thus, they were unhappy with me! The CM knew that this was due to my performance, and that is why he congratulated me.

> When you do good work, you don't have to spread the word. It happens on its own.

Refreshing Retirement

I retired as the Director General of Police Anti-Corruption Bureau (DGP-ACB) in October 2013. Although I had thought that I would relax post retirement, I was pleasantly surprised. A month prior to this, in September 2013, I was offered the position of Governor on the board of IIT Mandi in Himachal Pradesh by the HRD Ministry, Government of India, which I immediately accepted.

This period of my life has been interesting, challenging as well as refreshing. We have had to set up the Institute from scratch, addressing all its varied aspects in great detail starting from the planning and construction of the whole Institute. Getting good faculty in the Himalayan region is also a difficult task. But our hard work has paid off, and this Institute is now equipped with state-of-the-art equipment by international standards. I have enjoyed all the challenges this work has brought and continue to work at this position.

Heart-Questing

On 25th February, 2010, (Meher Baba's birthday), I started Heart-Quest.org. Heart-Quest.org (Happiness for all) was founded as a charitable trust in India. On 15th August, 2014, we started Heart's Quests Association in the US. The idea is that anyone can use it as a brand for anything and everything from his/her heart. The deeper concept is to shift our focus from our minds to our hearts, which is the need of our times (more empathy). Who can save humanity except the Great Grand Director General of the whole Universe who silently resides in our hearts as His abode?

Heart-quest is the tapping of one's inspirations in life. Further, it is about formulating aspirations based on these inspirations and one's value systems. We analyze and study people's inspirations and aspirations and based on these, we can create partnerships of mutual interest.

Heart-quest works at providing meaningful interaction towards meeting the individual needs of all human beings in their search for divine meaning, sharing and helping each other on our spiritual journey, and experiencing the thrill of leading a spiritual life together on Earth. In the most practical sense, it means helping victims of crime, accidents, social and self-abuse in all possible ways, to promote the reformation and rehabilitation of criminals rather than punishment.

Heart-quest is a continuous process. It has tremendous potential for practical research, academic work, social projects, and awareness campaigns. My American friend Jonathan Borough coined the word 'Heart-questing.' It also means attempts of the heart. It is an effort. One must increase the efforts of the heart – for self as well as others. What drives you decides what your quest is. Heart-questing is a psycho-social movement that will boost confidence in humanity. Let me explain the concept of Heart-questing with a few examples.

It was 14th April, 1988 – the day of Ambedkar Jayanti. My son was born and I was away in Nagbhir, handling a major law and order situation. My policemen had opened fire at the offenders from both, the upper castes and the lower castes who were pelting stones at each other!

After the situation was under control, I addressed my police officers saying, "Why do you get your salary?" Confused, they gave me all kinds of answers. I told them, "We get a salary to face the stone pelting. So we shouldn't lift rifles and kill people. Take a *lathi* (a long wooden stick) in one hand and a first aid box in another. The Police is not against people; it is only against the miscreants. We ask the Chief Minister for funds for the Police Force. But the impression about the Police in the minds of the people is not at all positive. Can't we show people common courtesies? When a person comes into the Police Station to lodge a complaint, can't we offer him/her a glass of water? By being courteous and polite, we can win over people and earn their trust. Then, there shall be no need to use rifles." This is one of the best examples of heart-questing on the job!

*

In 2010, I was invited by a few industrialists to the Taj Hotel in Mumbai. They were looking for a police officer with experience. They wanted me to resign from IPS and work for them. At that time, I had the ticket for my visit to Stanford, US in my pocket. Since theirs was a tempting offer, I told them that I would let them know once I got back. I was pondering over this question throughout my flight. I decided to ask Meher Baba in my heart because, the place that can hold God is the heart. Heart-questing is like the cultivation of the soil. The heart becomes fertile for the Lord to awaken rationale. The answer that you get when you ask the Lord who resides in your heart is the right one!

*

As the Superintendent of Police, I was invited to social gatherings to address people and guide them. I told them that the only guidance one can get is by heart-questing. After my lecture, during high tea, people who had invited me came up to me and said, "You don't look like a police officer." I replied, "I am sitting in a police station where different people come with different problems. In order to solve their problems and treat them fairly, I will have to look at their problem from their perspective. So if I look at the problem from the victim's perspective, how can I look like a police officer?"

In Retrospect

I was never a typical police officer. In fact, I had no idea what I was getting into when I joined the IPS. I was a simpleton. Police work is a challenging profession and more so, if one happens to be straightforward and simple.

Although I worked hard with sincerity, I never tried to hog the limelight or blow my own trumpet or hobnob with those in power. Nor did I have a godfather who would look out for me. As I look back over 35 years of my Indian Police Service, I see that I wasn't ambitious enough to chase the hot assignments and the glory they could offer me. However, I have no regrets. I know I did the best I could, considering all the factors that came into play at those times. While I worked in various leadership positions, there were others who got more visibility than me, but I think it's all a part of the game.

At the beginning of my service, when at times I would feel disturbed about what was going on, I got two pieces of advice. One was from my father who said, "Son, look upon your job merely as a *khaki* uniform and 'remove' it off when you are off duty." What he meant was that a sense of detachment would stand me in good stead, and it indeed did. The second advice was about marrying the right person. I think, I am more than satisfied on this score as well. In fact, my life and my job have been a testing ground for trying to keep up to the expectations of those who mattered and matter the most to me.

Meher Baba is the foremost in this list. He said, "Nothing is real but God; nothing matters but love for God." My life has been an experience in attempting to realize the importance of these words while living my daily life.

Meher Baba also used to say, "It is all a passing show," and "It is all nothing into nothing." This left a deep impact on my psyche. His words have helped me glide through the challenges in my life effortlessly.

I have traveled widely in Asia, US, Europe, New Zealand, Australia and feel fortunate to have been born in India. In spite of all problems, India has a very strong spiritual base. I am very sure that God is partial to India.

Life Lines
- Heart-questing is the biggest learning. One should always be heart-questing. It can be done 24x7. Heart-quest is my advice to everyone.

- One should take up at least one thing and do it religiously – whether it is fasting on specific day/s or reading specific books or going for a pilgrimage.
- If God brings you to it, He will bring you through it!
- People may speak about you behind your back. But, if you are true to yourself, what they say shouldn't matter.
- Even if you do not receive credit that you feel is your due, remember that God is watching you and taking note of all your deeds. He will give you what you deserve when the time is right.
- Make an effort to love everything, hate nothing!

> ### Words of Wisdom
>
> *Discipline and Spirituality are two important factors that can take you towards success. While the first keeps you grounded to continue to do your duty, the second prevents you from getting bogged down by failures, setbacks or by becoming overconfident and selfish due to success.*
>
> *I am proud to be a citizen of this country (India) that has a strong spiritual base since ancient times. The only thing we must do is to utilize this spiritual power that lies dormant within us, to make a positive difference in our lives as well as to those around us.*

7

A Cheerful Crusader

Vandana Jadhav

Dear Vandy,

You are an epitome of courage, determination and self-belief. I have seen you transform from a timid, demure woman into a confident and strong-willed lady chef today. Your life has been full of trials and tribulations, but you have stood tall through all of it – taking care of yourself and your children single-handedly. Focussing on your skills and strengths in spite of not being educated, your resolve to lead a respectable life and support the education of your children is truly remarkable. The famous saying by Maria Robinson, "Nobody can go back and start a new beginning, but anyone can start today and make a new ending," is a befitting adage for your life and spirit. Every time I meet you, I ask you, "Kasa kai, Mumbai?" (How's it going, Mumbai?), and no matter what situation you are in, you always respond with a chirpy, "Bari ahe, Mumbai!" (Everything's fine in Mumbai!)

Yours Affectionately,
Aparna

About Vandana Jadhav...

Vandana's story is one of great determination, undying courage, and unending positivity and optimism. Born in a lower income family, she was married off at the tender age of 16 without proper education and the slightest idea of the turn her life was going to take. Absorbing life's shocks and enduring the pain and suffering with a smile, she has emerged victorious with her mantra of 'Never give up.'

She has earned a good name for herself among cosmopolitan families in Thane (a suburb of Mumbai) with her cooking and the various snacks she dishes out with ease and expertise. Be it Indian delicacies such as *Theplas, Puranpolis, Modaks* or Chinese food, her snacks are very much in demand, and she is busy round the clock fulfilling these orders and ensuring gastronomic delight within the committed time. Dashing off from place to place on her little Scooty (a two-wheeler), she also provides people food for thought with her positivity and infectious smile.

"When you face a situation that you can do nothing about, it is an opportunity for two things – one, to test your faith in God and two, to teach you acceptance. When you accept what is, you clear your mind to think about what can be..." – Vandana Jadhav

I park my Scooty in the guest parking of Hiranandani Estate. Mrs. Patil is waiting to receive me and her order of 200 steaming hot *modaks*. "Greetings for the *Ganesh Chaturthi* festival," she says, giving me a hug. She coaxes me to come home for *darshan* (to pay a visit to the Lord at her home). Promising to visit them soon, I rush home on my Scooty to prepare my next two orders of *Puranpolis* and Chinese fried rice. The festival season is at its peak!

As I roll the dough to make my special *Puranpolis*, my mind wanders off somewhere into the past. It's been 16 years of doling out delicacies, and it's a hectic but good life! But it was not so always...

Young Years

I was born in the year 1976 in Santacruz, Mumbai. We are three sisters and one brother. My father worked at construction sites and my mother worked at the many houses that surrounded ours, as a household help. My parents belonged to the old school of thought where daughters were looked upon as a burden, to be married off at the earliest, with or even without minimum education.

Marital Miseries

In 1992, I was 16 years of age and in Class 8 when I was married off to the son of my father's first cousin sister. They lived in Thane, and we didn't know them well. But such are our customs and traditions that we trusted my aunt and her family who confidently told us that my would-be husband had a steady job and was a teetotaller. My parents were so trusting that they didn't make enquiries about the boy's character. By the time I came to know the truth, it was too late!

To my horror, the day I got married, I discovered that my in-laws had blatantly lied to us! My husband was an alcoholic! Neither was he working, nor did he have any source of income! I bravely packed my bags before I had even properly unpacked them and decided to walk out of his house and his life forever!

But alas! I was too inexperienced to know that it was not easy. My in-laws threatened me saying that before I ventured out of the house to leave my husband, I must think of my unmarried sisters. Who would marry them? My parents would be humiliated if I acted so irresponsibly. What would people say? My maternal home was fraught with financial problems, and my sisters were not yet married. My in-laws' words were powerful enough to stop me in my tracks. I had conveniently assumed that I could go back to my parents and get on with my life as though nothing had happened! Sadly, that's not how things work in our society.

My in-laws were confident that my husband would definitely improve now that he was married to a nice girl like me! Once the household responsibilities fell on him, he would certainly turn over a new leaf. After all, who did not have problems in their married life? Everything would be sorted out soon!

Right from Day Two of my marriage, I went to work to earn us a living. I did variety of jobs to earn any money I could – transported bricks or sand on my head for Rs. 25 a day, swept the roads for Rs. 30 a day, worked in a small company for Rs. 15 a day… and so on. A year after my marriage, I delivered my first child, a boy, and continued to work hard at these jobs. However, this knocked the stuffing out of me. My husband did nothing to support us financially. When a posh township called Hiranandani Estate came up near our small hutment, I got work as a household help, washing clothes and utensils, cleaning houses etc. During these years, I gave birth to three more children.

That was my husband's only contribution in my life! Those were truly difficult days. My married life had all the drama of a Hindi blockbuster film. My husband was wasting his life drinking. There was absolutely no one to support me. I couldn't go to my parents' house. My in-laws paid no heed to my worries. Many times, I had no money to buy food for the children and myself and would eagerly wait for my husband to return in the evening, hoping against hope that he would take pity on us and buy us some food. One day, when he returned, I found that he had bought himself drinks, but no food for us! The question of whether there was any food for us to eat never crossed his mind. Many were the days when my children and I went to bed hungry. To top it all, my husband hated it if I talked to anyone, accused me of having affairs with various men and even threatened to throw me out of the house! If I argued, he would beat me up. A woman whose husband doesn't support her is vulnerable to unwanted advances from other men, and I had my share of difficulties from that quarter too. Yet, I forced myself to remain calm for my children's sake.

My husband had seven brothers and two sisters. But no matter how desperate our situation was, neither did they bother to enquire how we were doing, nor did I ask them for help. I did ask my sisters-in-law to lend me water and electricity, but in spite of paying them for these necessities, they would shut off the supply at night, knowing that I wouldn't come knocking at their doors at that time of the day. So on most days, it was no food, no electricity and no water either. After eight years of putting up with such behaviour, when my youngest son was born in the year 2000, I decided that enough was enough, took my children and walked out of my husband's life forever. I stayed at my mother's place for 6-8 months.

> I decided that no matter what my karmas were in my past life, I DID NOT deserve such a horrible life!

Depths of Despair

Although I had walked out of my husband's life, I didn't know what my children and I had walked into. We needed a roof over our heads, and it had to be a *pucca* (a solid, permanent) house. I joined a chit fund and took a loan at ten percent interest and was able to build my own little place under the sun. I saved every penny I could. I was also firm that no matter what, I would send my children to school and see that they completed their education. They would never suffer the indignity of not being educated, like I had!

But as hard as I tried, I was unable to make enough money to pay back the loan on my house. Creditors would stalk me, making my life miserable. Finally, tired of this harassment, I let it go! I gave up my dream of having my own house! I had to sell off my house and I did it to pay back every penny I had borrowed.

> You need to rethink your goals with the passage of time.

This was also the time I lost my elder son. My world collapsed around me. I couldn't understand – Why me?! Neither I, nor my other children could understand what was happening. It seemed as though there was simply no hope for us. While earlier, it was survival which was a struggle, now it seemed as though just staying alive was a big challenge. But when you face a situation that you can do nothing about, it is an opportunity for two things – one, to test your faith in God and two, to teach you acceptance. When you accept what is, you clear your mind to think about what can be…

It wasn't as if thoughts of ending it all didn't occur to me. They did. But my acceptance of my son's death helped me to stay alive. I had lost one of my children. But my other children were alive and dependent on me. My family looked up to me for courage and determination. How could I let them down? That's when I realized that first and foremost, I was a mother.

> Motherhood is a great strength. It can help a woman overcome the greatest of challenges to make sure her children are safe.

I did not want my children to be orphans, and so I decided that I had to live. I would not let them be bogged down by my worries. I would give them a safe and secure environment. That's when I learnt that I had to keep smiling always for the sake of my children. And slowly, it became a habit.

A Champion Cook

One day, one of the ladies at whose house I worked, suggested that I start cooking for people instead of cleaning. "You cook for your family, don't you? So why not cook for others? At least give it a try. How long are you going to stick to cleaning, and how much can you earn this way?" she asked. She gave me the first opportunity of cooking a daily meal for her family. They were very happy and liked my cooking. She suggested that I take orders and prepare simple snacks and dishes for people. I did so and got an encouraging response from them. I also worked at people's houses and helped in the cooking when they had get-togethers and parties.

Soon, I realized that cooking was my strength and people liked my dishes. So, I decided to take it one step further. I bought a TV and began to watch cookery programs and learnt to make all kinds of food – Punjabi, Kashmiri, Maharashtrian, Gujarati, South Indian, Chinese etc., and was able to cater to the tastes of cosmopolitan families. I began to watch programs like 'Masterchef' and 'Food Food' and tried those recipes too. To my delight, all the ladies encouraged me to prepare something new for them. I also bought cookery books and learnt recipes in my spare time. I added various flavours, and experimented with various ingredients and spices to make dishes more delicious and interesting. Gradually, I picked up speed and was able to turn out dishes quite fast. The ladies called me 'Superfast Express.' Soon, I became so efficient that I did not even need to taste a dish to see if it had turned out well.

But then, I realized that walking to the various houses where I worked was a time-consuming and tiring process. If I could overcome it, I could add a few houses to my list and increase my income. So I decided to save money and bought a two-wheeler. It took me six months to learn to ride. I had never ridden even a bicycle till then, and here I was zooming across town on a Scooty.

Change in Circumstances

My life changed for the better in the last five years. I repaid all my loans. I began to enjoy cooking, experimenting, searching for recipes and creating something new. I worked at 13 homes and also took orders for various dishes. People from London and America who visited the families I worked for often placed orders of 200-300 *theplas* to take back with them. I happily provided them the dishes they asked for.

Many times, they even offered me employment abroad, stating that I could earn much more if I went there. I knew that was true. But I was living only for my children. How could I leave them behind? So I never explored the idea further.

> People who know me say that I am much better than a man! I often lost battles, but never lost courage.

Fateful Failures

I had always wanted to study, but did not get the opportunity to complete my education. Getting married without completing my education was my first biggest mistake. Not leaving my husband's house when I had decided to, was the second. When I realized that my in-laws had cheated us and that my husband was never going to improve, I should have cut my losses and walked out, instead of being afraid of what people would say. In spite of holding on to a disintegrating marriage, people talked behind my back and no one came forward to help me. While I have no complaints, I did realize that we are ourselves responsible for our fate and cannot afford to give others the freedom to choose for us.

I still feel appalled that in spite of 70 years of independence, there are parents who choose not to educate their daughters. They still believe that women's lives should be restricted to *chulha* (the hearth) and children.

Here Comes Happiness!

Now my elder daughter is married and has a two-year-old daughter. I am satisfied that I was able to educate her and got her married only after she completed her education. My younger son studies in Class 10 and younger daughter is in Class 12. I shall make sure that my children get good education. I have decided to be the beacon of light for my children – to be the support for them that I never had. I shall stand by them no matter what. I have always encouraged them to tell me the truth no matter what happens, instead of telling others.

Clients who know me are always surprised about how I can keep smiling and never show any anxiety and worry. My happy face inspires them to forget their own worries too. All my clients treat me like a family member. I may not have my own house, but this is my biggest asset that I have created – caring and loving people.

Future Pavilions

My children are my strength, my inspiration. They are the reason I am alive. I still haven't lost hope of building a house for them. I am working towards it and am sure I shall be successful. Once I do so, I would also like to start my own cookery classes and register my catering business. I am sure that with God's blessings and my determination, it shall definitely happen!

Life Lines

- No matter what the problem, never get bogged down by it. Keep your cool and try to find a way around it.
- Be positive and keep smiling. Never let people know what has befallen you.
- Never give up. It solves nothing. The situation can only change if and when you decide to take action.
- Do not be afraid of what people will say. Most people have no interest in others, and those who do, will say what they want to anyway. Neither of them will help you solve your problems.
- Trust in your ability to work hard for what you want.

- Do not take education lightly. Formal education is important. Also, one must keep learning new things in order to grow.
- Believe in God. Everything happens for a purpose.

> *Words of Wisdom*
>
> *Life is a combination of good and bad, happiness and sorrow. So, when you are faced with difficulties, remember that it is a temporary phase. Rich or poor, everyone has problems. Tolerance is a quality that can take us through any challenge. So, try to increase your tolerance; your problems will become smaller. Life is precious, and it is up to us to make it so. Believe that you CAN and never, never, never give up!*

8

Transforming Tresses the Tanveer Way!

Tanveer Shaikh

Dear Tanveer,

You are an awe-inspiring, grounded person. Always filled with warmth and positivity, your optimism towards life is contagious. Given your humble beginnings, you believe in giving your 100 percent in every walk of life – personal and professional. One can never know if you are having a bad day, since you are always committed to giving the best possible service to your clients across age groups and treating each one as 'special'. Your belief in all-round excellence rubs off on everyone you meet. Every time I meet you, I come away learning something new… Do you have a magic wand, my friend?

Yours Affectionately,
Aparna

About Tanveer Shaikh...

Tanveer is the Chief Creative Director and founder of the well-known brand TAS (Tanveer's Hair Studio and Academy) whose buzzword is 'Transformation.' Although his father insisted that he join the family hairdressing business, which he was not at all interested in, he decided that he would do so only after being formally trained in this art. Realizing the need for customized and systematic training in this profession, he decided to teach young, would-be professionals this creative skill. He is well-known in the film (Bollywood) and fashion industry alike for creating sensational looks, skilled styling, teaching as well as the excellent service he provides to his clients. He was an integral part of the prestigious Lakme India Fashion Week for ten years. The miracle maker that he is, he turns bad hair days into great hair for life!

"Hard work is my guru mantra. There are no shortcuts to success."
— Tanveer Shaikh

"It's gorgeous, Tanveer! I never thought I could look so beautiful!" gushes Kumud, an upcoming Bollywood actress after her hair 'transformation.' "You're the best in the world! God bless you!"

"Okay friends, today we learnt how to transform unruly hair into lovely locks! Any questions?" I turn to address my students of TAS (Tanveer's Hair Studio and Academy).

"That was a miracle, Sir! Will I also be able to do this?" quips wide-eyed, eighteen-year-old Rahul.

I laugh. "It's no miracle. What seems like a miracle is born out of sheer dedication and lots of hard work."

"Everybody loves the way you 'transform' them with a simple haircut. You must be getting blessed many times over, isn't it?" asks Kabir.

I laugh again. "Sure, I do feel I am blessed! But you would be surprised to know that the first time I cut someone's hair, she cursed me, and my career is a result of that curse!"

They look at me bewildered and in silence. "Tell us all about it. In fact, tell us everything about yourself," they say interested.

"Okay…" I begin…

Beginnings in Bombay

The eldest of two brothers and three sisters, I am a small town boy from Bijnor (in the state of Uttar Pradesh). Although my grandfather's father was a teacher, my grandfather came to Mumbai (then Bombay) in search of work and opened a barber's shop in Bombay's Fountain area. That was the time of World War II. The shop enjoyed the patronage of the British officers and my grandfather earned handsome tips as well. Gradually, he became financially well-off. After I was born, my father who also carried on the family profession brought us to Bombay.

Teething Troubles

Throughout my growing years, academics and I played a game of hide-and-seek! We had just begun to attend an English-medium school when my younger brother Imran was afflicted by polio. So, we went back to our village for his treatment. Here, I was enrolled in the Arya Samaj School where I studied till Class 2. This school was quite different from the one in Bombay. We had no notebooks, so we studied on slates (a sheet of thin, hard rock in a wooden frame, used to write in schools). My parents spent all their money on Imran's treatment. However, they realized that there was no hope for his ailment and also no opportunities for him in the village.

Once more, we shifted to the land of opportunities – Bombay. My parents were able to find a school for the physically challenged where they enrolled Imran. I began to attend the Municipal School (which was till Class 7). This was my third school.

My father rented a small shop in the Kalina area near Santacruz in Bombay. Our accommodation at Shastri Nagar in Kurla was far from comfortable. Water would flood our house in the rains. As compared to the huge spaces in the village, our house was cramped. Gradually, my father bought 125 sq. ft. of space behind the Kalina Masjid lane and we went to stay there in the year 1988. It was a lane where small entrepreneurs like barbers, washermen etc., lived and worked. I guess, this is where the seeds of entrepreneurship were sown in my mind.

Honestly, I was not at all an academic person. In fact, I failed in Class 3 and such was my disinterest that I often bunked school as well.

Teenage Tales

After Class 7, I joined a private Hindi medium school called Pathak Technical High School (which was till Class 10). Here, apart from studies, students could also learn useful professional skills and train to become blacksmiths, carpenters, electricians etc. I was fond of electronics and loved to play around with appliances like radios, televisions, fans, and wished to become a technician. This was where I found something that I liked for the first time. My teachers suggested I take up carpentry and I found that I was in my element while doing Engineering Drawing. Drawing and its symmetry attracted me and studying it for three years almost made me half an engineer. I use the views, patterns, and symmetry I studied then in my designs even today.

> When you study something with a great deal of interest, it stays with you forever.

Although I discovered that I was fond of and good at technical things, my father was constantly persuading me to learn hairdressing from him. He used to say, "If you have art in your hands, you will never suffer! No matter what the economic situation, you will definitely be able to feed yourself." However, I was dead against this!

I got 75 percent marks in my Class 10 exams. (I got 10 percent extra marks due to my technical education.) I decided to become a Mechanical Engineer. However, when I went to Saboo Siddiqui College at Bhindi Bazaar with my mark sheet, the watchman refused to even let me in. "You can't get into this college with that score," he said. He ruthlessly dashed my hopes to the ground and the simpleton that I was, I took his words to heart and came back home. As there was no one to guide me, I didn't even try to achieve my dream. I then decided to take up Commerce and got admission in Rizvi College in Bandra.

Father's Firm Stand

Despite my taking admission in Commerce, my father did not give up on his dream of making me a hairdresser. In 1994, after Class 10, he would send me to work in his friends' barber shops to learn hairdressing during the holidays. They would pay me Rs.10 per week which I collected as pocket money. My father was the inspiration behind my finally choosing this profession.

> He did not give up his dreams for me, although I had very easily given up mine!

The reason I didn't want to join this profession was that in those days it did not have the prestige that it does today. People would look down on barbers although it is a fact that everyone needs someone to cut their hair. It's as simple as that! But the social stigma at that time was unnerving. I remember the day we had to introduce ourselves in the first year of junior college. When asked what my father did, I said he owned a hardware store. It rankled that I had to lie about my father's profession although he was a hardworking and honest person. Later, when some of the students came to know the truth, they ridiculed me. This made me feel even worse, and I was sure that this was something I would never do!

However, I had underestimated how firm my father could be. After a lot of coaxing on his part, I told him that even if I did enter this profession, I would do it in a professional manner. He however, couldn't understand why I needed to learn elsewhere, when I could learn my family business from him.

I somehow managed to pass Class 11. But, since I came from a Hindi medium school, I could not overcome the language barrier and failed my Class 12 exams.

> In spite of not clearing the exams, I had learnt an important lesson! No matter what I chose to do, I knew that I just had to learn and be able to communicate in good English. My education had finally begun!

Exploring Education

After my failure in Class 12, I was at home for some time. My mother persuaded me to study seriously. However, caught up with my father's idea, I did some research about this profession. I did not want to become 'just another barber!'

I explored Mumbai and also visited New Delhi. People like Shahnaz Husain and Jawed Habib had turned this profession into an art, given it a good name and earned fame and respect. This was an upcoming field, and I found that there were academies that offered professional training. I came back to Mumbai in 1997 after my survey.

I wanted to join a reputed academy and get trained professionally. However, my father had no money to enroll me in such a place. So, the only thing left for me to do was to join my father's barber shop and learn from him. Within two months, I learnt everything he could teach me. However, I was still not satisfied. There was much more that was missing. Since my parents were not sure about my commitment towards this profession, and going by my past performance in academics, they refused to send me for a professional course.

That's when I decided to earn money and do the course myself. I joined my relative's barber shop. For three months, I started my day at 7 am and worked continuously till 12 am. Although, I was to get between Rs. 1500 to Rs.1800 per month, my relative did not pay my dues of three months. In spite of all my hard work, I could not join my course! It looked as though there was no way out of this.

> As they say, every cloud has a silver lining.

The three months of hard work in my relative's shop was enough to convince my parents of my commitment towards learning this profession. My parents gave me the money I needed for the three-month course, which was a Diploma in Hairdressing. My mother pawned her jewelry for the first installment of the fees. I was the only one to complete this course within two months!

This course was the first turning point in my life. It gave me inspiration and opened up new opportunities before me. It changed me. I was caught by the 'artistic' bug and also became interested in teaching. I now looked at this profession as an art and at myself as an artist. I also decided that I would take this art ahead and become the best teacher in the world! I would train young minds to transform others and create new looks, new styles and new personalities!

Career Carnival

I was young, enthusiastic, presentable, and good at my job. Thus, the academy where I did my course recruited me as a Hair Stylist. I was transferred to Cochin in Kerala and was to work at the salon in Hotel Trident, donning several hats like manicurist, pedicurist, hair stylist, manager and so on. Suresh Gopi, who was the star of Malayalam movies was my permanent client. So was an actor called Rahman. I had become a well-qualified professional. In my twenties, I was beginning to gain respect for what I did. Although I had learnt soft skills, I was still not fluent in English. Being in Kerala, I had the opportunity to improve my English. I became well-known due to my expertise and people began to specially come to me to get their hair cut. My confidence was at an all-time high!

The Tale of a Transformation

Now, such are the times when one has to be careful! Once, a South Indian lady called Ms. Diana came to me for a haircut. She had waist-length hair and in my quest to give her a great haircut, I inadvertently ended up reducing the length of her hair upto her neck – shorter than a bob. Although she was quite disturbed, I managed to convince her that she was looking good. At first, she was convinced. However, when people told her that this haircut did not suit her, she began to cry.

I was perplexed. How had this happened?! I imagined the worst and thought that I would either end up losing my job or being sent to jail. I almost swore that I would never reduce the length of anyone's hair again! To top it all, 'Malayala Manorama,' a leading newspaper covered this incident and I became the talk of the town overnight!

To my surprise, I was inundated with phone calls from people who wanted me to shorten their hair! The lady too, came back to me later for a haircut and also got her friends along. The haircut had transformed her and she was happy! The incident had been good for business! This is when the word 'transformation' came into my head.

In the year 2000, I was transferred to Chandigarh and in 2001, to Mumbai where I became the Salon Director. However, when I saw that there were no opportunities to grow further, I knew it was time to leave. To grow, I had to branch out on my own.

> Nothing grows under a banyan tree.

Lakme Lever

I had my own ideas by now and wanted to try them out. In 2001, I joined 'Lakme,' Hindustan Lever's salon in the Churchgate area in Mumbai as a Hair Stylist. Till then, Lakme was only known for its cosmetics. I was the first hairdresser for women in Lakme's branches. This was a speciality. I drew a good response from the clientele. They became accustomed to my communication style, my personality, hygiene, care, and quality of work. I carved my own niche and was promoted to the post of Manager.

Working with Lakme, I was at the right place at the right time! I became Lakme's experiment – their Creative Stylist. They charged a premium for my services. I developed their Hair and Services section all by myself. It was hard work without holidays, but I loved every minute of it.

Then came the great opportunity of Lakme India Fashion Week. I was proud to be a part of this event since its inception. Lakme was promoting its salon to fashion designers, actors, and the who's who in the fashion and film (Bollywood) industries. I became famous as both, a trainer, and a creative hair stylist. This was the first time we launched new haircuts. My team collaborated with the well-known hair care brand Wella and created six new haircuts. We trained people from all over India. I derived a lot of satisfaction by teaching people.

By the time I was 25, I had already made a name for myself in the industry. I was an asset for the company as I was their highest revenue earner. But I was still not satisfied with my education.

> After a certain point, it became clear to me that people were looking up to me and asking for my advice. But what about me? Who was there to advise me? Who would help me to fulfill my dreams? My quest for growth was on.

Learnings from Landmark Forum

There is a famous dialogue in the Hindi film, 'Om Shanti Om,' which goes – *"Kehte hain agar kisi cheez ko dil se chaaho…to puri kainaat use tumse milane ki koshish mein lag jaati hai."* (If there is something you strongly desire with all your heart, the entire universe begins to conspire to manifest it for you.) I realized how true this was when my client Marina Kapur (Executive Vice President, Head of Private Banking – Yes Bank) told me about Landmark Forum. It was exactly what I was looking for – a course that would change my life forever, make me decisive, and give me direction for the future!

Needless to say, I enrolled for this course. It gave me the power to harness my strengths and gave a new direction to my life. It also gave me the profound understanding that what I was searching for, was lying inside me all the time. It freed me to do what I wanted.

It's wonderful how things fall into place once you decide to change your life. One of my friends had been telling me to do shows independently for quite some time. But I was not mentally prepared for it. When I met this friend again, he suggested that we organize a small show on a holiday and gauge the response. I agreed and we began planning the show. However, my company came to know about it. Obviously, this was not acceptable to them.

Leaving Lakme

I realized that doing shows was a prime opportunity for me to grow and now there was no holding back. It was the Landmark Forum course that gave me the courage to resign from Lakme. Although they refused to accept my resignation, we did arrive at a midway that I would do my show, but would come back and join them as a consultant.

It's Showtime, Folks!

My first show held in Jaipur was a new step in my life. It turned out to be a huge success with 350 participants. I achieved a totally different height by doing this show. Although I was ill on that day, I was brimming with the power of love and confidence and was on the top of the world!

Fateful Failures

On the backdrop of my first success, I decided to do 100 shows in a year and concentrate only on doing shows. This was the biggest mistake of my life! I didn't realize then that 100 shows a year meant doing a show every three days!

When I was on the top of the world after my first show, I felt that I had become popular and that everyone knew me, and this would result in great success for my future shows too. People would eagerly invite me to do shows in their cities. But I was wrong. Shows are expensive to do, and I hadn't taken into account the fact that no two cities respond the same way.

The end result was that after my first show, I couldn't get an opportunity immediately for the next show. I had no money left, was out of a job, had lost my confidence and to top it all, I was supposed to get married very soon!

It was a tremendously stressful time. But somehow I managed to hold myself together. "Be patient," I told myself.

Picking up the Pieces

One of my friends had opened a salon in Colaba, Mumbai. When I left my job, she had offered me a place to practise. I hired her salon and used a part of it for training. I registered a company called Tanveer's Hair Education and Services and started a diploma course. I got ten admissions and gathered enough money for my wedding. By this time, I had thought that I would only teach, but when you have been associated with people for most of your life, it is difficult for you to suddenly stop meeting them. So, I started taking hairdressing appointments in Colaba at my friend's salon. Finally, things began to run smoothly again.

Ironically, I discovered that my show in Jaipur had made me famous in the north, especially in Rajasthan and I started getting requests for shows from Uttar Pradesh, Bihar, Gujarat, Himachal Pradesh, Punjab etc. Of course, I did shows there but this time, I made sure that I concentrated on my other activities as well. From then on, there has been no looking back.

> Most problems can be solved if you keep your cool and keep doing your best in the circumstances!

Loss and Life After Loss

I lost my father to diabetes, the silent killer disease in 2004. I had wanted my father to be able to see my show but sadly, this was not meant to happen. His death made me more responsible, as I was the eldest sibling and also had to look after my mother. My siblings were studying, and the survival of the entire family depended on me. During this time, I let go of many opportunities that came my way – going abroad, starting a new business etc., due to my inability to make quick decisions.

When I look back today, I realize that had I taken the risk then, I would have done much better and risen to the top much faster.

> Although fear is useful for survival, it will only keep you alive. It will never take you to the top.

It was only after doing the Landmark Forum course that I was able to get out of the rut, start life from scratch again, and set up on my own. I realized that if big stars were earning based on my talent, my talent was a brand in itself, wasn't it?

I lost my mother in 2011. I wanted her to attend my shows as well but she was unable to do so due to her health. While she was seriously ill, I left my work to be by her side for about a month, just before her death. Although a part of me died with her, I still had to be strong for the sake of my family. Now, I was all alone and the responsibility of the entire family was on my shoulders.

That took its toll on me and I fell ill with diabetes and cholesterol. But not being one to give up, I decided to educate myself about diabetes. Education is a lifelong process and is the best advantage you can have. I learnt to take good care of myself and my health so that I could endure the hard work and pressures of my profession.

Exciting Achievements

I was thrilled when my dedication and passion for excellence were rewarded! I was awarded the iDiva Young Achiever Award for four consecutive years by iDiva, a magazine on the beauty industry. I was also awarded the Young Achiever Award for being the most preferred hairdresser. In September 2017, I did a very important show in collaboration with a top Indian brand. This show, called Professional Beauty India, is one of the most prestigious shows with the presence of major Indian and international brands. This was a milestone in my life where I created my own new seasonal looks before a huge crowd of around 1500 people.

Future Pavilions

I am truly passionate about teaching, and it's something I can do all my life. Everyone... yes, everyone should have the right to education. Till the time people are not educated, they will keep discriminating against others on the basis of caste, profession, and so on. But education can change all this.

Hairdressers make people look beautiful. Our job is to transform the ordinary into the extraordinary. Our mission should be to make India beautiful in all possible ways. How can we do it without education? Education is the difference between 'good' and 'great.' Without education, one will only do hard work, yet get nowhere.

My aim is to encourage young, professional hairdressers to get educated in a customized and systematic way so that they can go ahead, do greater things, and bring fame and respect to this creative art.

*

"But who was it who cursed you? You missed telling us about her," says Rahul.

"Oh that! Yes... it was when I was five-years-old. My neighbor had come to meet my mother. When no one was looking, I took a pair of scissors and cut her long, beautiful hair! She was extremely furious and in anger she cursed me, saying, "Cutting others' hair at such a young age! Mark my words... you won't do anything else from now on... all your life, you will only cut people's hair!" say I with a chuckle.

*

Life Lines

- You can develop yourself to become a renowned brand.
- Be passionate about achieving your goals.
- Health is wealth.
- Be very careful about your choice of words. While words can build bridges, they can also build walls.
- Be focused and earn respect.

- Money is important, but it is not everything in life.
- Never stop learning.
- Never think of yourself as superior to others.
- Be tech-savvy. Technology is a must for success.

> **Words of Wisdom**
>
> Each one of us should have a dream. To achieve that dream – passion, patience and persistence are essential. Past accomplishments are only milestones in your path to achieve bigger dreams. So press on – dream on!
>
> Decisions should be made wisely, but quickly. Opportunity never waits for anyone. When you make the first move, the horizon is wide open and the sky is the limit. I have learnt this the hard way because I couldn't implement a few decisions quickly and therefore, missed opportunities. But I wish that my team and my students learn this at an early stage and achieve their goals faster.

9

A Tale of Turnarounds & Transformations

Ashwin Pasricha

Dear Ashwin,

You are a genuine soul, a trusted friend, a professional with in-depth knowledge of human psychology and of course, an expert on Leadership Assessment & Development. From the time I have known you professionally, I have been intrigued by your understanding of human behavior and your ability to analyze any challenge from various perspectives, often ones that don't occur to most of us. This makes you an excellent coach – I have personally benefited by your sound coaching.

Your approach to tackle tricky and tough situations calmly is really noteworthy, Ashwin. Thanks for being my sounding board always!

Yours Affectionately,
Aparna

About Ashwin Pasricha...

With a wide experience across multiple industries, Ashwin Pasricha is an HR person with a difference! Given his philosophy of touching lives, he has the unique distinction of turning around not one or two, but four businesses, and that too, at the beginning of his career. While doing so, not only did he focus on results, he also managed to meaningfully engage people in the process of business transformation. Having a deep connect with nature, building and nurturing relationships, and touching lives positively everywhere he goes, this entrepreneur truly lives up to the name of his human resource consulting firm – 'Human Network & Associates'. His insatiable quest to consistently break the mould and learn anew gives him the zeal to come up with pathbreaking interventions that lead to personal and business transformations, along with giving back to society.

"My life reflects the lines from Robert Frost's poem:
Two roads diverged in a wood, and I –
I took the one less traveled by,
And that has made all the difference."
– Ashwin Pasricha

Childhood Commemorations

I still remember the peace and serenity of the Jammu valley where I lived as a child. Although I was born in Mumbai, my father was posted in Jammu where I spent my early years. Having seen the best of Kashmir in all its pristine glory and experienced the peace and tranquility, which comes with being one with nature, I developed an intense love for scenic landscapes, snow-clad mountain valleys, brooks, rivers et al. Staying in a small neighbourhood where the entire community was one extended family gave me a deep sense of belonging and being a part of a tribe.

One of the most defining moments of my childhood took place during the India-Pakistan war of 1971. The Pakistani troops were one night away from crossing the river Chenab and entering Jammu. If our troops were unable to stop them, the Pakistani troops would storm into Jammu city the next day. Although our well-wishers told us that we should evacuate, my parents refused. Worried, I asked my mother if there was a chance that Pakistan would enter Jammu. She replied, "There is no reason for us to leave our home. I have complete faith in our Army." This incident impacted me deeply.

> From my mother, I learnt optimism and courage to stand by my beliefs and decisions. It also developed in my mind a deep respect and admiration for our Armed Forces.

Enlightening Education

Later, we shifted to Kolkata where my sister and I went to the same school. I remember an important incident at school. I had qualified for what we called 'Heats' for the 100 meters (which was a trial run for the school's sports events). My teacher insisted that I wear white canvas shoes for the event. But at that time, I had only leather shoes. My parents couldn't understand the need to buy white canvas shoes which I would wear only for a day. But

I insisted that they buy me the shoes and they gave in reluctantly. Unfortunately, I didn't win in the final event. I was dejected and felt that I had let my parents down. Although I had pestered them to buy me what I wanted, had I given my 100 percent to it? I knew I hadn't. This was a big lesson for me.

> I learnt that I must do my best at every given opportunity and not take anyone for granted.

When I was in Class 3, we shifted to Bombay. I was quite a shy and diffident child. My sister, on the other hand, was a brilliant academic student, who would always top the class. So by Class 7 and 8, I began to wonder what was so exceptional about her. Now in hindsight, it is clear that she had both, learning ability and superior analytical thinking skills.

Tired of being a second citizen, I decided to challenge the *status quo* and more importantly, my self-concept.

To be like her, I had to work really hard at my studies, usually 4 – 5 hours a day after school. I did so and graduated from the bottom ten percent to the top five percent of my class. My teachers were amazed with my progress.

However, this turn of events didn't last long and in the crucial year of Class 10, I ended up with 53 percent marks and as a result, I had to take admission in an evening college for a year. Faced with this eventuality, I studied as hard as I could to get into a regular college and after performing well in the first year, I took admission in a regular day college in Class 12. However, due to various disturbances on the personal front, I did not do well in Class 12 also.

Considering my performance in academics, my father advised me to take up a professional course. After looking at the alternatives, I finally selected Hotel Management as a viable career option. As a child, I was a dreamer and had the tendency to visualize the future. I kept wondering what I would do. At this point in time, one day, while I was traveling in an auto rickshaw, a voice inside me said,

"Do your graduation and go to XLRI Jamshedpur for your masters in Human Resources."

> There are times in your life when your intution will speak or try to connect with you. If you tune into your intuition, it will tell you what is right for you.

But we generally tend to suppress or ignore this inner voice of ours. I too, ignored my inner voice and instead, filled the form for the Hotel Management course. To gain admission, I had to appear for the All India entrance exam which had 30,000 students that year. I had decided that come what may, I had to clear it, so I began studying in full earnest. I practically lived with the hotel management entrance guide for 3 – 4 months, carrying it with me 24x7, studying whilst waiting for a bus, at home, and anywhere I went.

When I cleared the exam, my self-confidence, that had taken a beating due to my Class 10 and 12 results, revived. I was given admission in the Institute of Hotel Management (IHM), Ahmedabad. This meant that I would be staying away from home for the first time in 18 years. Though I was excited about this new phase, I was also apprehensive about moving to a new city and leaving behind my family and friends. Would I be able to cope with the new environment?

College Katta

Given my academic scores, I didn't get accommodation in the hostel. So, I took up a rental room, 30 kilometers away from the Institute. My day would start with a cup of milk, washing my clothes and catching a bus to the Institute. If I missed the bus, I had to walk. It was a punishing regime, but I braved it for 45 days. Later, I shifted closer to the Institute as a paying guest. At college, I developed a good bonding with fellow-students and a lifetime friendship with my best friend, Nihal Wagh.

Although I had limited income, this was a blessing in disguise. It was here that I learnt to stretch every rupee I had and to make it count. My lessons in budgeting were learnt here, which have stood me in good stead so far in life. After a year, I got an opportunity to apply for a transfer back to the Institute of Hotel Management (IHM), Bombay.

I joined Taj Hotels as part of my Industrial Training for 6 months (in the second year). It was truly a warm place with old world charm. After I finished my studies, I was chosen by Hotel Holiday Inn, Juhu, Bombay, as a Management Trainee. Thus, I started my career in 1990 at the budding age of 21.

Career Course

The first 18 months of my job were very difficult. We were supposed to work with various departments. The hotel had a strong union. Although they were nice people, I found that to survive and thrive, I needed to build lasting relationships with the staff, the union and the management. Slowly, I built a network. One of my memorable achievements has been transforming four different food & beverage outlets in terms of customer satisfaction, sales and profitability and achieving my budgets consistently for eight years.

Here's how it happened. Although I was to be given independent charge of at least one food & beverage outlet after training, I was not given this charge because the management thought I was too soft and would not be able to manage the Union. I was very upset with this decision. Luckily however, Mr. Paul Peter came into my life as our new Head of the Department. He was my first mentor. He entrusted me the charge of the 24 x7 coffee shop, with a clear mandate to turn it around in the shortest possible time.

> In life, you will face many challenges; each of these is designed to help you become a better version of yourself.

Turnaround Tales

For the next 14 months, I worked very hard, put in my best and turned around the coffee shop. Customer complaints decreased, customer satisfaction increased to an all-time high, and so did profitability. I reached a point where the shop was running on autopilot and I actually had no work to do!

As soon as Mr. Paul heard of this achievement, he came over to meet me. He told me that I seemed to be relaxing. I replied that I had earned it. He said, "You are way too young to take it easy. Let's go for a walk." We went to a Chinese restaurant called 'Sampan.' This restauarant had a very strong union. Mr. Paul said, "I want you to take charge of this restaurant and do what you can." So it was going to be a cycle of hard work all over again. I rolled up my sleeves, built a strong rapport with the Union and put together a plan to revamp operations. Within 12 months, I once again managed to turn it around. Tested against all metrics, the results of the restaurant were at an all-time high. Turnover went up 1.5 times and our discerning clientele rewarded us with their continued patronage. Once again, I found that the pressure had eased and I could sit back and relax a bit.

> My experiences made me realize that business is about people. People are made up of feelings and emotions. You have to take care of them, engage them, understand their hopes, dreams, aspirations, and align them to a common vision.

Juggling Jack

As my education in Hotel Management was only a diploma, I decided to pursue a three-year degree in Psychology from Mumbai University. I finished my degree while working and enrolled for a part-time two-year MBA program. However, the minimum attendance of 75 percent was necessary to complete the course. My classes were scheduled from 7-9 pm. So I requested my boss to allow me the flexibility to attend them. He said, "I will allow you, provided you meet the following conditions:

1. You should exceed the target
2. There should be zero complaints
3. Ensure that the staff is motivated and engaged
4. Don't ever get lax

The day you don't perform, your privileges will be revoked." I remember saying, "I will not let you down." And then, as a gesture of his confidence in me, he handed me a new assignment to turn an Indian restaurant around!

Managing my classes and work together for two years was a tough challenge. I worked from 12 pm to 4.30 pm and then again from 9.15 pm to 1.30 am. I used to get really tired, but my passion and zeal to excel gave me the zest to start afresh every day. I completed my MBA while working, with good attendance and good scores. At the same time, I managed to turn around the Indian restaurant. This led to a recurrence of the oft-repeated scene – a walk with my boss and a new assignment to transform a newly launched coffee shop. I did this for the next two years and repeated my past successes once again.

> Once you have given your word, there is no looking back. Your word is a sacred promise and defines who you are as a person.

Building Bonds

Though my repeated successes may seem like plain luck, there was a lot of hard work in the process. I made it a point to find out details about the people I worked with – their families, their important festivals, their anniversaries etc., and invested time in them. I made sure that they were comfortable, they had time to spend with their families and were excited to come to work.

> People have hopes, dreams and aspirations. They want to make a difference and feel valued. It is the leader's responsibility to understand what makes them tick.

I generally used to have two meetings a year with my direct reports and my supervisors. The agenda would be, 'How will we live and work together as a team for the next six months?' We created ten commandments for this purpose. The first principle was always the same, "Thou shall always keep thy word. Words once spoken cannot be revoked. Promises are sacred."

This principle was followed to the 'T.' Even during the riots, when bus services were disrupted, people would come to work walking because they knew I would be waiting for them. But to gain this confidence and trust from the people, first, I had to be a role model for them. I was at work during every festive occasion and also on every Sunday. I had to hold myself accountable to a higher standard to inspire others. I also empowered my team to run the department and make decisions based on shared principles.

I told my people, "You can sanction your own leave, subject to certain guidelines. According to the forecast, you know the days of peak volume, the staffing pattern, the risk, how we are doing as per the budget – the surplus and the shortfall. So if you want leave, take it, but first look for options to reschedule or accommodate each other and then make your decision." The results were unbelievable! Around 98 percent of the time, this approach worked like magic.

I always encouraged people to be honest. Working in the hospitality industry is tough. The continuous work even on weekends and during festivals takes a toll. I understood this and told my people that they could tell me honestly if they did not feel like coming to work for whatever reason or if they had missed filing for leave earlier and something urgent came up. I would willingly sanction their leave, but they were not to lie. If we found out they were lying, they would be taken to task. My people understood the value of transparency. This novel approach made people feel at ease and helped maintain a healthy work-life balance. They reciprocated by taking ownership of the department's budgets and targets and helped in creating a service and marketing strategy to achieve the monthly targets.

> Leadership is about creating a context that inspires and empowers people to take ownership in service to a greater vision.

I was also blessed to initiate an 'Alcoholics Anonymous' (AA) program. Alcoholism is rampant in the hotel industry, and the Union came up with an idea to tackle it. I gave the Union my office space and brought the AA local chapter to facilitate the meetings in-house. This effort reduced absenteeism, increased employee engagement and was a unique opportunity where the Management and the Union came together for a good cause. We were successful in saving three people by de-addicting them. One of them went on to become the Employee of the Year.

After eight successful years in Operations, my boss asked me what I wanted to do next. I told him I was interested in Training. So, from Operations, I went on to become the Head of Training at the same hotel. The Training Department was basically an extension of the Personnel Department. I correlated the impact of training initiatives with profitability and sales, which was quite revolutionary at that time, through certain tools and programs. I demonstrated the impact that training makes and quantified the rupee value associated with it.

Thus, having spent a glorious decade in this wonderful industry that had given me so much. I now had a feeling that I had 'been there, done that.' In order for me to grow as a Training & Development professional, I had to work to broaden my horizons and explore new frontiers.

ITES Innings

I decided to move on from the Hospitality industry. In 2000, I got a call to join the training department of a company that was venturing into ITES space. It was an international call centre called Global Telesystems in Mahape. The interview went off well and the VP HR said, "I would like to make you an offer, but why have you asked for a 100 percent rise in CTC (cost to company)." I replied politely but firmly, "The hospitality industry doesn't pay much. But if you benchmark my ten years' experience and my skill sets and compare it with this industry, what I'm asking for is quite fair."

I got the offer with a 100 percent rise in CTC. I was given charge of different processes and campaigns. In this company, training was not just a support function. We didn't just measure how many people were inducted and trained. The management was interested in knowing whether these people were actually performing on the job and making the business profitable. So, my focus was to create value for the business. Our performance was rated on how well each business did. We had to take ownership for business outcomes. Here, I learnt two important principles –

1. Always create value, in whatever role/function you are in.
2. Value can only be created when it translates into a business impact in a positive sense. You can see it, feel it, hear it, and measure it. As Peter F. Drucker, the well-known American management consultant and author has said, "If you can't measure it, you can't improve it."

Once, an important million dollar campaign suddenly fell through because we were not meeting the Service Level Agreement. This was a telemarketing process selling credit cards to the US, which was a part of our business. This was the only campaign where our clients wanted to do the training themselves because they felt we would not be able to create value. So even though we were handling other campaigns for them satisfactorily, they didn't allow us to train their people. According to them, this campaign was exclusive. However, they began to face problems with it. The Vice President asked me if we could help them in any way. I met the client and did a diagnostic study. The campaign was suspended and within 72 hours, we started training people on the floors for a week.

The training had a very interesting 'Fish Bowl' Design. There were three concentric circles with the participants in the centre, followed by managers and senior managers in the next circle and finally, people from the client's side in the outer circle. All the stakeholders were picking up live feedback and identifying strengths and improvement areas. I did the Behavioural training, and my colleague did the Sales training. Within two weeks, the campaign was back on track. After four weeks, the client asked us to resume the telemarketing campaign. This was a huge achievement. This victory got us a lot of credibility as it was about service recovery, where we had taken on a challenge and had been agile enough to start training at a moment's notice and deliver results.

HR Innovations in IT

My next important assignment was in Mastek Ltd., an IT firm, as Head of Training. At Mastek, I understood the true meaning of the phrase, 'Culture eats strategy for breakfast.' Culture is about how you mould people, inspire them, make them feel a part of the organization, and get them to move towards one goal. This company had a highly employee-centric culture. Thus, it was the ideal environment to learn, grow, and contribute.

An important project we were working on practically failed as the project managers were not able to manage it end to end, although they were technically qualified. I did a diagnostic study and found that although the Project Managers were good at managing projects from a technical perspective, they lacked the ability and foresight to manage projects from a behavioral perspective.

To address this gap, we designed a pilot program for three days. This program was so successful that it ran for 5-7 years, and was called 'Managerial Excellence Program – Art and Science of

Managing Projects from a Behavioral Perspective.' The CEO was very impressed with the live feedback. The COO personally tracked the progress of all participants after the program, and now interestingly, all the project managers demonstrated the ability to manage projects far more holistically with all the dashboards in green.

The new technical trainees joining us were intimidated by our culture, which was largely entrepreurial. We were facing attrition at the end of 14-16 months. After diagnosing the problem, I designed a two-day experiential program for understanding the organization from a cultural perspective – Pravesh, which had a huge impact. This program helped people understand the company's values, its vision and guiding principles through experiential learning, i.e., through powerful simulations and guided discussions. I also realized that just training the trainees wasn't enough. When they got back to work, the project managers and leaders had to engage with them in a personal way.

> Change happens at an individual level, at the team level, and also at the organization level. But before change happens, you have to create an ecosystem to sustain the transformation and the new-found awareness. Only then can you lead change. I understood this important lesson through my experiences.

This successful program ran for 5-6 years. Attrition reduced markedly and some people even stayed on to become long-term employees.

I realized that when I saw a problem from a future perspective (e.g., how to reduce attrition), I needed to go into the future and see whether today's solution would serve the problem in the long-term. The nature of the problem is continuously evolving. When one looks at a problem from a future perspective, one realizes that some problems are such that they can only be solved in stages, while one is trying to find an immediate and absolute solution.

Aparna Sharma

Another issue was hiring talent. The bigger companies in the industry would take the cream of the talent and we needed to ensure that we would still get the best out of what was left. So we defined our technical recruitment process in a manner that gave the best results in the shortest possible time.

It was a great learning experience for me for three-and-a-half years. But I found myself thinking about what would be my next step. I find that after every few years, I get restless. For me, its very important to reinvent.

> If you are stationary, you get obsolete. If you are moving, then you are learning and growing. So, just like a snake sheds its old skin, one needs to reinvent oneself anew, periodically.

Venture with Vodafone

Next, I got a call for an interview with the telecom giant Hutch, which later became Vodafone. I worked there from 2006 to 2008. I joined as Head-Employee Development and was responsible for Leadership Development and Employee Engagement on a pan-India basis. My role was about leadership and capability development, strategic interventions, and talent management.

The Telecom experience was about managing ambiguity, complexity, and uncertainty in a fast-changing environment. This assignment taught me various things. One of them was anticipation – What's next? Once when I had gone to Kerala for a program, I went to a bookstore in the hotel. There was a book that caught my eye. Its title was, 'What's Next After Now?' by Steven Harrison. This phrase hit me very hard. It is a phrase that can be interpreted in many ways. If you are doing good, what's next after now; if you have lost it all, what's next after now? Although I didn't read the book, its title had me transfixed. It truly transformed my thinking and my life. It accelerated my pace of thinking. In today's world, you could be satisfied and contented, but what is good and relevant today, could be mediocre tomorrow. I include this quote, 'What's next after now?' in all my programs.

I did a very successful program on leadership called 'Lead' which was declared one of the best leadership programs. It got international recognition from the Vodafone group. I launched programs in 2007-8 for Employee Recognition called Vodafone Star, Mega Star, and Superstar, which I believe still exist. I also designed an innovative program on Customer Centricity, which recognized employees who went the extra mile and their stories were captured as 'Vodafone Tales' and a coffee table book was printed, published, and circulated to all circles in the country.

Entry into Entrepreneurship

In 2008, I was doing quite well heading Employee Development at Vodafone. That's when the title of the book popped into my mind once again – 'What's next after now?' It was time to move. I decided that it was time for me to start something on my own.

During the handing over phase at Vodafone, I found, for the very first time, that I was all alone. Until then, apart from the brand I represented, I had no identity. Now, I had nothing else except for who I was. For all entrepreneurs, this first step is the most difficult. In a job, one has a designation, a title and a defined scope of work with a fixed remuneration. Becoming an entrepreneur, however, calls for moving out of one's comfort zone and stepping into the unknown. It is about going deep within and asking yourself existential questions.

> The life of an entrepreneur is not easy. You have to walk the talk, be optimistic, look for the silver lining – and there may not be a silver lining for a long time. So, you have to look deep within, search for a purpose, and live your dream till it becomes a reality. If your intent is powerful enough and you back it up with hard work, dedication, application, and upgrade yourself, then you can add value to your customers.

I started my consulting practice in June 2008, which was a recession year. When I started off, I didn't really have a plan. In my first interaction, while pitching to a client, I found myself fumbling. That is when I realized that while I had experience regarding business, I didn't have hard-core selling experience. I had to learn to sell through trial and error. For the first two years, I was finding my feet, understanding what I wanted to do, pitching to clients, and also realizing that initially you have to take whatever comes your way because you need to prove yourself.

I saw that I needed to reinvent myself continuously. By reinvention, I mean starting each day as a new chapter and asking myself – What can I learn today, what can I create today? Reinvention is really about the mindset because as humans, we tend to hold on to things that have worked well in the past. But our entire journey of life is about unlearning and re-learning. Fortunately, I realized quite early that what I was doing today would become extinct tomorrow.

I rebuilt my entire business model. And today, in the 9th year, there is a properly planned strategy in place for the next 15 years. I am doing the kind of work that resonates within me very deeply, is very transformational and very challenging.

An important insight in this entire journey was that although you may have a plan, you need to revisit it regularly, changing and adapting it according to the situation.

> As an entrepreneur, your idea or concept of your product or service has to be redefined hundreds of times to stand the test of time.

After nine years of being in the consulting business, I now know experientially about strategy, positioning, differentiation, marketing, sales etc., and more importantly, how businesses work, after having catered to all industry verticals.

'Human Network & Associates' and its Horizons

My mission is to partner with organizations to unleash human potential and accelerate business performance with a clear ROI (Return on Investment).

It was with this in mind that I started 'Human Network,' which is a learning and development consulting firm focusing on -

1. **Leadership Development:** Building leadership capability to accelerate business performance.
2. **Executive Coaching:** As a tool to develop leadership potential and top executive talent for future business needs.
3. **Custom Interventions:** Designing capability-building solutions to accelerate performance.
4. **Talent Transformation:** Creating a development track for high performers and building a talent pipeline.

As a coach, I work with the best of executive talent and diverse businesses, and one thing which simply amazes me is the zeal and yearning of the human spirit to aspire for more – a deeper sense of purpose, bigger dreams or a far more fulfilling life. I am grateful that I am in a position to be of service to them, and the joy which one experiences seeing them achieve their goals is the biggest reward for me personally. For this purpose, I track their progress for two years even after the program has formally ended, to see how they are doing and if they need additional support.

A Power Program

Wisdom generally comes to us in hindsight. But what if you have the power to convert your hindsight into foresight? How would one do that?

I would like to share with you a very interesting way to do this – by writing your autobiography in the reverse!

I found that a powerful way to shape and co-create your destiny is to write your autobiography. But one must go into the future and write it in the reverse. Say, if I were to start by writing ten years from now, I would mentally step into 2028 and start writing my autobiography in the reverse order... 2027, 2026... and so on.

We all have a sense of what we want to see happening in our lives. But we never put our thoughts on paper. As one does this, one realizes how one would really like one's life to unfold. This exercise embraces all areas of your life namely, career, relationships, lifestyle, hobbies, social causes etc.

This process helps one to find one's purpose and actually begin to consider the possibility of shaping one's life story.

Doing this gives one a travel plan or roadmap – where one is, where one wants to go, and the distance one needs to travel to get to the final destination.

> With this excercise, you can get clarity about your future and how you would like it to be. You become conscious of the fact that you need to make the most of your life starting from right now! Life is about shaping and living every moment for the better. The power of this exercise is that your hindsight becomes your foresight. You will know in advance how you need to prepare for the future.

In Retrospect

The central themes of my life till now have been –

1. What's next after now - Reinventing myself – The journey of life is about evolution, not taking things for granted, valuing life, and evolving to become a better person, better professional, better parent, spouse, or companion.

2. Discovering my purpose, discovering my gifts and sharing them freely with the world. The principle of giving back affirms my faith in humanity.

Looking back, I feel that these were the crucial years of my life. The opportunities that I got taught me many important lessons. The work I do today as a Certified Executive Coach and a Leadership Consultant is based on the principle that Business Transformation is all about People Transformation. When we look at the world of business, we need to understand that it is all about people.

I am excited because today I am on the threshold of whatever I want to manifest in my life and am consciously shaping each chapter in my life for the better. What I am doing now and what I intend to do in the coming years will cause massive transformation within people and organizations. There is a bigger world out there, and I am ready to step into it!

Life Lines

- Even though you may make mistakes, don't be disheartened. Remember that the universe has a better design for you. When the time is right, things will fall into place. There are no failures; it is just the Universe going about its way of making sure that you become wiser and stronger.

- When you are committed to excellence, take nothing for granted and keep on reinventing yourself. Then the sky is the limit!

- Use the mantra of 'What's next after now?' and don't get complacent.

- Working with people means working on yourself too; otherwise, your work will not cause transformation. You need to keep on doing your inner work regularly.

- The importance of role modelling cannot be undermined in any leader's success story. Only if you walk the talk will people believe you, respect you, and follow you.

- When your dreams are beyond you and you embrace a bigger purpose or calling, you will experience true, authentic power.

Words of Wisdom

The universe has a certain role to play in your life. It will give you various opportunities. It is up to you to recognize which of these opportunities are right for you and to act on them.

People want their lives to drastically change in the future. But our life will change only if something changes in the moment today. We need to see what needs to change within us. Most of us have an outward focus. When we begin to have an inward focus, we realize that we ourselves are the change. As Mahatma Gandhi said, "Be the change that you wish to see in the world."

If you want to change, there is no place for complacency. The mantra is, 'What's next after now?'

10

Doing One's Duty the 'Shant Advait' Way

Dhyanshree Shailesh
(Mahamandleshwar Shaileshanand Giri)
(Guruji)

Dear Guruji,

I feel so blessed to have met and known someone so profound, yet so simple. Your depth of knowledge, your ability to convey the essence of existence and the philosophy of life in an easily understandable manner, and your spiritual consciousness are unmatched. Even though you are my senior from our school in Ujjain, your unassuming persona and ability to connect with less evolved souls like me is remarkable. You have shattered all myths about spiritual leaders that I grew up reading and believing through your genuine concern for all. I often wonder what led you to the 'road less traveled' and to find your calling in spirituality.

May you continue to guide and lead our souls towards their true purposes!

Yours Affectionately,
Aparna

About 'Dhyanshree' Shailesh...

'Dhyanshree' Shailesh or Mahamandleshwar Shaileshanand Giri is not your typical Swamiji, wearing a formidable expression and preaching from religious textbooks. A young seer educated in a convent school, he talks about the practical application of religion in one's daily life. An all-rounded personality who plays the guitar and loves music, he has been a student leader at Vikram University, a spokesperson of the State Youth Congress, has played cricket as well as acted in plays in his youth before turning to spirituality. He emphasizes the importance of performing one's duty, irrespective of one's path in life. His widespread campaign, 'Kartavya Kranti' or 'Duty Revolution,' aims to revolutionize society by urging people, especially the Gen Next, to focus on their duties, rather than rights. Guruji had joined the Sadbhavana Mission in 2002 with the late veteran actor-turned-MP Shri Sunil Dutt. His message of harmony and mission of world peace has been appreciated by people everywhere.

The Shant Advait Ashram set up by him sees people of all nationalities visiting and staying at the Ashram, to get a perfect vision of humanity and its religious and spiritual evolution. The flags of the Boddha religion (Buddhism) that were installed by Lama Paljor on his visit to the Ashram are a testimony of Guruji's belief in the oneness of all religions and his philosophy of 'One God – many paths.' An ardent nature lover, Guruji has taken great efforts to promote water conservation. He also espouses the cause of women's rights and gender equality. He is the Chief of Mahayog India Foundation, New Delhi. He continues to inspire the youth of today through his efforts to bring about a positive change in society, despite having renounced it.

"The mystery of life is that it is celebrated only when one is ordinary, although a majority of humanity is in the race to prove itself exceptional." – *'Dhyanshree' Shailesh*

Inspiration through Inner Wisdom

The knowledge revolution has overloaded minds with information and the real self has got lost in its web. Humanity has built massive infrastructure, but is lacking in simple humaneness. The animal instincts of humans are testimony to the fact that although physically the most evolved species, in terms of emotional refinement, humans are lagging behind in the evolutionary process. We have made great leaps in science and technology, but there are many unexplored horizons and secrets of the inner world yet to be uncovered. We may fly to the moon, but are yet to discover the universe within our own bodies. Undertaking this journey of exploration into the Self, I present to you my varied experiences hoping that they would inspire you to begin your own journey of self-discovery.

Early Experiences

Born in 1970, as Shailesh Vyas, I was an exceptionally bright student and was directly promoted from Kindergarten 2 to Class 2. My mother, an English teacher, taught me forgiveness and inculcated the virtue of respecting gender equality. My father, who worked in the Central Government and retired as Director, Ministry of Industries, taught me discipline and to fight against injustice. These early lessons shaped my personality and have stood me in good stead throughout my life. Since my father had a transferable job, I went to different schools at Ratlam, Jodhpur, Durg, and later at Ujjain.

I remember that once, a magician had come to my school with his child. After his show, he appealed to us, saying that he was a poor man and that he too wanted his son to get educated in a school like ours. I felt really sorry for him and gave him the quarterly school fees that I was to deposit with my teacher. I was honored by my Principal in the assembly the next morning for my benevolence.

As a student, I wondered why there was a need to earn money when Mother Nature already provides humans with basic needs like food, shelter, and warmth. The currency system seemed to me to have done more harm than benefit to humanity. In contrast, the barter system seemed more appealing.

The Drama of Dharma

During my visits to my grandfather, Pandit Laxmi Narayan Vyas, I learnt a lot about religion and rituals. The more I learnt, the more it infuriated me, as all of it made me feel distant from God, rather than feeling closer to Him. I found that I could never accept discrimination on the basis of religion and caste. It made me a non-believer of this most ancient concept of the world – God. I slowly began turning away from God, and my discussions with my family in this regard disheartened them.

During one of my summer vacations, I had visited my village. A person from our village was very popular as his predictions and blessings were said to come true. I enquired with my neighbors about how he did his predictions. They glorified him as the vehicle of the divine soul of the god Bhairav, who communicated through his body. At the age of 12, this seemed like a joke to me. I decided to see if this was indeed true.

I kept fresh semi-liquid cow dung in a basket and covered it with flowers, as an offering to this man. I went and touched his feet. I kept the basket on a table before him on the stage, where he was sitting wearing huge garlands. There was a queue of hundreds of people and everyone was eager to see the entry and expression of Bhairav Maharaj through this man's body. Soon, the man started getting fits and his head started moving in a circular motion. (This happened only after the desired number of people had gathered around him.) After equal intervals, he used to speak a few things to some people, then bang his forehead on the table in front of him. As expected, very soon he banged his forehead on the basket of flowers that I had kept on the table before him, resulting in a cow dung facial! Taken by surprise, he yelled and abused everyone present, and Bhairav Maharaj disappeared from within him instantly! I was happy that this drama had raised questions in the minds of the villagers regarding the authenticity of such imposters.

> This incident reinforced my belief that dramas of dharma were exceedingly causing harm to our society.

The Seen and the Unseen

As I was growing up, I began questioning the concepts of God and religion. However, even as a child, I found that I had visions that differed from those of other people. While people lived in the here and the now, I had the sights of the past, present and future. I could see the 'unseen' and could know the 'unknown' which was not possible for others to understand. At first, this scared me quite a bit. When I shared this with people I could trust, they rubbished it saying, "You think too much!" But I did realize through these incidents and visions that there is much more to life than what humans believe and perceive. The past, the present, and the future are all linked.

Sports and the Concept of Sahaj Siddha

I played cricket in the 9th and 10th classes. Little did I know that playing cricket could lead one to yogic realization. In spite of continuous bowling practice, I couldn't land the ball on the coin placed on the pitch. My coach watching me made me extra cautious, and I was unable to concentrate. But one day, I closed my eyes, took a deep breath and focused only on the ball, the coin, and the pitch. And lo and behold! I bowled 18 times in succession on the same coin without much effort!

> My experience gave me a purely yogic lesson – ignore the self, ignore time and the universe as if none of them exist and then perform all karmas as an observer and as a witness of the flow of incidents.

> To me, this is nothing but meditation. It will make you a *Sahaj Siddha*, one who lives a normal life, but decodes the secrets of spirituality in a very common and realized manner. This is your inner journey and is beyond time.

Having realized this formula, the next match was a cakewalk for me and I was awarded the Man of the Match, with a record of 9 overs, 11 runs and 7 wickets. This was the joy that meditation had brought into my life. But I soon acquired an ego and had to pay the price of my arrogance. Within six months, I had to leave the team. Although this incident should have been a wake-up call, being immature at the time, such wisdom did not come easily to me and I decided to give up cricket forever.

To Pray or to Perform?

When my friends and I played cricket around the Mahakaleshwar temple in Ujjain, the police stopped me from playing there to avoid disputes with devotees visiting the temple. I tried to logically explain to them that sports and playgrounds are better options for people to visit than a place of worship. After a long debate, I was strictly disallowed to play there. Though I was not able to persuade the authorities, my view still remains that rather than trying to please God by visiting Him in temples, one should try to make one's inner God happy through ethical deeds. We may be offering prayers to God while our neighbor may be ill, alone and helpless or a starving child may be crying out for help. What then, would be the best course of action? Would it be right to keep on praying? Or would it be more right to get up and serve those who are needy? Swami Vivekananda has answered this question when he said, "Where can we go to find God if we cannot see Him in our hearts and in every living being?" Reaching out to people in any way we can, stopping to smile at someone, counseling those in despair, or helping one who is ill are a few ways to lead a fulfilling life.

> It is said that, "Extending one hand to help somebody has more value than joining two hands in prayer."

Education, Insights, and Entry into Politics

Mid-way through my 9th class, my father got transferred to Ujjain. Despite this being a routine affair over the years, the transfer to Ujjain left me quite disturbed since my studies were interrupted in between the school year. However, one of my classmates helped me in completing all my assignments and encouraged me to achieve the top rank in my school. She would say, "You can achieve everything on your own, Shailesh. Do not depend on me. What if I die?" However, her words turned true faster than either she or I had expected and she met an untimely death. Though shocked by her death, I never cried for her because even as a child, I believed in life after death. I knew that we are never far from our loved ones.

> Today, this belief has turned into conviction as I am able to connect with many past, present, and future living beings and non-living things.

I entered politics in the year 1989-90 quite accidentally. I had gone to my college to pay the admission fees. A gang of boys threw me out of the queue mocking me and insisting that they and their protégées would pay their fees first. They were similarly harassing others. I was aghast and complained to the college teachers, but it was of no use. Finally, it was up to me, and I single-handedly revolted against these boys. After a tough fight, they realized I was not one to back down so easily. This gave me a lot of popularity. Other students began looking up to me as a leader. I became involved in solving problems and gathered a lot of clout. A time came when I found that in order to continue to make a difference, I needed political backing. That was when I officially entered politics.

Who am I?

In 1992, during the *Simhastha* festival (held every 12 years), I led a massive campaign against disturbing the infrastructure of Ujjain. I believed that new residential areas must be developed on barren lands rather than on productive, fertile ones and that old infrastructure should not be disturbed for a two-month gathering of religious saints and devotees. My public speech was appreciated by everyone, except for the higher authorities. Unsurprisingly, I was arrested for the strong stand that I had taken. During my arrest, a saint was watching me steadily. Before sitting in the police jeep as a protest surrender, I asked him, "Why are you watching me so keenly? Who are you?"

He replied, "First, do you know who you are?" and left, smiling.

His answer gave me a jolt!

The Enigma of Existence

For four days, his words kept echoing in my thoughts. Who was I – a famous student leader who had created a record in politics by becoming a Joint Secretary, the Secretary, and Vice President of the Students' Union of Madhav College for three consecutive years; a spokesman for the National Students' Union of India; a dynamic orator and good actor; or a good sportsman? I was unable to find a satisfactory answer to this question.

I asked my senior leader what difference it would make to the lives of those who always surrounded me if I left the city. He replied, "Many have come and gone. Your place will be occupied by somebody new, and people will forget you in a few years. Nothing changes anything!" His abrupt answer was like a slap on my face. I stood there, reeling with the realization of my inconsequential existence.

Sometimes, it takes something momentous to happen in order for one to change one's path. This incident was to prove the turning point in my life on the path of my journey within.

> If my existence was perishable and so easily replaceable, then it meant that I was nothing, and my being nothing wouldn't change anything! What then was the aim of my life? A vacuum started forming in my inner self. My ideas about my life, my place in society, my accomplishments, all of which I had taken for granted, and which I prided myself on, were shattered. My sense of self-importance went for a toss. I felt that I was completely alone in this journey of life, and so was everyone else.

I searched for answers in my own way. I went to a slum of beggars who were leprosy patients in the Hamukhedi area of Ujjain and stayed there with them for 32 days, lived at a five-star hotel at Delhi for 10 days, and also sat before the Shivalingam of the Mahakaleshwar temple in Ujjain to meditate. I stayed overnight at the Haji Maulana Saheb Dargah near the Kshipra river at Ram Ghat (Ujjain) and also visited my village to meet my grandfather. I tried to understand the purpose of my life through various means. But I got no answer from anywhere – neither from outside, nor from within. I bought all available books of philosophies across the world, but could not read them beyond a single page. I visited professors, gurus, pandits, and people who claimed to be clairvoyant. None of them could answer my questions satisfactorily. However, I did observe one thing – every book or learned person laid stress on performing one's duty.

Career and Campaigns

I did B.Com, M.Com and M.A. at the Madhav College, Ujjain, and completed my education in 1996. After this, I volunteered my services to the Vikram University, Ujjain, as a Coordinator for the Marketing, Advertising, and Concept-selling course, from 1996 to 1998. This was my learning ground where I learnt many an important lesson about communication.

> I also learnt that it is not enough to just be a good person oneself. It is also one's responsibility to try and put a stop to the bad things happening around us.

I started using this wisdom for my socio-political campaigns. In 2002, India was undergoing a change in the employment market. Everyone, from graduates to highly qualified youth, was harassed due to lack of employment opportunities. I held politicians and law-makers responsible for this situation and decided to start a begging campaign to awaken them. This time, I was not fighting against the government, but was persuading them to perform their duties towards the nation. I started the 'Bheekh Mango Abhiyan' (begging to make public representatives realize that youth needed employment) and the 'Boot Polish Campaign' (where I polished the boots of passersby with a huge crowd of youth). The voluntary contribution of money collected from these two campaigns was given to the administration to pass on to the Prime Minister of India and Chief Minister of the state.

Communal Chaos

Slowly but surely, my personality was beginning to be shaped now. But just as when a yogi moves closer to attaining *siddhi*, the prevailing negative forces in nature get overactive, a similar incident took place in my life, where things took a negative turn. Besides, I was just a beginner, that too, by destiny and not by choice. I did not possess the requisite strength to overcome these negative forces.

One day, after a political meet, some groups of boys clashed and the chaos took on a communal hue. Either deliberately or by chance, I was framed in this incident. Although I had tried to save an injured man by intimating the police and doctors to give him urgent medical attention, the government was biased on political grounds. I refused to take bail as my intention was to reveal the truth and I wanted to prove my humane approach before the world. But this being *Kaliyug*, evil initially prevails over good and I was destined to remain in jail for 29 days.

Although I had suffered as a victim of politics, I also had the good fortune of meeting a divine soul during this time. While in custody, an old man approached me and counseled me to continue being a good human being always. He also suggested that I resign from the political party I was associated with. He asked me to convey to the media that the Chief Minister would have to leave his post within 15 days, because a yogi like me had been framed politically without any wrongdoing on my part. This was another tense and serious turning point in my life. Was politics really not my cup of tea? If I gave it up, would it mean that I was shying away from tough times due to a one-off negative incident? These and many other thoughts ran riot through my mind. After a lot of internal churning, however, I eventually decided to go along with the old man's suggestion. Miraculously, on the 14th day of my announcement, the Chief Minister had to leave his post! I was bailed out and won the case too, within seven months. Till date, I always wonder who that old man was. Had God taken pity on me and sent him in the form of a messenger? I will never know. The hand of God works in ways unknown to us. Although I emerged victorious, I had lost all interest in materialistic things.

Counseled by a Clairvoyant

I left Ujjain and went to my father's home at New Delhi to give myself a break. One day, I went to a nearby shopping center for a walk. I bought a cigarette and started smoking. At the same time, a short, old man came up to me and started talking. I was least interested in conversing with him. This 74-year-old man, Dada Vahab, was a clairvoyant and told me about my past, present, and future. Speaking to him, I was reminded of Maharshi Kapil Advait, whom I had met in 1987 after he became a saint. He had advised me to become a saint too. At the time, I had turned down his advice with grace and respect. And now, here was this elderly man, speaking exactly the same words. I was alarmed and tried to disrupt the talk and say goodbye. But ignoring my attempts to close the conversation, the old man continued until he had finished all that he had to say. Then he himself ended the conversation and parted with the final words, "You are the chosen one. Whether or not you believe in God is not a matter of concern to me, but rather than the unseen, you must at least study deeply the seen. Just as land, fire, water, and wind have an impact on the body, mind, intellect, and soul; and the sun and the moon can be seen with your eyes, feel the other side of the unknown powers. I know you will do this against the assumptions of society. Be prepared for such an adventurous life, Guru Maharaj!"

He left me there spellbound, with the cigarette between my lips. I tried to fathom the meaning of his words. Did this mean I was to take up a spiritual life? Finally, I returned to Ujjain and met Dada Vahab once more coincidentally. After Maharshi Kapil Advait, Dada Vahab has had a long-lasting impression on my research on spirituality and God. He lived with me for four years before leaving for his heavenly journey, teaching me his Arabic and Hebrew techniques of messaging through nature.

I experimented with the *tantra* of telepathy under the guidance of both these Gurus. Through this *tantra*, I succeeded in getting in touch with people who had disrespected me in the past. They accepted that they had behaved unfairly with me. Through this experience, I realized that there is life beyond common human knowledge.

My Mentors

I had first met Maharshi Kapil Advait in 1987, after he became a saint. He was the one who explained my experiences on practical and logical grounds. Maharishi Kapil Advait and Yogmata Shraddha have played a vital role in my life so far. Maharshi Kapil is popularly known as Pilot Babaji because he was a pilot with the Indian Air Force before he turned towards spirituality, and his *akhara* is called Mahamandleshwar Somnath Giri of Juna Akhara. I met him again during the *Simhasta* in 2004, became his disciple and took *deeksha* from him in 2004. This was another turning point in my journey. Although Maharshi Kapil has supported me in my journey, he has at times, also opposed me. Initially, I had to face his gruff behavior after I started spiritual discussions with him. It was as if he wanted me to face and overcome every worldly illusion and other challenges on my own. However, I was not always able to comprehend this purpose of his. In my dissatisfaction with him, Yogmata always appeared to be an amazing power unto herself. It was as if she were answering questions, both, on my as well as his behalf. Later on, I renounced the world and took *sanyasa* in 2004. My guru renamed me Swami Dhyanshree Shailesh. The years 2009-2016 were a journey of self-exploration. As a renunciate, I slept in the Cantonment Garden at New Delhi, traveled to Sikkim where I meditated for hours at a stretch and completely lost track of time, and also visited the deep Himalayan regions to search for *siddhas*. It was during these years that I found my connection to God in my solitude and through my conversations with Him.

> On the path of truth, one needs selfless love and surrender to nature. Only then does nature unfold her magnificence and secrets before one.

The year 2016 was a landmark year, which marked the fusion of material and spiritual journeys for me, as I was invited by Pilot Baba to his camp at the *Simhastha Mela* in Ujjain. In this human gathering of lakhs of devotees, I was appointed the Mahamandleshwar of Juna Akhara of Naga Sampradaye, after taking the Mahamandleshwar pledge *deeksha* from Acharya Mahamandleshwar Avadeshanandaji Maharaj of Juna Akhara. I was renamed Swami Shaileshananda Giri (Mahamandleshwar is the title for the Head Warrior of Dharma for Nagas in Sanatan Dharma (which is the origin of all other dharmas). It is a high-dignitary post of Hindu Sanatan saints).

Media Mayhem

During this time, I had promised one of my close family members to help their children in their education. During the *Simhastha*, this family conveyed the good news of the selection of their son in an engineering college and of their daughter in a management college of New Delhi. We decided to go to Indore to purchase the necessary things for them. On the way, we stopped for a break. It was raining and the mud spoiled my *chola* (orange robe), but as we had to go anyway, I decided to change into a shirt and trousers and we proceeded to the mall. I think some tragedies are just meant to happen. Earlier too, I had been to malls in Indore with them, but this time, someone clicked my photograph as I was in a casual dress and made it viral. They portrayed me as though I were a traitor of the nation, or as if I were roaming naked in the mall. The local media wrote a story peppered with spice and printed it in the newspapers and on social media as well. Not to be left behind, some national TV channels too telecast the story.

All these educated and responsible people could have also looked at this incident positively as my efforts for the 'Beti Bachao, Beti Padhao' Movement (Save the girl child, educate the girl child), but they didn't. A few saints also treated this incident as anti-religious behavior as if the very foundation of religion had collapsed due to my going to the mall in casual dress and not the saintly robes. What hurt me was that no one even bothered to enquire whom I had gone with and what the purpose behind it was. At that time, no one seemed to remember the many lives that had been saved by my campaign against depression. But that is the way the world works.

> It takes a lifetime to painstakingly build a reputation and just one inconsequential event to ruin it. However, to save humans and humanity is the karma of Sanatan Dharma. The duty of a saint is to work towards everything that fulfills the responsibility of God towards His creation, irrespective of the fruits it brings one.

'Kartavya Kranti' Campaign

I initiated the Kartavya Kranti Campaign in 2016 after I was appointed the Mahamandleshwar. The path of *Karma Yoga* has been beautifully explained in the 'Bhagavad Gita'. I believe that it is best if both, *Karma Yoga* (the path of action) and *Bhakti Yoga* (the path of devotion), are practiced at the same time, and one can obtain the *siddhis* by chanting and praying, while parallely performing one's duty. I realized this secret *tantra* in the later years of sainthood. The 'Kartavya Kranti Campaign (Duty Revolution)' of which I am a part, runs in 121 countries today.

Through my studies, I have come to believe that as humans, we have no right to anything. One can only do one's duty *(Kartavya)* in one's life. A father thinks he has to the right to be looked after by his son in his old age. But he has no such right. All he can do is to fulfill his duty towards his children. A son feels that he has the right to his father's property. But all he has is the right to do his duty towards his father. Yet, we go about staking claims to what we feel is our right and live with the sorrow of unfulfilled expectations. Today, everyone talks about their rights, but no one talks about duties.

> Rather than focusing on one's rights, one should be alert towards one's duties. None of the religious scriptures talk about rights; all of them speak about duties.

Shant Advait Ashram

To be 'Shant' (calm) is in itself a miracle. When one is calm, one can go beyond the concept of time and become neutral – a witness *(sakshi)*.

The meaning of 'Advait' is one God. In my journey towards spirituality, I have studied many religions and found that most religions say that God, The Supreme Power, The Source is only One. I want people to realize that all of us, no matter who we are, what religion we belong to, where we live, come from only one source. This is why, I have named my ashram, the 'Shant Advait Ashram,' where people can experience calmness and meditate on this oneness irrespective of their religious beliefs.

I wanted this Ashram to be an oasis of peace, which people visited for succor, to get their bearings and rediscover themselves and also one which would be the centre point of the revival of the importance of Karma. The Ashram is a place in whose serene atmosphere one can converse with God and realize the Self through *Advaita Dhyan*, a meditation for the energy that rules all living and non-living entities. People from all over the world come here to meditate. Together, we work on issues concerning humanity as a whole – be it the availability of clean water, providing education to children, or helping the needy. The Ashram is a place where one can meditate without the insistence on rituals.

However, as is the case with most good initiatives, this too met with several obstacles. Though I had bought land for the ashram in 2006, I was deceived by a greedy realtor and cheated in the construction by engineers and could start construction of the ashram only in 2011. But far from deterring me, these events fueled my determination to build the ashram. I am still in the process of developing it and soon hope to finish work on it.

The Importance of Inner Understanding

To travel within, to pursue one's inner journey, is the supreme karma of each person. This journey is very adventurous – it is the feeling of inner peace and spiritual happiness. It is only 'Love' that gives one spiritual happiness. Whatever I learned from Dada Vahab, I have always tried to cultivate and highlight in my talks and teachings about the inherent character of human beings and love, and will always continue to do so, because it is important that love reaches the soul. The feeling of 'Sarve bhavantu sukhinah…', or praying that every person should live happily, is 'Mahayoga.' Only when one becomes a 'Love-yogi,' will the God within one speak. Selfless love is the only glorious thing and the greatest feeling in this universe!

> The truth is that any deed done out of love and compassion, by itself, fulfills every dharma and brings one closer to the highest ideal.

In Retrospect

I am truly thankful to my guru, Maharishi Kapil Advait, and his guru, Hari Baba, for the wisdom that they gave me. From my experiences, I have understood that the purpose of one's life can be achieved if one focuses on one's inner journey, rather than concentrating outwards. To conclude, I found God and accepted His supreme judgments, not because He was mentioned in the books of religion, but because my own research made me feel His presence in everything, living and non-living. The name of my ashram, 'SHANT ADVAIT,' reflects my understanding of the Divine and His Divinity.

Life Lines

- It is not age, but the edge of your efforts that counts.
- It is the female who nurtures the next generation… go beyond gender differences.
- Bow only before the truth.
- Learn to respect the visions of others and try to arrive at mutually acceptable decisions.
- Believe in the oneness of God – Advait!
- Accept criticism and honor – remain humble in both circumstances.
- Nurture leadership in others. Your role is not to rule but to guide.
- One must practice being neutral and take everything in one's stride. What we have is good; what we do not have is good too.
- In spirituality, there is nothing like 'worth doing' or 'not worth doing'. Everything one does is definitely of value.

Words of Wisdom

Unless one considers one's body as an accessory, one will not be able to sense the soul. The body is like a package in which one's existence is wrapped. Though it is important to take care of the package, if one only gets caught up in the package, one will never be able to unwrap it and behold the beauty of the gift within. Then one's birth will have been in vain. The most important purpose of birth is to know the soul. We need to realize that the needs, necessities, and luxuries, which the body demands are different from those of our soul. We need to understand how important and powerful we are, and that there is much more to life than just running in the rat race.

Our possessions are not our identity. They do not define who we are. Once we realize that we are distinct from our material possessions, we will stop identifying ourselves with them, and then will begin the search for our true identities, our true selves.

I encourage and invite all of you to undertake this journey into the self and experience this divine oneness by creating your own path and not by following the ones made by others! Best of luck to you for your life's journey!

11

Lessons from a Life Well-lived

Shri Pheru Singh Ruhela

Dear Sir,

I often wonder what I would have done without you. For someone like me, who was scared to go to school, since I was mocked by classmates for not knowing Hindi, you laid such a strong foundation by teaching me Hindi so well that winning all the inter-school Madhya Pradesh Hindi language and literature competitions was a cakewalk for me. Elocution, delivering lectures in Hindi, and now a book translated in Hindi – it's an absolute dream come true through your efforts and blessings. Above all, you sowed the seeds early on by instilling a sound value base and sincerity of purpose. I feel so indebted to you for who I am today. I seek your continued guidance and blessings!

Yours Affectionately,
Aparna

About Shri Pheru Singh Ruhela...

An M.A., B.Ed in English literature, Shri Pheru Singh Ruhela started his career as a teacher, rising to the position of the Headmaster (Principal) of the ACC Ltd. School, Lakheri (Rajasthan) due to his outstanding performance. His ability to engage with students endeared him to them and motivated them to perform better. His passion for teaching and the satisfaction of seeing young minds blossom into mature adults motivated him to constantly improvise his teaching style, to make the subject matter more interesting and easy to grasp. To this end, he ensured that he too upgraded his knowledge and qualifications. A dedicated educator, he did not limit his interactions to his classes alone, going out of his way to ensure that deserving students completed their education, which helped shape their future. Though retired, he continues to guide his students, who remain connected to him even today.

"Do your duty sincerely, without worrying about the results. The results of hard work may be delayed, but are never denied."
– Shri Pheru Singh Ruhela

A Bundle of Bliss

It's a wonderful feeling to know that before you came into this world, your parents and relatives were eagerly awaiting your arrival. A year prior to my birth, my parents had lost their ten-month-old son. The sudden demise of Jagdish (my elder brother) had left my family depressed and aggrieved. So, a year later, when I was born on February 28, 1937, their happiness knew no bounds. My family truly believed that Jagdish had come back in my guise. Hence, I was named 'Pheru' (someone who has returned).

I was brought up in a princely manner in this middle-class family. My nostril and ears were pierced to save me from bad spirits. A little bit of flesh was cut from both the ears. The signs remain to this day.

School Stories

In July 1943, at the age of six years, I was enrolled in the Government Primary school, run by the Provincial Government. The medium of instruction was Urdu. Post-independence, in 1947, it was upgraded to a middle school. This proved a boon for all of us since we could now study upto Class 8, which, in the past, used to be a nightmare due to the lack of schools nearby. I completed my Class 8 in 1951. There was no electricity in the village in those days. I used to study under a neem tree during the day and in the light of a lantern at night.

The nearest high school from my village, Binauli (U.P.), was at Baraut. It was very far, and there was no means of transport. The students who attended that school had to live in a hostel. So, only sons of landlords or moneylenders could afford to study there. Since the expenses for boarding were unaffordable for my family, the idea of my further education was dropped.

However, destiny paved the way for my further education. By chance, my maternal uncle Girwar Singh Thakur came to visit us and took me with him to study in an Inter College in Asara

(U.P). Everyone from his family was well-educated. They were an inspiration to me. He provided me with a background that was favorable for education. Although Asara was a remote village, it was prominent for its good education. I passed my High School 'Matriculation' (as it was known in those days) examination from the Board of High School and Intermediate Education, U.P, in 1953. This village was located about six kilometers from my village. Every day, I used to walk 12 kilometers to attend classes! What seems unbelievable today was a reality during my childhood!

> However, far from deterring me, this struggle for a basic education only increased my dedication and determination. Although this physical hardship tested my endurance, it was worth it because it developed in me the innate strength to accomplish seemingly impossible tasks.

High School Heartbreak

I got admission in the Science stream. My maternal uncle, who was a lecturer in the college, taught us Mathematics. After a few days of classes, he gave us some homework. Taking it lightly, I did not complete the assignment. The next day, he called my name in the class to check my exercise book. Seeing the work incomplete, he scolded me and slapped me before the class. This made a huge impact on my mind. Till then, I had always been the apple of everyone's eye! I had never anticipated such punishment. I felt extremely humiliated. I refused to study Mathematics further. My family tried all kinds of persuasion, but to no avail. My uncle too, tried to stop me from taking such a hasty decision. But no matter what anyone said, I didn't agree. I was transferred to the Arts stream the next day.

> Had I demonstrated the maturity to admit my mistake and to take things in my stride, my future would have turned out differently. But, by the time I realized my mistake, it was too late to make amends. To this day, I sometimes wonder what the course of my life would have been, had I continued in the Science stream.

The Certificate of Teaching Course

My maternal uncle noticed an advertisement in the newspaper for admission to a Certificate of Teaching (C.T.) course, published by Gandhi Vidya Mandir Rural University, Sadarshahr, in Rajasthan. Acting upon his advice, I applied for admission to the course. After a fortnight, I received a call letter to join the training. My father escorted me to the place. Here, we came to know that mine was the first batch. There were no tuition fees or hostel charges. Books were to be issued by the college library. We only had to pay for our meals and the cost of stationery.

After a month, the management declared a scholarship of Rs.15/- for each of us. This noble gesture was initiated by Seth Kanhaiya Lal Duggad of Sardarshahr, Rajasthan, who had dedicated his life and property for the upliftment of the masses. This move was a big support in helping the students meet their expenses.

During the year, a panel came to inspect the college. It was then that we came to know that the college was not recognized by the government. This was a huge shock to all of us, who had, in good faith, invested our time and money for the course. We collectively approached the Registrar and complained that the college had put our future at stake by their false claims. Some students threatened to sue the college authorities. However, we were assured by the authorities that the college would get recognition by the end of the year. Despite the assurance, four students left the course.

The college was based on the pattern of Gandhiji's Ashram. It was a novel way of learning and teaching and was very different from the prevailing education system. Wearing khadi was compulsory, smoking was not allowed, pure vegetarian food was served, and we had to spin the *charkha*.

The ashram also wanted to imbibe in the students the thought that people of all religions are equal. They only had different ways of living. No one was inferior, and no one was an untouchable. The college authorities also taught us the *bhajans* (prayers) sung by Gandhiji. There was no compulsion, yet everyone followed these teachings voluntarily.

> Gandhiji taught us the mantra of 'Simple Living, High Thinking'. This mantra influenced me then and is relevant even in today's times.

During this period, an incident occurred that left its impact on me forever. I was returning home during the Diwali holidays, with a friend from Rohtak. We stayed at his relative's house in Delhi. Sohrab Modi's film, 'Jhansi ki Rani', was being screened at a theatre nearby. I requested my friend to come with me to watch the movie. But, he preferred to go home. Since my train was at night, I went for the movie alone. In the intermission, a tea vendor entered. I called him to provide tea. He had nothing with him at the time. Just as the movie was about to start again, he came in with a tray of snacks and a teapot. He moved swiftly, handing over the tray to me. The snacks were tasty and being really hungry, I gorged on them. He then charged me one rupee and ten anna (an old currency unit in India), which was a big amount for me! However, there was no alternative, but to pay up. My mind whirled. I had only enough money for the railway fare home and had not factored in this expense. The only choice I had, post this indulgence, was to walk about 20 kilometers from the railway station to my village, with the luggage on my head and shoulders.

I am happy that this incident occurred during my youth itself, and taught me the eye-opening lesson of living within one's means.

> Life teaches us in various ways.

Our college eventually got recognition from the Education Department of Rajasthan, but with a change. Now, instead of a Certificate of Teaching, a Basic Senior Teacher's certificate was to be awarded to the students on completion of the course. In due course, in 1954, I passed out as a trained teacher.

Parellely, in a crucial development, the services of my maternal uncle and seven other teachers were terminated. Losing one's job was considered to be a calamity in those times! On the threshold of my career, I too was haunted by the fear that something similar would happen to me. However, rather than ruminating on their fate, my uncle and his colleagues remained undeterred. They took this up as a challenge and started a new school, the DAV School, from the sixth class onwards. The Arya Samaj helped them to set up and run this school.

> I learnt the important lesson that no matter what circumstances one has to face, one should not lose hope and should keep moving ahead.

My uncle, who was the Principal of this new school, called me to join the school. Thus, in 1954, I embarked on my professional journey as a teacher.

Intermediate Innings

In 1955, I filled up the form for the UP Intermediate Examination Board (12th class in today's times). Occasionally, I used to read Hindi novels. One day, one of my colleagues gave me a novel called 'Chandrakanta', written by Devaki Nandan Khatri. I started reading it and finished it soon. The novel was full of romance, thrill, anxiety, horror, spying, and loads of excitement. At the end was a footnote, 'To know the further developments, read 'Chandrakanta Santati.'

I found the novel so gripping that I could not resist reading it, although I knew that I had to concentrate on my studies. I read the complete series, which had 28 volumes. I was so enthralled by these novels, that I was not able to prepare for my board exam and ended up wasting a year. Aghast, I realized my mistake, but it was too late. I decided then that never again would I let myself be swayed from my goal. I resolved to reappear for the exam and clear it. I studied hard and finally passed the Intermediate examination in 1956.

> I realized that hard work, consistency, and focus were crucial to achieve any goal.

Missed Missions

In response to an advertisement, I applied for the post of Education Instructor in NEFA (North-East Frontier Agency), then a Union Territory. I attended the interview and a week later, went to a village with my father to seek a suitable alliance for my younger sister. A pandit had come to meet the host. During the conversation, my father asked him about me, without giving any details or reference. After thinking for a while, he said, "Most probably, he is your son. He has a stomach disorder. He is working in a private job. He has applied for a job recently. He will be selected, but will not join. After some time, he will get a permanent job where there is fire and water." Hearing his prediction, we thought that this job would be with the Railways, as locomotive steam engines were in use in those days.

About 20 days later, I received an appointment letter to join NEFA. On knowing the location and the political situation there, my mother wept bitterly and opposed my decision to go so far away. Hence, I dropped the idea of taking up this job. The pandit's prediction was right!

Marriage Memories

Another amusing anecdote brings a smile to my face whenever I remember it.

During my holidays, I had gone to my maternal grandfather's (Nanaji's) village. Some relatives had come to meet him with a proposal for my marriage. They were already acquainted with my family, but were seeing me for the first time. My grandfather asked me to get the hookah. Although I was getting the hookah ready, I was busy thinking of the girl in question. So, I forgot to fill in the tobacco and put only burnt dungcake. Rotationally, they drew the pipe. But, smoke did not come out even after two rounds of inhaling. Irritated, Nanaji glanced at me and said, "Did you forget to fill in tobacco?" His words reminded me of the slip. I hastily took away the chillum and ran away saying, "I will just be back." Seeing my face red, my cousin sisters and aunts laughed at me. I kept mum and enjoyed all the attention. Filling in the tobacco properly, I returned swiftly and they enjoyed the smoke.

Those days, the 'purdah' system was strictly followed. Couples were not free to chat before the elders. They had to play hide and seek to avail of an opportunity to meet each other. Imagine that I was able to see my wife only after our marriage! Today, this seems impossible!

A New Frontier

In 1958, I noticed an advertisement in the 'Hindustan Times' for the recruitment of teachers in the ACC Ltd. School in Lakheri (Rajasthan). The advertisement mentioned that to and fro rail fare would be paid to those called for the interview. I had never heard of the place Lakheri, but I applied for the job. My application was shortlisted, and I was called for the interview. The interview board comprised of seven members.

During the interview, the Chairperson asked me, "After joining, if we terminate your services, what will you do?" I replied, "Sir, this is a very surprising question. If you feel pleasure in recruiting and terminating the services of employees without any fault of theirs, what can I say or do? I will decide whether to continue or not in such a situation. However, if I teach the students with full devotion and my overall performance is up to the mark, then I don't find any reason for my termination." My response evoked laughter from them. I was asked to wait in the conference room. After five minutes, I was called back and informed about my selection, subject to medical fitness. I joined the ACC Ltd. School in 1958, and was on probation for a year.

ACC is a cement manufacturing company with its own powerhouse. I recalled the predictions of the pandit, which were proved 100 percent true. I wonder how, without any reference, clue, horoscope, palm reading, or anything else, he had predicted my future. I don't know what to call it... face reading or perhaps something else? Even today, I wonder about this. But surprisingly, after this incident, despite my father going to that village several times, he could never meet the pandit again!

Teaching Tales & Tribulations

The staff in the school was well-qualified. There were specialized subject teachers. Education was imparted totally free, under the welfare scheme of the company. Punctuality was a must. Co-curricular activities were given prime importance. I too, worked hard to the best of my ability. Based on my good performance during my probation, I was confirmed in 1959.

Impressed with my teaching skills, my boss asked me to coach his children. Being the tutor of the Headmaster's children was indeed a matter of prestige. However, my seniors became envious of me because they were deprived of this privilege. They were hurt that the Headmaster had bypassed them and given such an opportunity to a newcomer like me.

I knew that I had to deal with their behavior before the situation blew out of proportion. I pointed out to them that although the Headmaster did give me this honor, he had not given me any concession in my duties at school. In fact, I had to work harder as compared to them. Although the Headmaster paid me a handsome honorarium, I had never asked him for any money. I humbly accepted what he gave me.

Soon, I was made the Convenor of cultural and literary activities. I participated in literary competitions for schools, organized by the ACC Ltd. workers, on topics like Safety, Organizational relations between superiors and subordinates, etc., and also won prizes. I was chosen the Club Library Secretary and also the Entertainment Secretary, over several terms.

I searched for potential in each of my students. I used to counsel and guide students to work hard. Many times, I contacted their parents to persuade them to continue the education of their children even if they had to face financial problems. I also counseled the fathers to give up drinking, smoking, and gambling for the sake of their children. Though all of them did not respond positively, almost 70-80 percent did pay heed to my advice. Their behavior benefited their children and they did well and got admissions in medical, engineering, and other fields. Most of them hold prominent positions today. I feel proud and satisfied to see that my efforts have yielded good results and that I was able to positively shape the future of these children.

It would be hard to believe that despite being a teacher, I never taught my own children. I only guided them to study the textbooks thoroughly and attend their classes attentively to understand the fundamentals and concepts well. I am glad that my children listened to my advice and have done very well for themselves.

Along with motivating my students for their future progress, I realized that I too, needed to enhance my qualifications. So, alongside working in the school, I completed my B.A. (graduation) and M.A. (post-graduation) in English Literature, as well as B.Ed. My colleagues were impressed with my qualifications, and I earned more respect with all these stripes on my shoulder.

> I believe that education plays an important role in elevating one's life. It is the key that opens up new horizons and paves the way to enhance one's position in life. ✎

Renumeration Roadblocks

In 1966, I was awarded a special increment, raising my basic pay from Rs.100 to Rs.110. The following year in 1967, I was promoted to Grade B (Secondary Trained Teacher). The letter stated my basic pay as Rs. 114/-. I brought this to the notice of the Headmaster, claiming that it was a demotion, as I got only Rs.4/- extra, which was Re.1/- less than my normal increment in the lower grade. He termed it as a clerical mistake that would be rectified in the next month's payment. However, it remained unchanged in the next three consecutive months. I desired to put up the matter in writing to the higher-ups. The Headmaster fumed and shouted, "Are you dying of hunger?" Feeling humiliated, I never raised the matter again. Though this may seem an insignificant amount in today's times, back then, it was a considerable amount.

At every further promotion throughout my service, I had to bear this loss. It affected my Basic pay, Gratuity, Provident Fund, and other benefits. Cumulatively, I bore a loss of approximately Rs. 1 lakh. The Headmaster too, retired in 1983, without rectifying the error. To add insult to injury, his successor leveled false charges against me that the previous Headmaster had awarded me three special increments during his tenure, amounting to favoritism.

This added fuel to the fire and encouraged the hostile behaviour of my adversaries. Their taunts compelled me to approach the HR Head of the plant. He asked his assistant to bring all the relevant records. Finally, after thorough scrutiny, the error was traced. He said, "Your story is worthy of being published in the ACC Newsletter." But he communicated his inability to pay the arrears. However, he assured me a special increment as compensation, and to his credit, he kept his word. He shared that the Headmaster had never raised this point. Many years later, when I happened to meet the retired Headmaster, I asked him regarding this matter. He confessed that he had not raised it with his seniors.

The problem was never rectified. It is said that people with high integrity are always fairly rewarded. However, the reverse was true in my case. I suffered a huge financial loss (it may seem like a relatively small amount, but it was big money for me) without any fault of mine. This has made a huge difference to my pension today. However, I am satisfied that considering my outstanding performance, the management promoted me from time to time and made me the head of the institution – the Headmaster, in 1989. I am also happy that not only well-wishers, but even my critics, notwithstanding their antagonistic attitude, acknowledged my ability to work hard and deliver good results.

I retired from active service in 1997.

> Persistence is a very important quality. Sometimes, you may find yourself on the receiving end of a mistake, but do not be deterred by delay in desired results. Be persistent and do your bit every day till the time the mistake is rectified.

In Retrospect

Throughout my career, I have never taught a single class sitting in the chair. My classes were always interactive. Only when the students feel that the teacher is genuinely interested in teaching the subject, will they be interested in studying it. One of my strengths is that I can blend very well with people of all generations. I also took the effort to remember the names of each of my students. This created a personal bond with each of them and brought me very close to them. Even today, most of my students are in touch with me, and it gives me great pleasure to hear about their accomplishments and achievements. I am thankful that in my own humble way, I have been able to make a difference to their lives.

Life Lines

- Every child has tremendous potential. A good teacher must be a guru who can identify and harness this potential and guide the child towards what is good for it.

- Although it is not possible to go back into time and undo a wrong, once one realizes one's mistake, one should genuinely make amends and ensure that it is not repeated.

- Follow Gandhiji's mantra of 'Simple living, high thinking'. Greed is one of the causes of misery.

- Parents of today should not unnecessarily interfere in their children's life. They must do only what is necessary and leave the rest for their children to decide. That is how children learn to be responsible.

- Only having money is of no use. Children of poor parents may turn out to be brilliant students and do well in life whereas children of rich parents may turn out to be average. What is important is the spark within the child and how the child develops its own calibre.

- Bring up your children such that they understand their responsibilities.

- There is no substitute for hard work.

- Keep putting in your best work, no matter what anyone says about you.

Words of Wisdom

I have always believed in doing my duty, my karma, no matter what the circumstances. I have never bargained with God, asking Him for this and that. I knew that I would get the results of my hard work sooner or later. Also, I knew that doing wrong things would lead me to the wrong path and the results that I would get would be disastrous.

Life is a great teacher, and there is a learning opportunity in each of life's incidents. Learning is a lifelong process that adds to our knowledge. Knowledge equips us to deal with conflict and handle situations tactfully to retain our peace of mind. A restless mind harms oneself. So, work calmly and develop the knack of getting things done. Then, you will be an asset for your organization.

12

An Unconventional Odyssey

Prakhar Sharma

Dear Prakhar (Sunny),

You are an intense person with razor-sharp focus on anything you set your mind to. Having known you since my stint in the Philippines, I have always admired your firebrand personality and your absolute no-nonsense approach.

You are a man of a few words for those who don't know you well enough..., as well as such a stunning writer! You surely have a way with words when it comes to writing essays or research papers. I often wonder how someone can have such clarity and definite points of view on such a wide range of subjects!

Happiness always, my friend!

Yours Affectionately,
Aparna

About Prakhar Sharma...

An MBA (Masters of Business Administration) from the Asian Institute of Management (AIM) and a Masters in Public Policy from the National University of Singapore (NUS), Prakhar Sharma is currently pursuing his Ph.D in Political Science in the US. He has traveled extensively from Jaipur to Japan, Philippines to Singapore, and Afghanistan to the US. His vast repertoire includes a stint as a visiting research fellow at the United Nations University in Japan, working as consultant to the World Bank and the UNICEF and managing a large research program for Yale University. His work in Afghanistan entailed designing and managing research on governance and its interaction with political violence. Observing them firsthand has given him a unique perspective on conflict at grass root levels and the complexities behind implementing development and governance initiatives in conflict-ridden areas. An opportunity to brief senior staff at the White House on the impediments to stability in Afghanistan is just another feather in the cap of this versatile individual. A prolific reader and an excellent writer, he was also the associate editor for the alumni magazine of the Asian Institute of Management. His motto of constantly exploring keeps him motivated to pursue newer avenues and excel at them.

My favourite quote is the one by J.M. Coetzee, 'Slow Man' – "...So that someone might want to put you in a book...So that you may be worth putting in a book...Live like a hero...Be a main character. Otherwise, what is life for?" – *Prakhar Sharma*

I feel uncomfortable whenever I am asked to take stock of my past, and count my successes and failures. Perhaps, 'uncomfortable' is not the right word. What once seemed to be 'success', often appears rather miniscule with the benefit of hindsight. Also, is 'failure' to be seen as a setback or is it an opportunity to 'try again,' in spite of all that's stacked against you? Thinking about the past, and accounting for it sometimes also feels like an attempt to hang on to 'what may have been.' Yet, I have a story that I can share, not because it is exemplary, but because it is rather unconventional. The story is still a work-in-progress and is devoid of the stereotypical notions of success and failure, but it touches upon themes that may resonate with the readers.

The Leaves of My Life

I was born in Jaipur (India) in 1977. The Jaipur where I spent my childhood and college years was neither a commercial hub, nor did it stand out as a city with a pronounced intellectual bent. Most of my college education entailed self-study as attendance was not mandatory and classes were not organized on schedule. So, I had limited opportunities to socialize with my cohort. The social and cultural environment in Jaipur in the 1990s, when I was in my formative years of personal and professional development, also seemed rather restrictive. Most people from my age group were either happy to take up the jobs that were easily available or wanted to leave Jaipur to pursue educational or professional opportunities in metro towns.

Tradition, of course, had a role to play – safer careers were preferred while non-traditional professional choices such as writing were routinely discouraged. While doctors and engineers were looked up to, civil services and business administration were also considered attractive career choices in my social orbit. I never considered becoming an engineer or a doctor – Physics and Biology were always rather low on my list of interesting subjects – but I wasn't averse to the idea of competitive civil services exams or pursuing a career in business management. Although, there was no one in my family or friend circle who was in the civil services, somehow, the idea of being in public service, of working towards the 'greater good', was appealing.

> I believe in what Thomas Jefferson said, "I feel that every human mind feels pleasure in doing good to another."

Visionary leaders in business and politics also seemed like convenient role models. After all, who didn't want to emulate a success story? I, however, found literary figures, especially writers, more inspiring. Not necessarily those who were successful, but those who looked at life differently, were not afraid to go against conventional wisdom, and who dared to entertain a deserving issue.

Abstract Ambitions

I wasn't born into a family of means. While the claim of being a 'self-made man' is misleading – several people, knowingly or unknowingly, have played a role in shaping my personality, my attitude and my goals – I had to work hard for most things in life. People often talk about chasing ideals, dreaming big, and then working hard to realize one's ambitions. I do not recollect having specific ambitions, except entertaining the vague and broad notion of wanting to be proud of myself, being successful, being recognized for my work, and so on. The only concrete ambition I had was to create an opportunity to be able to showcase excellence through hard work and strong motivation. That was it – no lofty dreams, no unrealistic or outsized ambitions.

Being wealthy was appealing because I wasn't financially well off, but it did not seem to me an ambition of substance. I felt wealth would be a by-product of pursuing my goals, and accumulating wealth by itself wasn't my aim in life. Chasing happiness also never appealed to me as a goal. I wanted to find meaning to my life. The

Austrian neurologist, Viktor Frankl in his book, 'Man's Search for Meaning' mentioned that happiness was besides the point, and that one's purpose should be to find meaning in life. I thus realized that the 'pursuit of excellence' was the meaning of my life.

> As A.P.J. Abdul Kalam has said, "Excellence is a continuous process and not an accident."

Although circumstances in my personal life – limited financial means, absence of role models, inadequate opportunities for career advancement in Jaipur – moulded me into appreciating pragmatism, I had a declared preference for indulging in seemingly abstract ideas. I gravitated towards the abstract over the real, read philosophy and literature when most people of my age read only what was immediately relevant to their studies or work, and maintained a strong preference for intellectual eclecticism. While reading books, I aspired to think like authors, to kindle my hope of leading the life of the mind someday – being able to identify my prejudices through my writing; seeing the shades of grey in human interactions through imaginary characters; appreciating how some realities became facts while others were reduced to interpretations; and cherishing living with self-doubt and yet remaining confident of one's place in the world. This was the world that I wanted to inhabit – a world of thinking and writing. Aspirations for material success played second fiddle to intellectual stimulation.

Career Conundrum

To move from these abstract conceptions to a concrete career plan, I did not have professional role models – people who could go beyond telling me what was good for me. I perhaps needed someone like a tennis coach, who would point out my strengths and weaknesses, help me chart out my goals, and enable me to realize my potential. While my mother always wanted the best for me, she had not lived in the world that I so desperately wanted to inherit. She lived with dignity and pride, faced life's tribulations with a smile and an endless supply of courage, and lived life on her own terms in a society that deliberately and systematically discouraged such an attitude in women. My mother remains my biggest inspiration in life – she may not necessarily have had the tools to guide me about my future, but she instilled in me a strong, uncompromising belief in hard work and perfection, and a set of core values that continue to serve me well in moments of jubilation and tribulation alike.

After graduation, I committed myself to prepare for the civil services' entrance exam. Soon, I realized that it wasn't a good fit for me. I neither had the patience to memorize facts for the exam, nor did I think I could realistically pursue public service as a career, because most civil servants whom I met while growing up seemed either entitled or self-obsessed. I thus walked away, and considered the idea of competing for the MBA entrance exam. I thought MBA offered me a way out – it offered me the potential to earn a living and the prospect of pursuing my interests once I had accumulated sufficient savings. A year later, I did not get admission into any college that I wanted to go to. Many of my friends who prepared with me got into decent colleges and left Jaipur to pursue their MBA. I swallowed my pride, tried again the following year, prepared infinitely harder, and was offered admission in a respectable business school abroad. Two years later, I completed my MBA from the Asian Institute of Management, Manila, Philippines, on a bank loan.

The Karthik Connection

The first year of my MBA was emotionally taxing. I was homesick, lacked confidence and suffered from low self-esteem. I had never lived away from my mother and brother, never put myself in a position when I would need to make decisions for myself, and had never been in a context where others' opinion of me could have a tangible impact on my future. The stakes were high, and I did not respond well initially.

> It is interesting how all your demons conspire in unison to uproot your self-belief when you are out of your comfort zone. But, perhaps, those are the moments that tell you who you are and who you don't want to be. ✎

The turning point was when I ran into one of my seniors in the MBA program – Karthik Saravanan – who played a defining role in my life. Single-handedly, he helped me evolve from someone who was shy and unsure of his place in the world, to someone who was willing to back himself regardless of the circumstances, and who was able to work harder than anyone to succeed. Karthik would take time off his busy study schedule to speak to me, motivate me, and take me out for a coffee or a drink when I would do well. In him, I found a family away from home. We were like brothers in an environment that incentivized cut-throatism and looking out for oneself. The most important aspect of Karthik's role in my life wasn't just his constant encouragement or the fact that he motivated me to excel professionally, but that he inspired me to become a stronger and well-rounded human being and that he walked his talk. He is the most motivated, self-assured, confident, and optimistic person I have ever met. In him, I saw a role model that I was dearly missing in life.

The Choice of a Career

I would like to believe that my transition from being uncertain about myself to becoming relatively self-assured today entails more choice than circumstance. Of course, to borrow from Steve Jobs, one can live life forward, but connect the dots only when looking back. While I was studying abroad for my MBA and was, by all means, heading towards a career in the private sector, I was also thinking about where I wanted to contribute after completing my studies. I enjoyed Marketing as a student of management but did not have the outgoing personality and the unceasing optimism to excel as a Marketing professional. Finance jobs were usually the highest paying and the most coveted among my classmates, but Finance was not my cup of tea. I also wasn't good at Accounting. A career in Human Resources Management (HRM) was a likely choice because of my interest in helping others realize their potential.

The Direction of International Development

Amid this thought process, I enrolled myself in a class on 'Development Management' in the second year of my MBA. The class focused on the evolving areas of public action for development. The Professor who taught the course – Juan Miguel Luz - invited us to apply our management skills to pressing issues in International Development. With that one class, my perspective changed.

The course on Development Management offered me a fresh outlook. I could use my training to make a difference! Despite billions of people living under abject poverty, deprivation, civil wars or political and social exclusion, the solutions on the table seemed woefully inadequate. Governments did not have the answers, either due to lack of resources or the absence of political will or policy incoherence. International development needed people with fresh perspectives, and energy and skills that they could use to address problems that concerned not individual corporations, but entire societies. I felt myself gravitate towards that world.

The Philippine Public School System

Upon completing my MBA, I pursued this interest in International Development and worked for two years as a consultant with the Department of Education, Philippines. I worked closely with the Department's Undersecretary for Finance and Administration, who, incidentally, was the same professor who taught the course on Development Management during my MBA. Since we first met in the classroom, Juan Miguel Luz has been an inspirational mentor to me. The unique experience of working with him gave me exposure to development at the macro level – participating in the decision making at the national level and facilitating the implementation of difficult decisions.

Some of these decisions entailed streamlining the procurement of school textbooks, decentralizing the financial management for payroll, and working on a spending plan for the Philippine public school system. We tried to introduce innovative thinking in a system that offered no incentive to do so. We faced bureaucratic inertia, coordination issues, and systemic resistance to change. But I realized that more than the coherence of policies and implementation plans, it was the political will to implement plans that helped us move forward. Both, the Secretary and the Undersecretary of Education marshalled their resources to focus on a 12-point agenda for the Department of Education, which included academic reforms, resource mobilization, and professionalizing the bureaucracy.

For around 20 months, I worked on one full-time job (as a consultant for a development consulting firm, focusing on the Department of Education, Philippines) and two part-time jobs. In hindsight, this brutal regime was partly a labour of necessity – I needed the finances – but I also thoroughly enjoyed my work. It gave me a sense of fulfillment that I was actually able to push myself to the hilt while positively contributing to improving people's lives and make a difference.

One of my part-time jobs was to serve as the associate editor for the alumni magazine of the Asian Institute of Management. The role gave me an opportunity to write, to edit, and to supervise the entire process from planning the substantive and stylistic aspects of the publication, to reaching out to prospective writers, to interviewing business leaders and getting the different pieces together for publication. I also took on other projects that entailed writing case studies on exemplary school administration, developing research proposals for liberalization of education in the Philippines, and so on. These roles gave me opportunities to nurture my passion for writing, and I cherished them.

During my travels across the Philippines to conduct workshops on capacity building of education managers, I was struck by the disparities in education and development in general. School construction in some provinces in southern Philippines was impeded by specific acts of violence against government institutions. Children were often not sent to schools for their own safety. Textbooks and furniture were rarely, if at all, provided to these schools for the same reason. Inadequate resources committed to education hampered progress in the short-term and the potential for change in the long run.

I realized that development was infinitely more challenging without security and that people needed to be provided an environment safe enough for them to entertain longer time horizons. A Time Horizon could be defined as a perceived point of time in the future.

> When people's basic, everyday requirements are met, they can entertain longer time horizons and plan for the future. However, when people face uncertainty over the safety of their lives and their ability to pay their bills and provide for themselves, they are often unable to look beyond their immediate needs and are thus trapped in shorter time horizons.

Short-term thinking fostered narrow self-interests that resulted in negative externalities. It shortened people's time horizons as people looked to cut corners. My interest in understanding the link between development and the concept of time horizons, i.e., how one's time horizon influenced her/his intentions and actions, took me beyond the Philippines as I followed specific developments in the Middle East and South Asia.

Interest in International Security

I developed an interest in international security to the extent of defining it as the area within international development to which I wanted to contribute. I acquired my second post-graduate degree, in Public Policy, on a full scholarship from the National University of Singapore. For my summer training, I traveled as a visiting research fellow to the United Nations University in Japan to study the effectiveness of the International Criminal Court (ICC) in Darfur, Sudan. I studied different frameworks to assess how the ICC's mandate was compromised when member states like Sudan refused to comply. Unlike national rules that are obligatory for citizens of a country, international rules need countries to voluntarily comply. If they choose not to comply, there is little that international regimes such as the ICC can do.

Afghanistan Accounts

Before completing my studies in Singapore in December 2006, I got a job offer with a defense think-tank focusing on research related to anti-national activities. My first assignment was as Head of Research for a local think-tank in Kabul, Afghanistan. Unlike a couple of analysts who refused the offer because of the dangers of living in Afghanistan, I did not hesitate. I realized that if I wanted to make a mark for myself, I was unlikely to do so as a desk researcher in Singapore. So, I accepted the offer and flew to Afghanistan. The experience of living with local communities under precarious security conditions, undertaking field research, and managing projects gave me a unique perspective on conflict at grass root levels. Training young Afghan analysts – who have always been compelled by their circumstances to take sides on issues as determined by religious sects or ethnic affiliation – to undertake objective research and write dispassionate analyses, was a considerable challenge. The experience tremendously enhanced my understanding of the critical developmental and governance challenges and the linkages among various developmental issues in Afghanistan.

I enjoyed myself working in Afghanistan and believe that I learned more by living there than I would have by reading any number of books on the country. I realized that the war in Afghanistan was not a single war, but multiple conflicts that seamlessly overlapped. People often fought for local grievances, but they found a way to attach those local grievances to national causes with the intent to legitimize their actions. The solutions that we usually hear from international conflict and development experts – provide livelihood opportunities, build schools and roads, improve healthcare, democratize local institutions – are largely well-meaning initiatives, but often counter-productive if we are not aware of the contexts.

> Oftentimes, we seem to define problems to fit the menu of solutions that we already have at our disposal.

I was amused at the realization that this was the same thought process that I had encountered in Jaipur – the choice of a career was limited to selecting one among the preconceived set of options that one could pursue – medicine, engineering, civil service, etc.

The main problem was that the notions of progress, development and governance are different in Afghanistan than what we had assumed, based on either our theoretical understanding of these concepts or practical appreciation of these concepts in other contexts. Afghans want development, but not necessarily the textbook development that we prescribe as solutions – roads, bridges, schools, and so on. The broader point is not about the uniqueness of Afghans or Afghanistan, but to emphasize that despite evidence pointing to the flaws of using one-size-fits-all prescriptions, we continue to use them in challenging contexts such as Afghanistan.

Between 2006 and 2016, I spent around four years living inside Afghanistan; traveled to several provinces to conduct research; worked as a consultant for the World Bank and the UNICEF and advised them on programming their services for the most vulnerable communities; managed large surveys for Yale University to understand and explain 'blame-attribution' and 'information-sharing' dynamics in civil wars; led the ground-up development of two local research institutions and trained Afghan researchers to analyze their political context; raised $4 million for a nationwide teacher-training program; and briefed development agencies, implementing partners, diplomats, militaries, and non-government organizations on the political evolution of Afghanistan. I feel proud and satisfied that through my work, I was able to make a difference, however small, in the conflict-ridden context.

Formative Fellowship

My work in Afghanistan was noticed abroad, and I was invited as a visiting research fellow at the Stimson Center in Washington D.C. The fellowship was a formative experience, as it gave me the opportunity to give briefings at the White House to President Obama's Chief of Staff, senate staffers at the Capitol Hill and a group of 30 non-government organizations working on protecting civilians in conflicts. I recently managed a research institute at Yale University, focusing on understanding micro level patterns of political violence.

Today, I am enrolled in a Ph.D program in Political Science in the US, pursuing my interest in acquiring training in research. I am writing my dissertation on explaining why communities living in fragile contexts are more willing to accept public services from certain groups and not others. Through these research experiences, I have learned about political violence and how economic, political, and social issues interact in different contexts. In this process, I have also learned a great deal more about myself, my interests, and future goals. Even though research is, financially, one of the least rewarding professions, I constantly get the intellectual kick of being knowledgeable about issues that I care about, having the ability to reason, and constantly trying to identify patterns where none seem apparent.

Book Buff

When I started reading about a diverse range of subjects, the writer that first caught my interest was Ayn Rand. I was fascinated with her philosophy of rugged individualism and the intensity of her characters. In a collective society such as India, where selfishness was (and is) socially frowned upon, I found myself gravitate towards any literature that equated self-interested action with heroism. I felt that the culture that I grew up in enforced the notion that family, community, and society came before the individual. Thus, the interests of my family, my community, and my society (often in an interchangeable manner) shaped my priorities.

Rand offered me a getaway, a respite, even if it was for a few moments. Reading her books felt like I lived two lives, one, as a reader of Rand's fiction and another, as someone who had to fit in a society that did not spare much room for individualism. When I first read her groundbreaking books – 'The Fountainhead,' 'We the Living,' and 'Atlas Shrugged' – I was taken by her reasoning. These books changed my worldview. I felt that I could lead a morally fulfilling life without resigning my interests to the will of the collective. In a strange way, I began to see my life choices as a binary; I could either choose to be a 'prime mover,' an original thinker, a man who cared to think, to reason and to doggedly pursue his own interests, or, I could become a 'follower,' someone whose declared thoughts were a result of others' validation. Now, after having read more widely and being able to think more critically, I can see the limits of Rand's reasoning. Rand forcefully illustrated her arguments by developing characters that either embodied her philosophy or contradicted it. As a reader, you were compelled by the sheer force of her words to identify yourself with one of those two ideals. You ended up stoking your ego when you aligned with her ideals and feeling incomplete, in a bizarre way, if you did not subscribe to them.

Another author that I enjoyed reading was Leo Tolstoy. I have read pretty much every major book that he wrote, before venturing into and being captivated by Bertrand Russell's philosophy, Dostoyevsky's psychology of human behavior, Albert Camus' existentialism, and J.M. Coetzee's post-modernist 'otherness.'

It relaxes my mind when I read about characters that I find interesting, contexts that I can relate to, or when the style and substance of writing are worth emulating. I still read more than what my profession or social orbit demands of me.

> I believe that reading refines one's creative thinking process. As Charlie Tremendous Jones says, "You will be the same person in five years as you are today except for the people you meet and the books you read."

In Retrospect

Looking back, I can confidently assert that I did not have a straight, one-dimensional career plan. I pursued assignments that I found interesting and believed that if I enjoyed something, I gave myself a better shot at excelling at it. I chose work that I found challenging regardless of whether or not it was good for my career. I continue to work long hours and work during the weekends because I love what I do.

> If you enjoy what you do, the rewards follow, sooner or later.

Future Pavilions

I am an optimist. I believe that I am going to continue to lead an interesting life that is intellectually rewarding and morally fulfilling. Writing remains my sincerest passion. Given my love for writing, I could have been a fiction writer. I may still pursue it someday. I just need to keep exploring, dreaming, and working to realize my dreams. Given the opportunity, I would like to work towards developing high quality research institutions in India that focus on social sciences.

Life Lines

- Figure yourself out.
- Examine the relevance of conventional wisdom in any context.

- Failure is not the opposite of success. It can often be the building block to success.
- Aim high and back your ambitions whether anyone else does or not.
- It is easier to figure out what you do not want to pursue in life than to know what you want to do. It is, therefore, important to keep exploring.

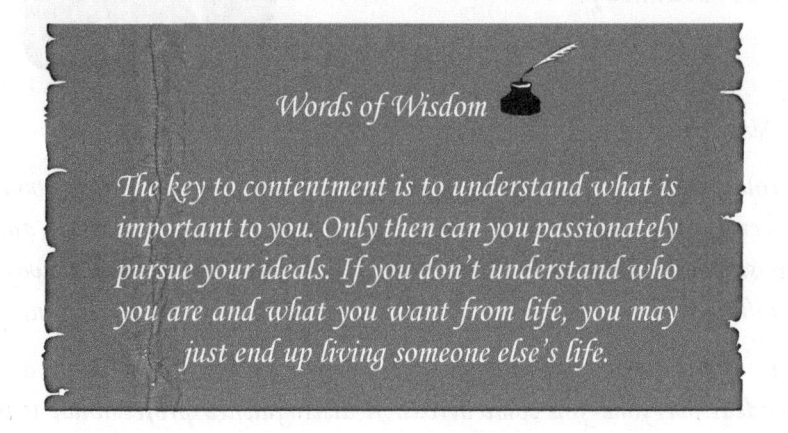

> **Words of Wisdom**
>
> *The key to contentment is to understand what is important to you. Only then can you passionately pursue your ideals. If you don't understand who you are and what you want from life, you may just end up living someone else's life.*

13

A Life Signifying Simplicity & Sensitivity

Arun Kaimal

Dear Arun,

You are an absolute bundle of energy – bright and passionate about everything in life, in fact, about LIFE itself. You ooze warmth and positivity and swear by the mantra of 'CAN DO' at all times. Always willing to lend a helping hand, you are truly a compassionate soul.

You have a way with people and words – verbal and written, and endear everyone you come across. A distinguished professional who is extremely hardworking, focused, and result-oriented; at the core, you are an inspiring being with a humane approach coupled with good words and deeds. I have seen you grow and evolve as a strong achiever and a caring friend.

Thanks a ton for always being there, Arun! You may be surprised, but it's true that I have learnt so much from you!

Yours Affectionately,
Aparna

About Arun Kaimal...

A Bachelor of Management Studies (BMS) from SIES, Nerul (Navi Mumbai), and Masters in Personnel Management & Industrial Relations from the reputed Tata Institute of Social Sciences (TISS), Arun Kaimal is truly an embodiment of a Senior Human Resources Professional (SPHR®). A certified Situational Leadership Level II trainer and Behavioural Competency Mapping Expert, his motto, 'Love people, nothing else matters,' reflects his passion to engage, empower, develop, and bring the best out of the most important asset of an organization – its people. His multilingual skills in English, German, Marathi, Gujarati, Hindi, and Malayalam have helped him connect with people across the board. He is also a visiting faculty at various management institutes. His stellar contribution to the field of HR has been recognized with the HR Warrior Award from the Indira Group of Institutions in India, in 2012. His publications include, 'The key to success is to bake your own PIE!' and 'Network Leadership.' Currently, he is leading the people priorities for the dynamic Water Quality Platform OpCos (Operating Companies) in the Asia Pacific region and working closely with professionals in the Water business and helping them realize their potential.

My favourite quote is the one by Mahatma Gandhi –
"I do not want my house to be walled in on all sides and my windows to be stuffed. I want the culture of all lands to be blown about my house as freely as possible. But I refuse to be blown off my feet by any." – Arun Kaimal

Tiny Tot

The early morning of 10th June, 1984, saw India's population count go up by one! This addition was made by the Kaimal family, second-generation settlers in Mumbai, living at the Railway quarters in Parel. A king-sized baby weighing 3.6 kilos was born to Geetha Kaimal, a housewife who had come to Mumbai for the first time less than a year ago, and Sukumar Govind Kaimal, an officer at the General Insurance Corporation of India. On the 28th day, the baby's maternal uncle (Mama) whispered the name 'Arun' into the ears of the child, and thus was christened Arun Kaimal, the protagonist of this chapter.

Early Experiences

I grew up surrounded by love, care, happiness, and sharing. Born in a cosmopolitan, middle-class Railway Colony at Parel, Mumbai, the lessons of adjusting to and accepting different languages, cultures, and customs had been ingrained in me since an early age. I attribute the success (whatever little) I have achieved today, to this nurturing and the early lessons in flexibility and humility during these formative years. It was in this secure and nourishing atmosphere that I began my life's journey.

I have always had a special relationship with God, inculcated in me as a child by my grandmother and nurtured in me as a young boy by my parents and the Chinmaya Mission. Chinmaya Mission's motto, 'To give maximum happiness to the maximum number for the maximum time,' has deeply inspired all my actions in life.

Detour to Dadar

The retirement of my grandfather from the Railways saw us moving from the Railway Colony to the Spring Mills compound at Dadar, Mumbai. Most of the people who lived in my housing complex in Dadar were employed in the Insurance sector. It was the late 1980's and 'LPG - Liberalization, Privatization, and Globalization,' were still unknown. The nation looked up to bankers, government employees, doctors, and engineers as demigods. Securing a government job was a dream held dear by the youth of that generation. As a child, I was however more keen on becoming a Police Inspector, thanks to the TV serial 'Karamchand' that was a rage with the young and old during those times.

It was in Dadar that I got to learn the rich Marathi language and also imbibed the rich culture of the state of Maharashtra that has produced many great sons like Chhatrapati Shivaji Maharaj, Lokmanya Tilak, Dr. Bhimrao Ambedkar, and others.

> Language, they say, connects many dots and opens many doors. Federico Fellini, the Italian film director and screenwriter, has said, "A different language is a different vision of life."

The doors to many associations, groups, and friend circles opened for me due to my knowledge of Marathi that I cherish till date as a gift from my stay at Dadar. I also believe that words have the power to make or break. The following verse beautifully summarizes the power of words:

Jivhagrey Vasatay Lakshmi, Jivhagrey Mitra Bandhava,
Amrut Chaiva Jivhagrey, Jivhagrey Marna Tatha!

These lines from an ancient Indian poem mean: On the tip of the tongue *(Jivhagrey)* resides Goddess Lakshmi (i.e., by saying the right things you can acquire prosperity); by saying the right things you can maintain good relations with friends and relatives; your words have the power to make you immortal and your words (saying the wrong things at the wrong time) can also bring you death! Hence, it is the tongue that can sway your fortune.

Living in Dadar also exposed me to a variety of festivals like Ganesh Chaturthi and Eid, which helped me learn more about Hinduism and Islam. I was also exposed to Zoroastrianism at the Dadar Parsee Youths Assembly High School, where I studied for seven years. These experiences helped me develop respect for all religions at a very young age.

> I learnt that all religions believe in similar maxims, and there is a lot that we can learn from all of them.

Currents of Change

In 1993, my father bought his first house and we relocated to Mulund, a suburb on the Central Railway line that marks the end of the limits of Mumbai city. Having lived in Dadar all these years, I was sad to leave behind my school, my friends, and many other small things that a young child has a special feeling for. I felt as I had been set adrift from the shore of my familiar world and cast into an unknown ocean.

My neighbors in the new housing society called me a 'Madrasi.' This was a strange feeling. I reflected on the fact that while in Dadar, I was a Hindu, in Mulund, I was a 'Madrasi,' and when I went to Kerala, I was referred to as a 'Mumbaiwala.' What was my true identity? Who was I? Although I didn't realize it at the time, later, these events helped me see the world as 'One Family' and understand that our affiliations and beliefs should not create boundaries but instead, should help us create bridges so that we can live in peace and harmony and prosper as one.

The change to a new location was a blessing in disguise as it forced me to come out of my comfort zone and adapt to my new environment. I quickly learnt that propinquity and affiliation are important aspects that affect group behaviour. My knowledge of Marathi, Malayalam, and a little bit of Tamil also helped me win many friends at my new school. My participation in various stage competitions and plays during my school days helped build my confidence and soon, I became the Class Monitor (in Class 6). Although the move to Mulund could have worked against me, since it came at a very young age, it gave me some good lessons in Change Management and prepared me better for living in this ever-changing world. All these happenings (moving to a new place, making new friends, becoming a class monitor) taught me an important lesson.

> One needs to change with the times and retain the core (values), but keep working on the peripheral and always go on improving. It is like an ancient Chinese proverb that goes: When the winds of change blow, some people build walls, others build windmills.

The Significance of Sociability

Another important concept that was deep-rooted in my mind since childhood was the saying, 'No man is an island.' Having observed my family's interactions and close association with the many families and people around us, I realized that man is a social animal, and social interactions and relationships would always be of great importance. This was probably why I always connected to and maintained large groups of friends wherever I went. Also, I have always held dear, my association with my faculty and all other professionals who have helped me in my journey. The sociability factor opened many doors for me in my personal and professional life – be it getting multiple offers on completing my education from college at SIES or the arrangement for accommodation when I went to Dubai for the first time in 2008 where my friend Ashley Fernandes (we studied together at SIES Nerul) insisted that I stay with him till I could find a place to live.

I also won the Best Student Award for Social Efficiency in school, was the elected Secretary of a politically affiliated Students' Union Body at junior college, and in my graduation days, I was the Class Representative and the Chairperson of the college events. All these roles have helped me connect to people from various walks of life and build deep personal relations with many of them. This is something that I value and cherish as my most valuable asset.

> A quote that I remember which emphasizes the importance of relationships is, "In an organization, you must always strive to have the Chemistry (relationships/team bonding) right; the Physics (rules, processes etc.) will automatically follow."

A Lease of Life

There is a divine hand above that blesses us all, be it Ram or Raheem, Jesus or Ahura Mazda, Wahe Guru or Lord Mahavir. Most people agree that there is somewhere, a force above, that oversees the well-being of us all, just as a mother takes care of a baby. My relationship with God that had started as a child was renewed as an adult by the experiences that I have had. I have made it a point to visit the temple of Lord Hanuman (Hanuman is an ardent devotee of Lord Rama and one of the central characters in the various versions of the epic 'Ramayana' found in the Indian subcontinent and Southeast Asia) every Saturday since 1998. It was in the summer of 2001 that I first had a *darshan* (glimpse) of the 33 feet tall towering statue of Lord Hanumanji, housed at the SIES College of Commerce, Nerul. The idol is imposing in its presence; yet, I have not seen any devotee, however hassled, leave the temple without being at peace. This idol, like many in the locality, is 'Navasala Pavnara' (wish-fulfilling).

It was on a winter evening in 2003 that my friend Jason and I were on the way to Vashi to have discussions regarding the sponsorship of 'Vibes' – our college festival, for which I had been elected as Chairperson. I did not have much experience of riding a bike and on that fateful day, my inexperience cost us dearly. A car rammed into our bike at full speed when we were negotiating a turn onto the Palm Beach road (infamous for a number of road accident-related deaths), and Jason and I were tossed into the air like a couple of rag dolls. Both of us lost consciousness. Jason regained consciousness before me and, along with a few good samaritans, helped me reach the hospital. The people who took me to the hospital told me that another vehicle had passed under me when I was up in the air. As they were at a distance from the accident spot, it appeared to them that I was held up in the air for an additional five seconds till the trailing vehicle passed after which, I landed on the ground. They said it was nothing short of a miracle – a person weighing 80 kilos being held up in the air for an additional 5 seconds, while Jason, weighing around 50 kilos, falling immediately towards the side and landing straight on the ground! It did not take me long to realize that the accident spot was in the direct line of sight of the idol of Hanumanji at SIES. That day, I realized the truth of the saying, 'Faith can move mountains.' My faith in God had seemingly bent the laws of gravity and saved my life! I am reminded of the following verse, which talks about the grace of God:

> *Mukam Karoti Vachalam, Pangum Langhayate Girim,*
> *Yatkrupa Tamaham Vande Paramanandamadhavam.*

Meaning: Even the mute can speak and the ones without legs can cross great mountains, and one's life will be full of happiness, if your mercy is showered on us, O Lord Madhava (Krishna), the giver of the ultimate Happiness.

(Source: From ancient Hindu scriptures in praise of Lord Shri Krishna.)

This accident proved to be the turning point in my life. I had been given a new lease of life and was filled with a deep sense of gratitude. Already religious by nature, this event made me contemplate further on the deeper meaning of life. My perspective underwent a radical change, and I developed a more philosophical approach.

> I realized that the cycle of birth and death is something that no one can escape from. We all have to depart one day and no one knows when. Like it is said in the Bhagavad Gita (the Song of the Divine), the Soul is indestructible and keeps changing bodies, just like human beings keep changing clothes. It is the actions and deeds of an individual that determine whether one (one's thoughts and memories) remains immortal or gets pushed into oblivion with the passage of time.

We all come into being with nothing and will leave this world with nothing. The race that all of us place ourselves in, to acquire, amass, or outdo someone/something is 'Maya' (illusion). If there is anything that is constant during all periods in our life, it is Change (what exists today, will not exist tomorrow). Hence, 'This too shall pass' and the joy of enjoying or being happy with nothing, are the ultimate learnings that one can have. Having mastered this, one can lead a very happy life in the midst of everything (or nothing). A Rajasthani saying captures this idea quite well:

> *"Khush reh jab tak hain,*
> *Kya patah kab tak hain,*
> *Agar kuch yaad rakh sake to sirf itna ke –*
> *Maaro so jaave nahi, aur jave so maaro naahi."*

Meaning: Be happy as long as you are here, for no one knows how long we shall live; if there is something that you should learn, it is a simple one liner:

What is mine will never go; what went, was never meant to be to be mine!

The Perfect Profession

All my early experiences contributed to broadening my outlook about people. As I was deciding on the next steps after my graduation, choosing HR as a career was natural as I understood that what I had loved doing for most parts of my life was working with people to achieve common goals. The energy, the fun, and the satisfaction of working with people and moving ahead with them is something I would not trade for anything else in this world. I was fortunate to have studied Personnel Management & Industrial Relations from one of the oldest temples of learning in our country – the Tata Institute of Social Sciences (TISS).

I have been extremely fortunate to have worked for some great organizations. My first full-time job was at Career Launcher, while my first job after completing my post-graduation at TISS was at Nokia. I worked with Nokia at different places like Mumbai, Gurgaon (now Gurugram), and Dubai. I also worked at Deutsche Bank, followed by GE, where I worked in two roles across Mumbai and Bangalore, and finally, at Danaher starting 2014. It has been a wonderful journey so far with rich experience and immense learning.

The Value of Values

After studying at TISS, I was selected by Nokia for their Global Graduate Program. In 2007, Nokia India was a Talent Factory with some of the best brains in the country passionately working to make the brand the most loved, in a nation where mobility was undergoing a huge transformation and 'Connecting People' was truly a need for a country so huge and vast. Getting a chance to work with some great leaders at Nokia, I quickly learnt that working for a company is all about maintaining a very high 'Say-Do' ratio. What you say is what you must do, and what you do, should always be in complete alignment with the company Vision, Mission, and Values and of a very high standard. If you can keep a very high 'Say-Do' ratio, your credibility will be high, and growth will surely seek you out wherever you are.

Next, the Chemistry part of working for an organization is as important (if not more) as the Physics part. The Chemistry part is the softer aspects that come into play at work, like trust, team work, relationships with peers, genuine care, and gratitude. This is what keeps the organization glued to the core purpose. If the chemistry is wrong, the reactions can be extremely harmful. The Physics part is about the policies, procedures, and rules that the company follows. These are often laid down by leaders/policy makers after observing trends, market practices, and recurring patterns in line with the law of the land. However, to throw the rule book every time there is an event may not be the best approach. Every situation needs to be understood in its context (with relevance to time, stakeholders impacted, and outcomes possible) and every decision/action needs to be inclusive and in the best interest of all concerned (*Bahujana Hitaya - Bahujana Sukhaya* – for the greatest good of the masses, akin to the win-win philosophy of the modern corporate world).

Working hard (in the face of every resistance/adversity) is also something that Nokia taught all its team members. The Nokia Values – 'Passion for Innovation,' 'Achieving Together,' 'Very Human,' and 'Engaging You' – taught me a term called 'Sisu', a Finnish word which can come closest to 'Resilience', when translated into English. The Finns are a very hardworking lot and the climatic conditions prevalent in Finland make every day a fight for survival in the extremely cold months of the year. In the corporate world as well, it is extremely critical to work hard and never fail to pick up the learning when one falls.

Another lesson that I have always cherished from my experience with Nokia is not compromising on one's values even in difficult times. A particular incident comes to mind here – a local labor inspector in the National Capital Region (NCR) near Delhi once threatened to cause trouble for us if we did not employ one of his relatives in our organization. We had two choices – to comply with his wishes and make sure we didn't run into trouble or to escalate this demand to the senior management for support. As a young professional, it was easier to comply with the request, but better sense prevailed, and I escalated this demand to my seniors, who promptly engaged the right stakeholders and ensured that we put an effective end to this situation.

Nokia India had a great set of leaders who always believed in hiring and growing people above and beyond themselves (leaders creating leaders, while making themselves redundant). This way, the organization would become an Organization of Giants – every leader growing people greater than oneself, as opposed to an Organization of Dwarfs, where every manager allows his/her subordinate to grow only up to a level or two below his/her level of competency. This logic is applicable to our personal lives as well. We must train our children in such a way that they become capable of taking their lives to higher levels than ours.

Travel Tales

At Nokia, I also had the opportunity to travel to more than 13 countries. Each travel is a tale and teaches one many things that can be cherished for a lifetime. Like author Anita Desai has said, "Wherever you go becomes a part of you somehow." Here are a couple of inspirational stories that I would like to share from my travels:

i) A colleague in Nokia, originally from Hyderabad, moved to Saudi Arabia almost 30 years ago. A matriculate from a family of seven, this devout Muslim lived a life full of hardships and challenges to ensure that his family lived in peace and happiness back home. Today, his brothers are all at very good positions, and one is based in Hyderabad and operates a school (Akshara Foundation), which provides education on a 'Charging what the Pocket Can Bear' model. Today, the school has more than 500 students and is an example to many. Young students, affluent and needy alike, benefit from the endeavor started from the earnings of an individual who started life with almost nothing, but today, is a loved and respected figure in both, Saudi Arabia and Hyderabad. What drove him to achieve these great feats was the hope to see his family and community lead a better life.

> When simple things are done with determination, they can lead to extraordinary results, impacting a much larger audience than originally intended or planned.

ii) A Lebanese colleague of mine who lost everyone in her family but for her mother in a gun raid, is another inspiration. She mentioned to me how she has forgiven the perpetrators of the crime because of her belief, 'An eye for an eye will make the whole world go blind.' She mentioned to me some of the teachings of

Mahatma Gandhi, which, honestly speaking, even I was not aware of. She shared with me how she sponsors the education of three children back in her hometown, in the hope that they will grow up with good education and lead better lives, ultimately bringing prosperity, which will lead to peace in her hometown and adjoining areas.

These and many more such individuals have enriched my life with their experiences and taught me lessons about humanity, compassion, determination, having a higher purpose in life, and much more.

Singapore Summons

In early 2014, I joined Danaher, a wonderful organization which believes in 'Helping Realize Life's Potential.' Again, I was blessed to have some great managers and leaders who helped me in my career journey here. The head of our company in India (my coach) and our HR Head (my manager and mentor) are two people who have left an indelible impression on my life and career. They have helped me with reflective feedback and inputs in the most constructive manner, helping me move into uncharted territories and to change behaviors that could possibly be limiting in the long term. One of the best inputs that I got from my coach is to manage time effectively. All of us have the same 24 hours in our day. The way we use these hours is what differentiates each one of us. The Deming Cycle (Plan-Do-Check-Act) is another insight that I picked up from my leaders here, along with the importance of having a plan (vision) for everything and instituting follow-ups/checks from time to time (actions) to ensure that the plan is progressing as envisaged. They say that a good plan mixed with strong execution is the key to success.

What better example of this than the island nation of Singapore (also called the Red Dot)! In early January 2017, I got an opportunity to relocate to Singapore. I found Singapore to be the perfect example of a well-governed and sustainable model of a successful nation. The founding fathers of Singapore, led by Sir

Lee Kuan Yew, set very ambitious goals for an infant nation as it gained a painful independence from Malaysia in 1965. Like true *Karma Yogis* (people who do their duty without attachment to the fruits of its results) as described in the Bhagavad Gita, though straddled with many challenges, the Singaporean leaders, along with the people, toiled hard (actions) in the right direction, with the zeal and enthusiasm to make Singapore what it is today – one of the best places to live in the world! I remember the last verse of the Bhagavad Gita (Chapter 18, Verse 78), a verse that I learnt during my Chinmaya Mission days, that captures the essence of success, on similar lines –

"*Yatra Yogeshvarah Krshno Yatra Partho Dhanur-dharah
Tatra Srirvijayo Bhutirdhruva Nitirmatirmama*" –

Meaning: Wherever there is Krishna (symbolic of Vision), the master of all mystics, and wherever there is Arjuna (symbolic of Action), the supreme archer, there will also certainly be opulence, victory, extraordinary power, and morality.

Today, my family and I are settled in Singapore for over a year now and I lead Human Resources for the Water Quality business of Danaher for the Asia Pacific region.

In Retrospect

The beginning, they say, has to come after every end, and the end, they say, is the start to a new beginning.

When a famous artist was once asked which his greatest painting was, without batting an eyelid, he immediately responded, "The next one." The pleasure of the journey ends with the catch.

> I am a firm believer that Life is a Gift, which you must enjoy in the Present and as a Present (Live to the fullest; live in the moment).

I am grateful to the force above for having gifted me with the best parents and a lovely extended family, the best brother and sister-in-law in the world, Sandhya – a soulmate who truly partners and collaborates in the journey of life, great teachers, wonderful friends and colleagues, and very inspiring mentors (Aparna Sharma – the originator of this initiative being one of my mentors whose guidance, love, and support makes me what I am). In October 2016, the arrival of Sriram (our baby boy) has made my life complete. All this is a combination that makes the left-hand side of my life's equation look terrific.

Fortunately, or otherwise, the right-hand side of life's equation will always be a mixed bag, as one can only control the inputs in one's life's journey. The output is always moderated by external factors and might vary from what one expects it to be. I have had my share of challenges – a couple of near-death experiences (the accident in Nerul and a heart related ailment in 2007), a few misses here and there, as well as challenges in my personal life related to campus love, among other things.

> Adversities help bring out the best in oneself. It is only when one is challenged that one gets out of one's comfort zone and tries to rise above the ordinary. I also believe in the saying by Hal Borland, "No winter lasts forever; no spring skips its turn." Life moves on. Life lies in movement.

Life Lines

- Do good to the world and good will come back to you in equal or more measure.
- Never do things with the end result in mind. Do things selflessly and trust in the Lord to give you the results. Sometimes the results may be delayed, but they are never denied – a learning that I absorbed from the Bhagavad Gita (Chapter 2, Verse 47). I consider myself really fortunate to have read and learnt a few verses from the Holy Bhagavad

Gita, thanks to the Chinmaya Mission and my grandmother's inculcation.

- Our achievements are not of our making alone. Various people, institutions, the community etc., contribute directly or indirectly to our success. Thus, we too, must keep the cycle going and give back part of what we have received.

> ### Words of Wisdom
>
> *I would like to share a story that continues to inspire me:*
>
> *Arthur Ashe, the legendary Wimbledon player, was dying of AIDS, which he contracted from a blood transfusion during a heart surgery in 1983.*
>
> *He received letters from his fans all over the world, one of which conveyed: "Why did God have to select you for such a bad disease?"*
>
> *To this, Arthur Ashe replied:*
>
> *"The world over, 50 million children start playing tennis, 5 million learn to play tennis, 500,000 learn professional tennis, 50,000 come to the circuit, 5,000 reach the Grand Slam, 50 reach Wimbledon, 4 to semi-final, 2 to the finals. When I was holding a cup, I never asked GOD, Why me? And today, in pain, I should not be asking GOD, 'Why me?'"*

14
Substance & Simplicity – A Powerful Duo

Smt. Sarita Deouskar

Dear Madam,

Your single-minded focus and dedication towards teaching made me a huge fan of yours since the day I attended my first History class in college. Your ability to explain the most complex historical events that one would otherwise remember only through rote learning made History truly an interesting subject. I looked forward to your classes every week – whether it was the history of the Mughal Empire or the French Revolution or World History. More importantly, your patience in spite of all the tricks of the students to derail the lecture was an absolute virtue. I was deeply touched by your motherly affection and genuine interest in helping students solve their doubts even after class. Even after so many years of having completed my college education, you exude the same warmth and concern for my well-being.

Words are not enough to thank you, Madam!

Yours Affectionately,
Aparna

About Smt. Sarita Deouskar...

Ever heard of a History teacher using the art of storytelling to ensure that students remember dates and facts? Smt. Sarita Deouskar was one such teacher. An M.A. in History and a topper from the Jabalpur University in the year 1960, teaching has been her lifelong passion and profession. She symbolizes the class of teachers whom one looks up to as gurus. Her charisma and dedication towards teaching infused enthusiasm into her students by bringing historical events to life! A strict disciplinarian with a humane approach, she was a perfectionist whom students looked up to. Her thoroughness in everything she did – teaching, handling students and peers, as well as her attention to her family are worth emulating. Like a true guru, she took genuine interest in her students, not just regarding their curricular life, but also going beyond it, which is evident from their attachment to her, so many years after her retirement. Even today, she continues to guide and inspire her students with her sagely and motherly advice on the twists and turns of life's path.

"Life is the best teacher. A teacher can teach you only so much. It is life's twists and turns that teach by experience, help assimilate the lessons learned and bring out the best in you."
– Smt. Sarita Deouskar

Aparna Sharma

The phone rings early in the morning on the day of *Guru Poornima*. It is none other than Aparna, one of my beloved students, who calls to wish me on this day since the last 25 years! Hearing her say that I have made a significant difference to her life is music to my ears even today. Her words take me down memory lane...

The long span of my life is full of both, good and bad experiences. But one must understand that both, achievements as well as failures, teach us some lessons. If achievements light up our lives, failures help us to mend our ways.

Teenage Toughness

My childhood was quite comfortable and smooth. By the grace of God, I was born into a liberal and educated family that believed in the proper education of their children without any discrimination. I was a simple and obedient child.

When I was in Class 9, my parents insisted that I should opt for Science after Class 10. They wanted me to become a doctor. However, they were terribly shocked when I informed them of my decision to study History and opt for Arts. I wasn't interested in becoming a doctor. As I came from a family of engineers and government servants, my decision to take up Arts was not welcome.

But even at such a young age, I stood firm and listened to my inner voice. This was the first time that I had broken the set mould in my family. I realized that my nature was not suited to either becoming a doctor or going into government service. Since my childhood, I had been fond of History. Unlike other students, I never learnt History by rote. My strength was that I could remember dates, which made it all the more easier for me to study History. Hence, I prevailed on my parents to let me take up Arts.

> The first step to getting the things you want out of life is to decide what you want. Then, life becomes a beautiful journey.

College Chronicles

I remember a humorous incident that occurred on the first day of my college. My friend and I were looking for our classroom. We were both new and knew nothing about the college. When we somehow reached the allotted classroom, we found only one student in the class. We enquired why the history class had not yet started. He told us that the class had been shifted to another room and gave us directions to find it. However, when we finally found the room, it was a toilet and not a classroom! How annoyed we were!

I graduated from City College, Jabalpur, in 1954. At that time, parents normally allowed their daughters to study upto graduation, but I was an exception. My parents willingly permitted me to do a post-graduation (M.A.) in History from Government Robertson College, Jabalpur.

During my post-graduate studies, I had wonderful and devoted teachers like Dr. Santlal Katare, Dr. S.D. Gyani, and Dr. R.M. Sinha who taught us a scientific approach towards the study of History. Dr. Sinha told us that to truly understand a historical event, we had to go into the causes of that incident. For example, in order to understand the Second World War, one must go into the reasons behind why the War took place. Through analysis, one could find that it was the loopholes and defects in the Treaty of Versailles that had resulted into the Second World War. There was no need to study History by rote if one had an attitude of analysis.

His teachings increased my interest in the subject. In 1960, when I secured the highest marks in the M.A. examinations of Jabalpur University, my parents realized that my decision of pursuing M.A. in History was correct. This was my first achievement in life.

Professional Posting

I decided to become a teacher because it would give me the opportunity to turn students into good citizens. I realized that this was my calling. After I completed my post-graduation, I got my first posting as Assistant Professor in Robertson College – my alma mater, just 15 days before I was to get married.

I enjoyed my job thoroughly. This was the turning point in my life, and since then, there has been no looking back. I devoted all my energy to give my best to my students. Their performance became my greatest satisfaction. Even today, if any of my students remember me as a good and sincere teacher, it gives me immeasurable satisfaction.

I never taught from books and notes. Once I began to teach, I realized that there were various innovations that I could bring into teaching History to ensure that students were interested in the subject. I believed that knowledge of Geography was important in order to study History, especially in case of World History. I started drawing maps for students to understand the areas where the various wars took place. I found that this made historical facts clearer to them and the events that occurred became interesting. All my classes were necessarily interactive.

Marital Matters

I got married in 1960, the same year that I was appointed to the post of Assistant Professor at Government Robertson College, Jabalpur. After my marriage, I had to strive hard to maintain a balance between family and work. Mine was a conservative family. My husband was a professor of Sanskrit. My in-laws lived in the village, and my brother-in-law and sister-in-law stayed with us. It was obvious that my in-laws did not want me to work.

However, my father insisted that I continue to work so that I could become financially independent, add to the family's income, and put my knowledge and learning to good use. Therefore, I had to make sure that my work would not disturb the family equilibrium.

> Although this may sound run-of-the-mill for working women today, our generation had no precedent of working women. Neither our mothers, nor our mothers-in-law had gone to work. Through trial and error, we tried to give our best to our families and professions.

Unfortunately, one of my brothers-in-law died in a rail accident. He had gotten married only 15 days earlier. Everyone in the family was devastated by this loss and worried about the future of his young bride. My husband and I asked the young girl to come and stay with us in the city. We got her educated and later, also got her remarried. Today, it gives me great pleasure to say that she is happily married and content.

I had multifarious responsibilities in the family, which I feel I have handled successfully. In return, I have received love and respect from all the family members. I consider this, too, as one of my major achievements.

> To take care of one's family, one must take up challenging responsibilities. However, this does not give one the right to claim all the credit.

Transfer Trials

In government jobs, one has to face sudden transfers. At the time of my marriage, my husband too was posted in the same college as I. But just after four months, he was transferred and posted at Government College, Durg. This made him and other family members think that I should discontinue my job. This caused me immense mental stress as well as disturbance in my family life. My in-laws were so insistent that I was on the verge of leaving my job. But my father intervened and advised us to bide our time and wait for a posting at the same college or at colleges closer to each other. Had I given up my job then, it would have proved to be the greatest blunder of my life.

> I feel that just like my father did at the time, parents of today must help their daughters to stand firm and prevent them from taking rash decisions under family pressures.

Again, when my husband was in Pune for his Ph.D, I had to stay alone with my three children because I too was working and couldn't leave my job to be with him. During this period, I had to undergo many unpleasant situations. This was a very stressful period for me. But I held on and told myself that this too would pass.

Teaching Tidbits

My selection by the Public Service Commission, Madhya Pradesh, to the post of Assistant Professor of History was my next achievement and a feather in my cap. However, my tenure at the Government College, Hoshangabad, where I was posted, was not very congenial due to the non-cooperative attitude of my male colleagues. I was junior to most of them and was the only woman in the teaching staff. Moreover, my posting was through the prestigious Public Service Commission, and this rankled them. Initially, I found myself lacking the innate strength required to get over this problem. Facing such challenges on a day-to-day basis was indeed a daunting task. However, with my perseverance and fortitude, I was able to overcome this problem successfully.

From 1979 to 2000, I was posted as Head of the Department of History at the Government M.L.B. Girls College, Bhopal and later also at Sarojini Naidu Post-graduate Girls College, Bhopal. In both the colleges, I had very competent and good colleagues and with their cooperation, I organized many state-level as well as national-level seminars and skits.

I had the opportunity of performing many administrative tasks such as admissions, conducting of University examinations, management of students' union and various academic and cultural activities. These were opportunities of learning. I understood how things worked and how to keep them running smoothly. I also learnt that it is essential for teachers to update their subject knowledge consistently.

In 1985, I was promoted to the post of Principal and posted at the Government Girls College, Vidisha (M.P). Though this was professionally a very lucrative and prestigious opportunity, I had no interest or aptitude for administrative work, especially

Accounting. My expertise lay in teaching, and I felt that I could better contribute towards moulding students positively this way, rather than as a part of the Management. That is why I decided to forego this promotion.

> You don't have to play every ball that comes your way... some could be wide or no balls... let them go!

I retired from service on September 30, 2000. I remember that even on the day of my retirement, I devoted one hour to prepare for my lecture, even though I was quite comfortable with the subject.

> Preparation is very important in everything you do, no matter what your profession. It is the first step to ensuring success in any venture.

Lost Horizons

There were other fields too, that I wanted to explore, but failed to do so. I had a keen interest in classical vocal music and was taking private coaching for it too. I had not only passed the examinations in music, but had also participated in youth festivals. My parents also wanted me to pursue music along with my profession, but compulsions of service and family obligations did not allow me to do so.

I must acknowledge that I had to face some setbacks that I failed to overcome. Bitter memories of them still haunt me. In retrospect, I find that I lacked sufficient courage to resist injustice in any form. I consider this to be the greatest weakness in my personality.

I could not pursue research work for technical reasons. Despite my keen desire and all possible efforts, I could not obtain a Ph.D. This has always pinched me. Research work is essential for one's academic career. I had very idealistic notions about research. With my brilliant academic record, I was keen to pursue research work leading to a Ph.D degree. However, when I applied for enrollment as a Research scholar, the Research Degree Committee turned down my application outright, on the grounds that I did not possess proper knowledge of the Sanskrit language, which is essential for pursuing any research project on Ancient Indian History. I consider this to be the worst failure of my life.

> Before taking up any important work, one should thoroughly examine all the relevant aspects of the work. Even then, if one fails, one should make continuous attempts to attain the goal.

In Retrospect

Upon reflection, I find that my achievements are not extraordinary ones. However, I have the deep satisfaction of having performed all of my duties to the best of my abilities. I was strict with my own children about their studies. As a mother, I believed in inculcating affection, discipline, and a sense of responsibility in my children. I made sure that I spent quality time with them.

Similarly, once I was at work, I was completely focused on giving my best to my students. I loved my students and was able to command respect, obedience, and love from them as well. I have always believed that honesty, sincerity, and good intentions pay in life. In my personal and professional life, I have always adhered to my principles and values without deviation and have found that people have also reciprocated in the same manner. In my professional life, I have earned a reputation such that people still remember me out of respect even after so many years of retirement.

My first love was teaching, and I enjoyed every moment of it. What hurts me the most is that today, we have very few good students who willingly take up the Arts stream out of genuine interest. Also, reading habits have reduced and reading beyond the syllabus is neither encouraged nor followed.

At the age of 80, I have the satisfaction that my children are well-settled and are responsible human beings. My experiences have been valuable and have enabled me to give advice to my children and grandchildren. Though retired, I now enjoy teaching my grandchildren!

Life Lines

- Life is all about learning.
- Successes reinforce our behavior, and failures show us where we should not tread, or alternately, find paths where none exist.
- Face your fears - Fears can hold us back from experiencing everything that life has to offer. When we give in to fear, we limit ourselves.
- Treat people the way you want to be treated.
- Ethical behaviour always pays off... if not immediately, then surely in the future.
- Follow your dreams. Take immediate action if you want to see you dream turn into reality, or it may never happen.
- Competence should be backed by perseverance and consistency. If you are capable of doing something, but do not put in the required hard work, then productivity will be compromised.
- Find a mentor who thinks about your welfare and gives appropriate advice.
- Education develops one's ability to make the right decisions for oneself.
- Every woman needs to be economically self-sufficient.
- Also, you must first deserve and then desire. This helps one to avoid frustration in life. Assess your potential thoroughly. Do not imitate others blindly.
- No matter what field you are in, update your knowledge regularly.

Words of Wisdom

The Indian social scenario is precariously grim today. The joint family system, which had been one of the strongest pillars of Indian society, is fast disintegrating, and the younger generation finds itself helpless. The emotional thirst among our youngsters propels them to traverse the slippery ground of life with no direction and objective in mind. They are so pressurized by their parents to score good marks and seek lucrative jobs that when they cannot fulfill these expectations, they get frustrated. This frustration leads them to take self-destructive steps. In this situation, it is the responsibility of parents and teachers to give them moral support. Being a teacher myself, I must emphasize that the Indian Education System should lay emphasis on moral values and enjoin the youth to be good human beings, instead of restricting them to becoming money-earning lifeless machines.

Only material prosperity and social status are not enough. Along with material achievements, one also needs indomitable inner strength. Love, kindness, and moral virtues are the perennial sources of happiness and inner strength. The next generation needs to imbibe goodness, honesty, and sincerity in their personalities.

15

Packing a Punch with Positivity & Persistence

Aparna Sharma

Dear Aparna,

My salutations to your fighting spirit, your positivity, and your unending determination! Your tenacity to come out on top of whatever has come your way, is noteworthy. No matter what happened (and a lot has), you have remained focused on your goals and yet, maintained the urge to do good to others as well!

When the world looked black and the future bleak, you have patiently waited for the sun to shine, knowing that it eventually will. From being discriminated against, ridiculed, and put down, you have only grown stronger, taking responsibility for yourself and your actions.

Of course, you have made mistakes. But I am happy that you looked at them objectively, with an open mind and worked hard to correct them.

You have used every opportunity you found, created one where none existed, and made a mark in your chosen field. Many have tried to stop you, upset your plans, and throw you off your path, but each time, your feet refused to budge, your eyes remained focused, and your hands refused to stop working!

When no one lent a hand, you put your faith in your own two hands! You are never lonely even if you are alone, because you believe that God is always with you.

The passion to create something new and to do something for others is the driving force of your life. Whether it is your coaching, your books, or the scholarship you started, you have given them all your 100 percent.

Along the way, you have collected treasures, not of material gains, but of people – brave and inspiring, who have added value to your life and have been a constant source of immense positivity. This is something that only very few are blessed with.

May the Almighty bless you in your journey ahead, with even more treasures in the form of such people and may you pass on their lessons to others and inspire them too!

Yours Affectionately,
Aparna

Every breath is a tenacious fight to live a worthy life!

As a child, I was unaware of the challenging scenarios that I would have to face in the future. I took life as it came and tried to make sense of what was happening around me. I developed the habit of looking at the bright side of things at all times, even when my chips were down.

The battlefield of life demands that we stand tall and face the scorching sun as well as the cold, harsh winds. There is no choice but to bravely face what comes your way. How we deal with this struggle and who we become in the process is what we shall be remembered for.

I have come across many people in this journey of mine. I observed the challenges they faced daily, their moments of happiness, the situations that brought tears to their eyes and also their struggles to overcome their problems. But there were some amongst them that stood out due to their uncommon determination, intellectual toughness and extraordinary mindsets. Unknowingly, they sowed the seeds of their unending positivity in my mind.

We hardly give credit to the 'ordinary' people we know, and that is like overlooking the treasure buried in our own backyards. These so-called 'ordinary' people have within them the qualities of determination, resilience, honesty, and optimism — qualities that we would all like to inculcate and that are necessary to shape our lives.

From Vandana (Vandy), who helped me keep my house (and my head!) sorted, to Tanveer, who creates magic with his hairdos, to Dr. Radhakrishnan Pillai, who has guided my efforts as a budding author, to Dr. T.V. Rao, who has been instrumental in shaping my thoughts and efforts as a Human Resources professional right at the start of my career, these 14 people have inspired me deeply.

In them, I found authenticity, sincerity of purpose, a down-to-earth attitude, and genuineness in all aspects of their personal and professional lives. These are the qualities that are common among us and bind us together.

I hope that the extraordinary lessons I have imbibed from these 'ordinary' people will also fuel your passion and inspire you to go the extra mile to fulfill your dreams.

Here's a peek into my life, my story!

I draw inspiration from the saying, "Life may not always give you the results you want, but it always provides you the lessons you need. There is no teacher like life!" – Aparna Sharma

Breaking Biases

My struggle to be accepted began right from the time I was born – no, not by my parents. It was my paternal grandmother, who was unhappy at the arrival of a second girl child. I am a living example of turning around with missionary zeal the perceived worth of a girl child, to create and live a fulfilling life on my own terms. It would have been easy for me to get deterred since, as a child, some of my relatives would not even let us play with our cousin brothers.

Even though I was written off and life started with rejection, the sense of empowerment and trust that my immediate family – my parents and sister equipped me with, was good enough for me to stand tall even as a child. My mother was my driving force. She has always believed in me, even at times when I have lost hope.

> In my view, it is important to have an anchor or identify one in one's formative years... this helps one to steer one's life in the right direction at all times.

Boarding School Background

I have had a memorable childhood! My father had a transferrable job. In Class 5, I joined the prestigious Maharani Gayatri Devi School (M.G.D.) in Jaipur as a boarder, to avoid changing schools frequently. This was the first time in my life that I had moved out alone.

The preparation and leaving for the hostel in Jaipur from Lakheri (where my father was posted) was similar to a *bidai* (the ceremony after marriage where the daughter leaves for the husband's house).

The routine at boarding school was rigorous – waking up at 4:00 am, group exercise at 5:00 am, the usual action-packed day in the school, with lights out at 9:00 pm! I learnt to take responsibility for myself at a very young age. We had bunk beds, and each student had turns during the week to sleep on the upper bed. Now, this had me stumped! I was scared to sleep there, and I knew I had to get out of this arrangement somehow. There was no point in telling the authorities of my plight, so I learnt to do what I had never done before – negotiate with my hostel mates for the lower bed! To think that I had started to learn the art of negotiation so early on in my life!

> Viktor Frankl, the Austrian neurologist and psychiatrist and a Holocaust survivor, has said, "When we are no longer able to change a situation, we are challenged to change ourselves."

Besides studies, I participated in sports and extra-curricular activities that helped to boost my confidence and develop my personality in an all-round manner. I learnt to play all the sports like cricket, football, hockey, throwball, horse-riding etc., that were taught in my school. Although life was moving at top-speed, in the second year (Class 6) I began to feel homesick. I would often weep for my parents. Many times, we tend to take our close relations for granted when they are around us. This separation from my family made me realize their worth and appreciate them even more. However, I consider myself lucky to have experienced shades of all familial relationships as well as friendship, love, and care bestowed on me by complete strangers!

> Life in a boarding school gives one a very distinct personality and helps one to appreciate one's family and become independent. One learns discipline, the value of time and money, and of course, the art of negotiating for what one wants!

Travel Tales

Upto Class 4, I had lived in several states and cities due to my father's transfers. After Class 6 at the boarding school, I went to Ujjain, where I studied from Class 7 to 12. For one who did not know Hindi till Class 4, I won the Madhya Pradesh state level Hindi grammar competition several times. The entire credit of this achievement goes to my teacher, Shri Pheru Singh Ruhela. Later, I moved to Bhopal for graduation (B.A.) and then to Mumbai for post-graduation (M.A.-TISS).

Most people find it difficult to constantly adjust to new surroundings. However, I took these frequent migrations positively, made new friends, and imbibed the good things from the various cultures I came in contact with. I also picked up local languages wherever I lived (even abroad), which helped me bond with people.

> Traveling helps break out of one's comfort zones and brings one into contact with new cultures. It thus broadens one's horizons and enriches one's experiences.

About My 'Aai'

Perhaps, she came into my life to teach me mental toughness and firm resolve! At Ujjain, I lived with Aai, my father's elder sister (Dr. M.D. Vyas), for six years. It was Aai, who had undertaken my mother's delivery, so the attachment with her was truly special.

Late Dr. Vyas, fondly known as 'Aai' by her family and 'Vyas Bai' by her patients, was a child widow, who painstakingly completed her education with distinction and also ensured that her siblings were educated in spite of no financial support. She managed to make a mark for herself at a time when formal education for girls was not encouraged. She was the first lady doctor (LMP from Calcutta) in the family! In spite of what had befallen her, she became a pillar of strength for the whole family and sacrificed her life and happiness to help them, without asking for anything in return.

Along with academic excellence, she was an ardent sports follower and won many trophies and medals. By virtue of being a gynaecologist, she was able to mold tender minds and thus became a role model, not only in our family, but also in the city of Ujjain. With her exemplary courage, strong moral values, 'can do' attitude, self-confidence, and hard work, she helped the needy and exhibited righteousness at all times. She passed on these values to all those who were part of her life, and especially to me, in more ways than one. Aai never came to my school even once in six years. If the teachers ever had to convey something about me, they sent a sealed envelope in her name. That was the level of trust and respect they had for her!

I was an all-rounder, from academics to sports to other extra-curricular activities, and Aai was always there to back me up! She nurtured my winning streak at every step. As one of my school friends recently said to me about her, quoting John Mark Green, "Life tried to crush her, but only succeeded in creating a diamond."

> Surround yourself with people who are positive, believe in you, empower you, appreciate you, and genuinely care for you. They will keep you motivated to overcome your limitations and create a mark for yourself.

Career Conjecture

Aai had wanted me to become a doctor like her; however, I took up Arts in college because I wanted to become an IAS officer. I moved to Bhopal for my Bachelor's Degree (B.A.). Here, I met two of my favourite people – my best friend, Faiqa (meaning - unique) and Professor Sarita Deouskar, who instilled in me the love for History.

My dream had been to get into the Civil Services. However, with time, civil services was no longer a preferred option for me. I did not want to get married early, like others in my family. I was determined to become financially independent first.

While thinking of financial independence as well as what I liked to do, I realized that being with people, understanding what made them tick and working with them, were all my areas of interest and with this in mind, I applied to the prestigious Tata Institute of Social Sciences (TISS) in Mumbai for a post-graduation in Personnel Management and Industrial Relations (PM & IR).

Training at TISS

The two years of study and training at TISS were intense and life-changing. What I learnt at TISS is the foundation of my professional success, and it made me confident and versatile as an HR professional.

During the campus placements, I turned the tables on the interviewers! I was offered a job by a sought-after employer. During the interview, I told them that I would consider joining only if they allowed me to begin on the shop-floor. They were shell-shocked! I could almost read their thoughts, "Is this girl crazy? She wants to work in one of the most unionized environments of our times!" But I was firm in my resolve.

During my training at TISS, I had been attached to manufacturing companies as part of the field work. I had realized that real jobs were not those where one merely sat in the office without a practical understanding of ground realities. Rather, they were those where one learnt to work with others, face tough challenges, and deal with the unknown, yet arrive at win-win solutions. The next day, I got my offer letter!

> Working one's way up the ladder in the formative years of one's career gives a thorough understanding of the function and business and helps one grow.

Professional Pathways

I joined as a Management Trainee, reporting to the Plant Industrial Relations (IR) manager. It may sound unbelievable, but I started out by doing administrative work like serving tea and coffee in the Union-Management meetings! This was definitely not what I had trained for! However, I decided to take it as a learning opportunity.

With a positive attitude, I grasped the fine art of negotiation and the practical aspects of arriving at agreements between differing viewpoints of the management and blue-collared union representatives. It was here that I realized that there are no textbook solutions to corporate problems, or to life's problems, for that matter. Looking back, I am glad I took this off-beaten path, which shaped the next 20 years of my career and helped me develop an open mind. This experience taught me what I could never have learnt in any class!

Meeting Dr. T.V. Rao and working under his guidance on Redesigning PMS (Performance Management Systems) at NOCIL for the merged entity was a high-point in my early career. He guided and mentored me as I coordinated and helped him conduct training on the new PMS for over a 1000 employees.

Throughout my professional life, I have volunteered for opportunities and assignments that seemed difficult and had few or no takers.

Take for instance, my stint in 2003 as an expat in the Philippines, based out of Manila, while working with Monsanto. It was an environment that was unlike any other I had ever seen or known! I felt completely alien in a place where I could neither connect with the people, nor the lifestyle! I missed India and longed for my family, my friends and yes, even my food!

However, once again I began to tackle the challenges I encountered, one-by-one. My penchant for languages helped, and I was able to speak Taglish and Tagalog within the first three months. This helped me connect well with people who did not trust foreigners easily. I endeared myself to all through my simple, focused, and straightforward nature. At work, by setting up robust systems and processes and coaching people internally for bigger roles, I was able to make a mark in Monsanto both, locally and globally.

> Taking risks mindfully gets one out of one's comfort zone and keeps one agile.

Reminiscing the time I lived in the Philippines, I would say that 'those were the best days of my life!' Philippines became a home away from home with my colleagues and their families. I also learnt to play golf, scuba diving, and gardening, and in my spare time, traveled extensively to most islands with my Filipino friends. I met Prakhar in the Philippines while he was studying and later, conducting research at the Asian Institute of Management (AIM).

I also did pioneering work in setting up the Research & Development Centre at Bangalore for Monsanto India. My career at Monsanto was extremely enriching and rewarding, from where I truly transcended geographical and cultural boundaries!

Courting Challenges

The biggest challenge for everyone today is managing their interpersonal relationships – with family, among friends and especially in professional circles. Although one may have a straightforward attitude, the world has many shades of grey. Not everyone is happy about another's achievements. Often, one encounters so-called friends or well-wishers getting in the way of one's success. I have tried to deal with such situations calmly and stoically.

I have always believed in challenging stereotypes – whether of gender or age. This has especially been true when I have had older professionals reporting to me. Traditionally, expertise and maturity are seen as functions of age, and I have always had to battle with this outlook. Also, being a woman leader, especially in the manufacturing sector, has its own challenges. I always had to work twice as hard, or even more, to prove myself each day. I have dealt with such situations by being open to seeking knowledge from senior people, being humble and genuinely valuing their inputs. There have been hits and misses; at times, people saw my humility as a sign of weakness. However, I have taken such incidents in my stride.

> It is vitally important, especially as an HR professional, to take people along, however challenging the process may be.

One of the unexpected challenges that came up was in the form of responsibility for a team member's safety, and that is how I met Mr. Raj Khilnani, a worried parent, whose daughter was in my team. I went beyond the call of duty to ensure and confirm that she had reached home safely, post a late night event. It was only a couple of years later that I came to know who he was.

Marital Memories

I repatriated back to India from the Philippines after a fruitful stint of two-and-a-half years since by then, my parents were extremely anxious about my marriage. According to Indian standards, I had missed the bus. As per my resolve, I was building a respectable career and was now open to the idea of marriage.

Marriage brought in more responsibility on the personal side. It taught me to walk the tight rope and balance the various fronts – career, my own desires and happiness as well as family life.

> There is nothing demeaning about giving in for a relationship you treasure. A few adjustments and compromises go a long way in maintaining love, peace, and harmony in the relationship.

Writing Repertoire

All through my school, college, and working life, I have kept discovering my latent talents and have nurtured them at every available opportunity. I had a knack for writing poems and short stories while in school. Years later, I started writing professionally for HR journals and magazines. A few years ago, I created my own website, www.aparnasharma.in, to reach out to people far and wide and to be able to help anyone who sought career advice.

A couple of years ago, I was approached by a publishing house to write a book on HR for students and early career professionals. It was a wonderful opportunity to contribute to the body of knowledge in the HR profession. Writing a book is an intense process. There has been immense learning in promoting the book within India and overseas. With all the hard work and support, the book has become a bestseller in the Management category. It has received wide acclaim from academia and the corporate world since it is extremely comprehensive and written without any jargon. It has also been translated into Hindi so as to reach schools and colleges in the Hindi-speaking states.

Personal Pursuits

For one to lead a wholesome life, one has to make time for everything – oneself, work, family, health as well as hobbies. So, when I needed to take a sabbatical, I already had a bucket list in place, which I had prepared a few years ago.

I was determined to learn to play squash, but nobody was ready to coach someone over forty. Undeterred, I kept trying and finally convinced a coach, who bet on me. Today, I have mastered the game.

I had a latent desire since the last few years, to undertake the challenging, yet fulfilling journey to Mount Kailash; however, I did not know when and how it would happen. With God's grace, my wish was fulfilled. The experience is still so fresh in my mind that I am still in a trance, although I am living in the real world. I still have plenty of things on my bucket list, so this is just the beginning for me!

> There is a time for everything in one's life. When the time is right, everything around you will propel you towards it – you just have to stay tuned, walk the path, make efforts for it to fructify, and go along.

In Retrospect

Looking back, I consider myself lucky that I inculcated many habits of successful people at a very young age. My habit of waking up at 5 am is one of them. Not just does it give one a head start, but one can also soak in the peace and quiet and begin one's day calmly.

My professional journey started 21 years ago and I feel a sense of pride in where I have reached. I have overcome difficult circumstances, converted the negativity from rejection into a positive guiding life force, and have stuck to the path I chose for myself. It has been such an incredible roller coaster ride… with extremely challenging ups and downs, joys and sorrows, victories and defeat. There has been much learning and also the immense satisfaction of being able to contribute meaningfully and touch not only the lives of the people one works with, but even their families.

I 'grew up' very early. Through my early experiences, I learnt to distinguish between good and bad, truth and lies, genuine and fake, and right and wrong. I have made use of these to propel myself forward with greater wisdom and positivity.

Although I am a spiritual person and believe in doing things selflessly, I have often been misunderstood, personally as well as professionally. The world considers me a success today, but this is a result of days, weeks, months, and years of hard work, perspiration, and perseverance. People believe that I have got things on a platter. But, they seem to forget that in order to get where I am, I have taken numerous rejections in my stride – from my childhood to my first job and even later on.

When I first came to Mumbai, I was ridiculed and despised for being a small-town girl. However, I am proud of being a small-town girl! Instead of responding to these barbs, I let my actions and results speak for themselves. Even when my parents were seeking an alliance for me, I was rejected by conventional families because I was considered highly educated and had lived overseas for many years. But, I did not let this depress me. If one is clear about one's objectives, one learns to focus on them and ignore such trivial matters. I am a combination of practicality and spirituality. Both these aspects of my personality help me to move on, no matter what.

I continue to draw inspiration from Aai. After she passed away in 2010, I initiated a scholarship, named 'UDAAN – Believe in

Yourself,' to promote education of the girl child in my school (St. Mary's Convent) in Ujjain. It is said, "When you educate a girl, you educate an entire family." Although we live in the 21st century – an age of apps and gizmos, there are still many small towns and villages in India, where differential treatment is accorded to male and female siblings within the same family. Boys are encouraged to take risks and girls are deprived of learning. The only way to bring in a sustainable change is by providing education to girls.

One receives a lot from society, one's parents, teachers, friends, relatives, and colleagues. One must realize that it is one's duty to give back so that the cycle of goodness continues. Since it was not possible for me to help every individual who has helped me, I started the 'UDAAN' scholarship as my way of giving back to society. This scholarship is a tribute to 'Aai.'

The Paragons of Positivity

I am indeed blessed to have met positive, hardworking, and determined people since my childhood and continue to do so. It is so satisfying to be able to bring them to you and make them a part of your life too.

My amazing help, Vandana (Vandy), has been cooking wonderful new dishes especially for my family, since the past so many years. I was introduced to Tanveer while he was transforming people with his exceptional hairdos, and his down-to-earth and cheerful attitude was something I couldn't forget. I kept in touch with him even while I was living overseas, and he is solely responsible for making my hair, my crowning glory! I happened to meet Dr. Radhakrishnan Pillai at Mumbai University. Chanakya has always intrigued me and thus, a stronger connect with Radha. Not only is he a best-selling author, but also a true friend, who guided me when I wrote my first book.

Dhyanshree Shailesh (Guruji) is my senior from school (Ujjain). I heard of him through a school friend and visited his ashram. I instantly experienced a divine connect.

My conviction that the world is a small place grew stronger when I met Arun Kaimal, my junior from TISS, at Deutsche Bank. We have been associated through various professional forums, and his dedication to work never ceases to amaze me. Ashwin Pasricha, a fellow HR professional, had set up his own consultancy and came to pitch his services to my company. Later on, he became a certified coach and coached me too. He continues to be a trusted friend and a true sounding board. I met Sarah when I was hiring scientists for the Monsanto Research Centre (MRC) at Bangalore and her contagious enthusiasm has left a lasting impression on me.

Sometimes, it just takes just a moment for people to click and that's what happened when I met Vimlaji. We bonded instantly, and age has been no barrier to our friendship.

Life wouldn't have been the same without the presence of these wonderful people. I am thankful to them for being a part of my life.

> Positive people are a gift from the Almighty. It is important to learn from them and ensure that we, in turn, infuse positivity into the lives of those we know.

Life Lines

- Each one of us is a package of many talents. We must nurture them at every opportunity and keep the process of self-discovery and learning an ongoing one.

- Challenging experiences in life must make one 'BETTER' and not 'BITTER.' They must be used to motivate oneself to explore all possibilities and work on one's self-imposed limitations.

- Life is full of opportunities, so believe in yourself and make the most of them.

- Unwavering determination and focus are extremely critical. Do listen to what the world tells you; however, become deaf to negativity.

- A clear vision, backed by definite plans, gives one a feeling of tremendous confidence and personal power.
- The world swarms around you when you are successful and are a name to reckon with. You can tell your fair-weather relatives or friends (personal and professional) from the true ones, especially when your chips are down.
- Stand up for what you believe in. You can do so by being assertive and not aggressive.
- Success is achieved by ordinary people with extraordinary determination.
- Difficult circumstances are God's way of testing you. Believe that if He brings you to it, He will also bring you through it.

Words of Wisdom

I have learnt a simple thing about life: IT GOES ON... Sure enough it does! But I urge each one of you to make your life COUNT! I always live life fully, packing 48 hours into 24! I have never held back and have always given my 100 percent to whatever I have undertaken, as though there is no tomorrow.

When one lives life in this manner, one does not have regrets. I firmly believe that nothing in life is unfortunate. As a saying by Victoria Holt goes, "Never regret. If it's good, it's wonderful. If it's bad, it's experience.

Acknowledgments

My heartfelt gratitude to the Almighty for His abundant blessings and guidance to lead a successful life by finding inspiration in the people around me. The coming alive of this book is a dream come true for me. I had dreamt of writing this for about a decade... but, I guess it was meant to happen at 'the right time'.

However, I was barely a writer. I became one with my first book, 'Reality Bytes – The Role of HR in Today's World.' I am short of words to thank Mr. Vishal Soni, CEO of Vishwakarma Publications, my Publishers, for unearthing the hidden talent in me and for transforming me into a best-selling, sought-after author.

I would like to wholeheartedly thank all the contributors – the authors of each chapter, who have put their heart and soul into sharing their life stories and moments of truth for the benefit of the readers. Many thanks to them for being open about all the incidents that the readers can learn from.

This book would not have been ready without the partnership and constant guidance from Ms. Yogita Vaidya of Word's Worth Literary Consultancy.

Thanks to my friend, Anshul Singh, for walking a few steps with me in 2012 and believing in my dream. Your belief in me inspired me to give my best.

I would like to thank all those whose assistance proved to be a milestone in the accomplishment of my goal.

Finally, I would like to thank my parents, Usha and Narendra; my sister, Manisha and her family, Ashish Jijaji, my nephews, Rohit and Ravi; and my husband, Sanjeev for their love and support. They kept me going in the toughest of times!

About the Author

Felicitated with the **'Woman Achiever Award 2018'** by Indian Women Convention (IWC), **'MTC Global Outstanding Corporate Award for Excellence in Human Resources'** during the 6th Annual Global Convention – SANKALP 2016, **'Women Achievers Award'** by World HRD Congress & Institute of Public Enterprise in 2013, **'HR Super Achiever Award'** by Star News at the 20th World HRD Congress 2012 amongst many others, Aparna is a passionate learner in her journey of **over 21 years** of intense and expansive HR work. In her diverse roles, she has successfully been a learning partner, mentor, and coach to leaders, leadership teams and organizations to build competencies, learning abilities, and nimbleness for achieving purposeful performance.

After completing her post-graduation in Personnel Management & Industrial Relations (PM & IR) from **Tata Institute of Social Sciences (TISS)**, Mumbai, Aparna made her foray into the corporate world through **Nocil** and moved into different roles in the HR function in organizations like **Monsanto, Novartis, UCB, Deutsche Bank, Lafarge, and Greaves Cotton.** Over the years, Aparna has learnt to persistently and passionately value freedom, authentic relationships, and the realization of people's potential.

Winner of many accolades like **'Women Leadership Award'** for BFSI (Banking, Financial Services & Insurance) Awards by Institute of Public Enterprise (IPE), Hyderabad, **'Achiever of**

Excellence Award' by Bombay Management Association (BMA) and Indian Society for Training & Development (ISTD, Mumbai), she is regularly featured as one of the **top women HR Leaders** in the country and quoted as a **Thought Leader** in HR. Under her leadership at Lafarge, many in-company Global Awards such as **'Digilearn Championship Trophy'** and **'WAVE' (Women Adding Value & Excellence)** have been received besides external recognitions like **CLO (Chief Learning Officer's) Award** consecutively for three years.

Beyond her corporate role as an HR Leader, Aparna also dons the hat of HR contributor through her associations with **Indian Society of Training & Development (ISTD), All India Management Association (AIMA), National Institute of Personnel Management (NIPM), National HRD Network,** and **Sumedhas,** where she actively participates in disseminating her acquired knowledge and building the HR fraternity by creating future leaders. She was the **Honorary Treasurer of National HRD Network, Mumbai Chapter (2012-2015)** and a member of the Executive Committee. She was also **elected as member of the National Executive Board of NHRDN for the period 2013-2015.** She has been an **Independent Director** on the **board of T.S Alloys Ltd. (100% subsidiary of Tata Steel Ltd.).**

A wildlife enthusiast and an amateur photographer, Aparna spends most of her leisure time close to nature. She also loves traveling as it gives her an opportunity to meet new people. Books are Aparna's favourite ally, and she dedicates some time every day to read something new. An avid reader, she has a collection of some of the best books of the century.

She launched her maiden book, 'Reality Bytes – The Role of HR in Today's World' in 2015 in English, which has received wide acclaim across the globe. The book has also been translated into Hindi and has been launched across the country. (Visit http://www.aparnasharma.in/reality-bytes-role-of-hr/).

Aparna has instituted 'UDAAN' – a scholarship for all-rounder girl students entering Class 10, at St. Mary's Convent School in Ujjain where she studied, as a tribute to her aunt, Late Dr. Mohini D. Vyas. She also spends time guiding and coaching students as part of the school's career guidance efforts.

She is also actively involved in adult education through various forums and dedicates time to old-age homes and orphanages in Mumbai.

To know more about Aparna, visit: **www.aparnasharma.in**